VESSEL

LOVE & DARK SERIES
Book 1

HINA MCCORD & BECCA C. SMITH

Published by Red Frog Publishing, a division of Red Frog Media

Visit our website at www.2nerdgirls.com

First published in 2014

ISBN 978-1949877243

Printed in the United States of America

Dedicated to our amazing grandmothers...

Hina McCord

To Lois McCord: I couldn't have asked for a more caring, nurturing, supportive grandma. You always made me feel like I was home. I was allowed to be myself in your house, and that is something I will treasure for all of time. I love you, I love you, I love you. Your beautiful soul radiates like the warmth of summer in my memories. May sunlight fill your bones with strength, and the stars guide your heart ever forward into the everything.

Becca C. Smith

To Grandma Anna: Thanks for being a badass woman who inspired me to write badass female characters. You were one incredible woman. I love you.

PROLOGUE
LUCIAN

The alcohol in her perfume was strong enough to burn my eyes. I sank my teeth in deeper as she moaned with pleasure. I was already full, but what was the point in leaving her alive? So that she could continue to wait tables at The Bargain's Inn, married to Floyd the town's drunk?

Not that he was of any use to her now.

I wasn't Lucian the Merciful . . . not anymore. But it was more convenient to kill someone who was already dead inside. Her eyes rolled back and I languished on the last few drops as her body trembled then orgasmed.

Would her dismal life have given her this sweet of a death?

I let her body thud to the floor. I wiped my mouth and straightened my back, kicking an empty beer can at Floyd's carcass. His severed head sat on top of the TV he'd been yelling at before he'd hit her.

My body surged, their blood filling my hollow cavities with

warmth. I wasn't supposed to stop in for a snack, but when I'd passed and saw what he was doing to her, I just couldn't resist cutting him open.

Things like that weren't men.

They were monsters . . . like I was.

I walked steadily out the door, their rocking chair creaking in the warm desert breeze as I gazed up at the quarter moon. Where was the Vessel hiding? It had been five hundred years since the last one, and he should be of age by now. I shifted restlessly. Waiting was an agony I'd become all too familiar with.

Adnachiel was probably keeping the Vessel from activating his powers so that I couldn't track him. As if that had stopped me before. Any mistake, any misstep, and I'd be at that dog's doorstep ready to rip him apart.

This game of ours had gone on for too long. My eyes were dull with boredom. If only I could bring Adnachiel enough pain to satisfy my rage. I couldn't fill this growing emptiness, even after a hefty feeding like tonight.

Maybe this time I'd end it and drag that Vessel, boy or man, to the depths of hell with me . . . to meet my maker.

CHAPTER 1
SHEA

"Shea Harper?"

Even the way the woman said my name made me want to punch her. I'd been sitting in the housing registration room for about three hours now. All this lady had done so far was tell me to sit down and shut up until my name was called. Of course, this was after I had asked her five times if she could help me. The room was empty for God's sake, and I could tell she was just futzing around on the Internet. She was making me wait on purpose, and now that she was bored, she was finally going to talk to me.

Seriously? Would anyone *really* mind if I punched her? Maybe a little slap? Kick in the shins? Anything to inflict some kind of pain?

All I wanted were the keys to my new abode. Was that too much to ask? Apparently for this woman, it was.

It wasn't like Arizona State University was my dream school, but I grew up in Phoenix, and my parents didn't want to pay out-of-state fees. It had taken every ounce of manipulation I could muster just to get them to agree to let me stay in a dorm!

So here I was.

Sitting in a room.

Waiting for condescending-annoying-lady to grace me with her time.

I should have taken care of my housing situation months ago, so I only had myself to blame. But that didn't justify the attitude from Ms. Dorm-pants over there.

I stood up and walked to the front desk. She sat behind it, ruffling through papers with an irritated grunt here or there.

Finally, she made eye contact and handed me a sheet of paper. "Fill that out, please," she ordered tersely.

"I already filled out an application. They said all I had to do was come here and pick up my keys." I told her what I'd been trying to tell her the entire three hours I'd been there.

She sighed and her nostrils flared a bit, but she didn't raise her voice. It was more of a gritted-teeth-I-freaking-hate-you tone. "This is not an application, Ms. Harper. It's a release form for your keys. I do know what I'm doing, after all."

Normally, I'd blush and apologize profusely, but this lady brought out the worst in me. "Got it, thanks," I said with a roll of my eyes. Pretty stupid since she was the guardian of my coveted keys, but I couldn't control myself.

"If you want to come back tomorrow, the office opens at noon," she threatened.

That did it.

Attitude gone.

I needed my room tonight or I was going to have to sleep at home, and since my car was already full of everything I owned, there was no way that was going to happen.

"Nope. I'm good. I'll just fill this out. Anything else you want me to fill out? Can I get you some coffee? Snack? Anything?" I went into full-on *sweet*-mode.

"Just the form will do," the woman said.

I thought for just a second I could see a hint of a smile. I was glad my pathetic-ness could entertain her.

After that, I was surprised at how quickly everything came together. I handed her the fully filled out form and she handed me the keys. I tried not to think about the fact that she could easily have done this hours ago. I just took a deep breath, smiled, and left before she could find some excuse to take away my new home.

The intense Phoenix September sun hit my body like I had stepped into an oven. It was 107 degrees today and that was nothing compared to the 120-degree summer days the city experienced all of July and August. 107 was actually a cooldown! I despised Phoenix. I couldn't really hate on Arizona completely since it did have pretty spectacular places like the Grand Canyon and Bell Rock in Sedona. But Phoenix? Phoenix I could loathe with all of my soul.

I'd wanted to go to UCLA for my undergrad degree, but every time I was about to get a loan, scholarship, or grant, it would fall through. It wasn't long after that I'd become convinced that there was such a thing as "the Phoenix gods." They never let anyone leave once they had them in their grasp. That was what it felt like anyway. When an opportunity came my way to get out of this city, something random and, frankly, absurd would keep me here. Why else would so many people live here? It couldn't be by choice! It had to be something supernatural. There was no other explanation, in my opinion. I was beginning to think Phoenix was stalking me, it wanted to keep me so badly.

I could barely breathe because of the intense heat, but I'd been dealing with this crappy weather my whole life. I just had to grin and bear it. First things first, I needed to cool down. I grabbed an elastic band from my jeans pocket and tied my pale blond hair back into a sloppy ponytail. I had been growing my hair out since last year, so it was just past my shoulders, making it a furnace on my neck anytime I went outside.

I took my sunglasses out of my purse and put them on. My eyes were extremely sensitive to the sun. They were technically hazel: gold some days, green others, and every once in a while they managed to be a boring brown.

I peeled off my small black cardigan. It was essential when I was in overly air-conditioned ASU offices, but outside it might as well have been a fur coat. Jeans and a tank for me. It was the only way I could survive.

I never had to worry about eating crappy food, at least when it came to weight. Digestion was a whole other story. My roll of Tums was a permanent addition to my list of essentials.

"Shea! Where's your car?" A voice sounded behind me.

I whirled around to see my very best friend in the whole wide world, Aidan O'Connell. You couldn't get a more Irish name than that! Aidan's roots may have been in Ireland, but he was born and raised in Phoenix as well. He'd been my next-door neighbor since . . . well . . . birth.

Our moms would always laugh about the fact that Aidan and I were born on the exact same day, minute, and second. I used to question the minutes and seconds part, until our parents showed us our birth certificates. Sure enough, it was one of those weird anomalies in life. We called ourselves the "spirit twins." Totally cheesy, I know, but we were four! Give me a break!

I suppose any other girl with a pulse would go all aflutter for someone like Aidan. He was pretty gorgeous. I wasn't blind, it was just that I always thought of him as a brother, so it was difficult to see him in a "hot" kind of way. But the boy was a stunner, that I couldn't deny, whether I liked him that way or not.

His hair was dark brown and short, with a swoopy kind of messy look that guys seemed to be into nowadays. It suited his sculpted face, giant blue eyes, and those crazy long eyelashes I was secretly jealous of. Though on the surface he could easily fit the title "pretty boy," Aidan was actually the toughest guy I knew. He wasn't "body-builder" huge, but he was a little over six feet and in incredible shape. That boy had a ten pack at least, if that was possible.

Yup, my best friend the hottie.

Sometimes I almost wished I liked him in a romantic way. It would be so much easier. I knew Aidan would die for me. He'd been my protector since preschool when the resident bully, Greg Chanto, had decided he wanted my Pokémon card collection and grabbed it at playtime.

When Aidan had found out, he'd had Greg in a headlock until he cried and gave me back my cards. Aidan had even made Greg apologize and promise never to do it again. This had been the first of about a million events where Aidan kicked someone's butt because he thought he was protecting me in some way. It was very "big brotherly" behavior, which was probably why I saw him like family instead of boyfriend material.

And to be fair, it wasn't like Aidan had confessed some undying love for me and I was choosing not to be with him. Aidan was just Aidan. We were best buds. That was that. As far as I knew, neither one of us wanted anything more.

Right now, he had this adorable, silly grin on his face, like seeing me had made his day. His sparkly, warm eyes looking at me like that always gave me a surge of fierce loyalty toward him. I was just happy we were both going to ASU so we wouldn't be separated. I wasn't ready to live life without my BFF yet.

"What do you mean where's my car? You parked it." I rolled my eyes as I reached his side. He was holding a large box that looked heavy for me, but was probably as light as a feather for him.

"I know, but I got all turned around. There are too many courtyards. They all look the same." Aidan shifted the box uncomfortably. "I just want to drop this off in my dorm."

"Is that seriously all you're bringing?" I asked incredulously. My car was filled to the brim with all my stuff. We'd barely had room for Aidan's one box. "And don't you want to know where the dorm is and not the car?" I was a little confused at his logic.

"I mapped out where the building was from where I parked the car, but when I forgot where the car was, I couldn't find the dorm. I've been wandering around campus since you went into housing registration," he admitted lamely.

"You've been walking aimlessly for three hours holding a

fifty-pound box in hundred degree weather? Didn't you think to ask anyone for directions?" I would have been appalled, but it was so Aidan to do something like that.

Aidan gave me a sly smile. "I don't ask for directions, you know that."

I sighed heavily, shaking my head in amusement. "Come on. I know where the building is."

Aidan was instantly by my side as we walked through the maze that was the ASU campus.

"You got into McClintock Hall, right?" Aidan asked with a slight worried tone.

"Barely. The housing lady was being such a jerk." ASU had what was called "residential living," which basically meant on-campus housing for students with the same major. Aidan and I still weren't sure what we wanted to do with our lives, so we opted for majoring in Liberal Arts and Sciences. It sounded good and we figured we could always change it later.

That left us a few options for housing, but since Aidan was way more prepared than me, he'd gotten into McClintock Hall ages ago. It seemed like the best place to be since it was near the library and central to campus. I was just happy Crazy-Lady had given me my first choice. It wouldn't have been horrible to be in another building, but Aidan was my security blanket at this point, and I was glad we'd be living in the same place.

It took us about ten minutes to arrive at our new home. It was an L-shaped building. One side was three stories and the attached side was two stories. It looked like it was built in the '70s from the blocky architecture and the brown-and-white paint job. But at least there were lots of windows. I hated dark houses.

I needed my space as bright as possible. Natural sunlight was the best and I was thrilled that I'd have that, but I had come prepared just in case. One of my suitcases was completely filled with every table lamp I could stuff in it.

"What room are you in?" Aidan asked as we approached the bottom level.

"What room am *I* in? What room are *you* in? You have to put that box down before you pass out." Just like Aidan to be more concerned with me than himself.

He half laughed and nodded toward his back. "I forgot already. It's on a slip in my back pocket. Could you grab it?"

I was about to grab the white piece of paper sticking out of his jeans but stopped myself. It suddenly occurred to me how intimate it was to reach into someone's pants pocket, even if it was just a piece of paper. And for the first time in our entire lives together, I felt embarrassed. Or at least self-conscious. "Um, why don't I take the box and you get the paper?"

Aidan's face turned a little pink, and it wasn't from the heat. "Oh, right, sorry." He didn't hand me the box, but simply placed it on the ground in front of him. He grabbed the paper and read his room number aloud. "222."

I felt horrible making a "thing" out of something that should have been so normal for us. I'd known Aidan since forever. We'd had sleepovers and campouts. We'd slept in the same sleeping bag, for crying out loud! We'd been eight, but still.

Officially, we were adults now. Standing in front of our dorm. In college! And suddenly, touching Aidan's butt, even if it was just to grab a piece of paper, was just weird. I couldn't explain my crazy logic. I didn't want to cross any lines. Not with Aidan. He was too important to me to screw it up.

He brushed the whole thing off as if it'd never happened. Picking up his box, he gave me a goofy grin that told me everything was fine between us. "Shall we?"

I smiled back, relieved at how he handled my insanity. "Maybe your roommate will be there already."

"Ha! I'm a single occupant, sucker!" Aidan teased as he walked up the small flight of stairs to the second level.

"What?" I punched him in the arm playfully. "How did you pull that off?"

"It's called filling out the request early. As in before the due date. You wouldn't know anything about that," he laughed.

"You suck," I grumbled, but I wasn't mad. I was extremely jealous! I was going to have to share my room with someone called Gerta Jones. Who would name their child Gerta? I had an image in my head: a cross between Godzilla and Jabba the Hutt. I just hoped I was wrong.

"Yeah, I know." Aidan had his triumphant-face on.

"You're still going to have to share the bathroom." I had to knock his victory down just a little bit. The way the floor plans worked, there were two people to a room and two rooms shared one bathroom. So basically, four people to every bathroom.

"True, but still. I win," he laughed.

We reached his room and he put his box down on the two-seater couch on the left. The rooms were all the same from the research I'd done. They were set up like a small one-bedroom apartment. The front room consisted of the love seat and two desks with chairs. The back room had two twin beds side by side, a sink, a closet, and a door to the shared bathroom. Pretty simple.

11

I took out my dorm slip and looked it over. "I'm a couple rooms down from you, 225. I'm going to unpack my car. I'll meet you back here when I'm done?"

Aidan looked at me as if I was insane. He placed his hands on my shoulders and his eyes met mine. "Do you honestly think I'm going to let you unpack your car alone? You practically brought your whole house!"

"Which is why you shouldn't be forced to help. I got this. No worries." Though I knew it was a useless argument, I had to try. I hated moving with every fiber of my soul, so to have my best friend help lug all my crap seemed like a horrible abuse of friendship.

"Um, you're crazy. Now, where's your car?" Aidan wasn't budging. He was going to help no matter what I said.

"You keep forgetting that you parked it." I grinned.

"Oh, yeah." He grinned back. "Follow me."

Two hours later I was finally done. It was early evening, so at least it was in the nineties now instead of the 107-degree madness. And after going up those stairs five hundred times, I was drenched to the bone in sweat. Okay, maybe it wasn't five hundred, but it certainly felt like it! And at least I was able to leave the heavy box of extra lamps in my car since the dorm was perfectly lit to my satisfaction.

Gerta had arrived and she was actually quite pleasant. She was a short, pretty girl with brown hair and brown eyes, and as far as I could tell, she appeared very sweet.

The only difference between Aidan's and my apartment was the fact that the furniture setup was reversed.

Aidan was currently plopped on our couch. Gerta didn't

12

seem to mind. She was eyeing him like a piece of prime rib.

I felt a pang of . . . something. I wouldn't call it jealousy, but it was definitely territorial. I suddenly had the need to sit right next to Aidan. He was so exhausted he leaned his head on my shoulder and I fought the urge to be smug to poor little Gerta, who looked like I'd taken away her favorite toy.

"Are you two a couple?" Gerta asked with a forced smile, but really she was hiding her disappointment that Aidan might not be available.

He took his head off my shoulder and immediately shook his head. "Nah, just best buds. We've known each other since we were kids."

I wasn't expecting the knot that abruptly lurched in my stomach. It actually hurt. Not because it wasn't true, but because I wanted Gerta to think we were a couple. What made it more confusing was the fact that I didn't actually want to be a couple.

What was wrong with me? I didn't want Aidan romantically, but I didn't want him to be romantic with anyone else. It made no sense, but I felt it as strongly as anything I'd ever felt. I was being so selfish! How much of a jerk could I be? What if Aidan was so quick to say we were friends because he liked Gerta? I couldn't be the a-hole friend who cockblocked him from every potential girlfriend.

I swallowed my feelings of . . . whatever the heck I was feeling and simply said, "Nope. Just friends." When Gerta's eyes lit up, I added, "Good friends. Best friends. As in, if anyone even came close to hurting him, they'd have some serious hospital bills."

Aidan laughed and nudged me with his shoulder playfully. "We look out for each other." He gave me a smile that made my chest swell with affection. I really would tear anyone apart who dared to mess with him.

Gerta leaned back against one of the desks across from us. "There's a party at Delta Delta Phi. You guys want to come?"

I wasn't normally a party person and neither was Aidan . . .

"We'd love to!" Aidan's face lit up with so much enthusiasm I didn't have the heart to disappoint him.

"Yeah," I said with as much gusto as I could muster, "that sounds awesome. Let's do it."

Aidan went to go clean up and I did the same. A quick shower to wash off all the moving-slime felt amazing, although I was super paranoid that our next-door neighbors would walk into the bathroom at any time. The shower was closed off, but people could still come in and use the "other" facilities. I wasn't used to sharing anything, being an only child, so splitting a bathroom was making me jumpy.

I dried off and got dressed at super speed. I decided on jeans and a tank top. Yes, pretty much the same outfit I wore earlier, but this was a different tank; it had black and white stripes. I called it my "Paris" tank.

Gerta was wearing a killer short dress that made her look like a movie star. I suddenly felt very frumpy.

"You're going to dry your hair, right? You're seriously not going to let it air-dry at a party?" Gerta looked downright appalled.

I was going to do exactly that, but from the look of horror on Gerta's face, I said instead, "Of course not. I just can't find my hair dryer."

"Here. Use mine. And I have a ceramic straightener so it won't fry your hair." Gerta loaded me up with an expensive-looking

14

hair dryer and flat iron. They were the kind that super swanky salons used. I realized then that Gerta was definitely a girly-girl and I'd have to adjust my personality accordingly.

"Thanks," I said with a grateful smile, though I felt more frustrated than grateful. I really didn't want to go to this party. I really didn't want to dry my hair. I just wanted to curl up on my new uncomfortable twin bed and read my Kindle until I fell asleep. Was that so wrong?

Despite my desire to be a hermit, I went into the bathroom to get ready. After all was said and done, I was impressed with myself. I looked pretty darn good. My hair had never been this straight in my life. Not that my hair was curly, but it had a natural wave to it that the iron completely flattened. The style really ended up suiting my oval face.

It was all worth it when Aidan arrived and his jaw dropped to the floor. All he could say was, "Shea."

I took that as a compliment, especially when he hardly noticed Gerta. And, trust me, he was going to be the only boy who didn't. That girl looked good!

Once the three of us started walking over to the frat house though, Aidan was back to his non-gawking self, talking about how excited he was to start school. We all gossiped about our classes and how lame it was that we had to take math and science as a requirement. Although, my heart was half into that argument. I actually liked science and math, but I didn't feel like being the lone sheep in the conversation, so I complained heartily with Aidan and Gerta.

When we arrived at the Delta Delta Phi house, it was already spilling over with people. Apparently, this was "the" party to go to, and from the looks of it, most of the campus had crammed inside. Even the lawn and porch were stuffed with students.

"I guess we came to the right place," Aidan observed. I looked over at him and could tell he was fighting the urge to leave.

I was about to suggest we do just that when Gerta wrapped her arm around his and pulled him toward the front door. "Let's get some alcohol in you."

I followed close behind them, not wanting to be stranded in a sea of people I didn't know. Aidan kept giving me smiles of encouragement while Gerta led him through the throng of drunk coeds. It was getting harder and harder to keep up with them until finally I realized I needed to grow a pair and let Aidan have fun.

I stopped in the middle of the room and watched Aidan and Gerta get swallowed up by the ocean of people.

Okay.

Here I was.

Getting more and more claustrophobic by the second.

I was about to become a human bulldozer and shove my way out of this hot, sweaty, crowded place when an ice-cold red cup was gently placed in my hand. "You look like you could use a drink."

I peered up at the guy who had handed it to me. I had to say, he was pretty beautiful. He had smoldering brown eyes, pale blond hair, and cheekbones for days. He was way too good-looking to talk to me. It must have been dark in here.

"I don't take drinks from strangers. Leave me alone." Why did I just say that? It was like I couldn't control what came out of my mouth. I mean, I'd uttered some pretty stupid things before, but I was fully aware that I was saying them. This was different. It was as if someone else was pulling my vocal strings and wanted to tell this guy to go away.

That was it.

My instincts told me Blond-Boy was bad news.

He looked at me as if he was butt hurt. Like it had taken all his courage to come up and talk to me and I had blown him off. The people pleaser in me felt like a complete jerk.

Maybe I was being crazy-paranoid-girl. It might not be instinct; it could be fear-of-hot-boys. I'd definitely been known to choke up when talking to a cute guy. They intimidated the crap out of me.

"I'm sorry. It's all these people. It's freaking me out a little." I lifted the cup to him. "Thanks." I didn't actually drink it. I still had unreasonable fears of poisoning and roofies, but I pretended to so he wouldn't feel bad.

"I'm Frank," he said with a shy smile. "We can go outside and get some air if it'll make you feel better?"

Okay. He was being sweet.

"Sure," I responded with what I hoped was a pleasant smile. "I'm Shea."

"Hi, Shea." From the relief on his face, I'd say I did my job recovering from my earlier nastiness.

We walked through the packed partiers and finally emerged into the night air. It was warm outside, but not nearly as suffocating as the frat house. There were almost as many people outside as inside, but somehow being in the open air made it psychologically better.

"Over here." Frank placed his hand on the small of my back

and led me to an outcropping of sycamore trees. They were in full foliage, making it hard to see anyone through the low branches. "See? Private, but still close to the party for an easy getaway if you decide you don't like me," Frank whispered charmingly.

The hairs on the back of my neck rose. Something was off.

"You know what? I completely abandoned my friend in there. I should go get him." I wanted to run from Frank. He was nice and I was probably acting like a scaredy-cat, but all I could think about was finding Aidan and being as far away from this guy as possible.

"How's your drink?" Frank ignored my statement completely.

I dumped it on the ground. "Excuse me," I said and tried to push past him.

He grabbed my arm. "That was rude." His face went from sweet and charismatic to angry in about a second.

I tried to shrug him off, but his grip was like a vise. And by vise, I mean I couldn't move at all.

Frank leaned down so his eyes met mine, and even though it was dark out, they constricted right in front of me as if someone had shone a flashlight in them. "You won't scream. You won't even remember this. Just relax."

I screamed.

I would never forget the creepy look in his eyes.

And relaxing was entirely out of the question.

But Frank's reaction was the opposite of what I expected. He was shocked. As if simply telling me not to scream would have actually worked. Did he think he was some kind of hypnotist or something?

The shock wasn't enough for him to release his hold on me

though. He pulled me closer, and I was pretty sure the guy was about to bite the back of my neck! Who did this guy think he was: Dracula? Freaking psycho!

I tried to move, but he was strong. He didn't look like he'd be that powerful, but the more I grabbed at him and tried to wriggle away, the more he just stood there like stone. I wasn't that weak, was I?

And you'd think with a party right next to us someone would have responded to my scream, but no such luck.

That's when I felt his teeth on my neck. On my neck! He was seriously going to bite me like a raging lunatic! I'd read about nutzoids like Frank in a magazine once. They really thought they were vampires. All I could think about was the part in the article that said it was a lot harder to bite into flesh than the crazies thought. For Frank's teeth to actually break my skin, he would have to bite down really hard and possibly take out a chunk of me.

Oh, God. This was going to be bad.

I tried again to move Statue-Boy, but he might as well have been rooted in cement.

I felt his teeth puncture my skin. The sensation of blood trickling down my back was surreal and terrifying. Not to mention the fact that Frank was moaning like he was having an orgasm.

Terror raced through me.

I was trapped.

No one was coming.

Something deep inside me snapped.

I screamed once more, but this time it sounded like a battle cry.

My eyes burned and I saw a flash of white.

Frank pulled back instantly, horrified.

The white was gone.

I felt like myself again.

I was about to run when I saw a blur of muscle beside me. Frank's body suddenly flew in the air and smashed against a nearby tree.

Aidan stood next to me. I could feel the rage flowing off him like waves of power. It was much more terrifying than Frank's attack. The fact that Aidan's fist had made a six-foot college student fly ten feet in the air and smash into a tree was a little mind-blowing. I knew Aidan was strong, but seriously!

Frank recovered more quickly than I expected. He pleaded to Aidan, "I didn't know she was yours."

Aidan snarled. He sounded more like an animal than a man. He leapt at Frank and grabbed him by the throat. "If there weren't so many witnesses . . . "

Aidan was right; we had gained quite an audience. He must have caused a scene by racing to save me. The only thing I could think of was that he had heard me scream. Out of all the noise and people at that party, Aidan had heard me above everything else. If I hadn't know it before, I knew it now: he and I were connected. He'd always be there for me, no matter what.

Frank was a blubbering mess and barely choked out the words, "I didn't know she was claimed!"

Aidan made sure Frank was looking him in the eye. "I'm not one of you," he growled.

I had no idea what they were talking about, but Frank's eyes went round. He choked. "What are you?"

Aidan didn't answer. He must have been amped up on adrenaline because he threw Frank by the neck like he was a rag doll.

Frank scrambled to his feet as if it had been a gentle shove. He knew better than to stay at this point and ran into the darkness.

People were asking me if I was okay and trying to high-five Aidan. I just wanted out of there. I needed to be in the quiet. I needed to be away from people. I needed a freaking Band-Aid.

Aidan ignored everyone's praise and lifted me into his arms, cradling me like a baby. I leaned my head on his shoulder and let him carry me. Normally my feminist side would tell him to put me down so I could walk on my own, but feeling his arms holding my body made me feel safe.

And I really needed to feel safe at the moment.

Aidan took me to his dorm room so that we could have some privacy. He laid me on one of the twin beds and gently examined my neck. "Not too bad. You won't need stitches. I've got a bandage here."

I touched his arm. "Thank you," I said. Talking made all my emotions flood to the surface. Tears streamed down my cheeks and I couldn't stop them. Everything that had happened hit me full force. I hated crying. I wasn't a crier. But being attacked on my first day was too much for me to process. I was completely overwhelmed.

Aidan's arms were instantly wrapped around me. He held me close. I clung to him like he was air. He had saved my life. My best friend. My Aidan. I couldn't love him any more than I did in that moment.

21

He pulled out of the embrace and smiled. "You're going to sleep here tonight." He left no room for argument.

I simply nodded and let him clean the bite marks and bandage them properly. I was exhausted. My head barely hit the pillow and I was asleep.

***

I awoke to the sound of someone knocking on the door.

Aidan was out cold on the twin bed next to me. I didn't want to wake him. From the light coming in through the window, I knew it was morning. Or, I hoped it was morning. I had been known to sleep in pretty late from time to time.

I tiptoed past Aidan and walked through the bedroom to the main living space where the desks and couch were. Cracking open his front door, I was not prepared for the hot guy standing there.

After last night, I didn't think I'd be interested in another boy . . . ever.

But . . . this guy?

He had a kind of half smirk, which made him ridiculously sexy, but he held himself in a way that pretty much told me he knew that already. I hated it when really good-looking people knew that they were really good looking. He had piercing . . . was it teal? Holy crap, this guy had almost turquoise eyes! But a deep, deep teal like they could be dark green or dark blue depending on his wardrobe.

His face angled in all the right places and his dark hair was short and perfectly in place.

He wore a simple black T-shirt and jeans, but he managed to make that look like he had stepped out of a modeling shoot. And from the look in his eyes, I could tell he thought I should be falling all over him.

Not going to happen.

No way was I going to let this guy know I was attracted to him. Not after last night.

"Yes?" I said as snarkily as I could.

It took him aback.

Good.

I liked bringing down egomaniacs a notch or two.

He took a moment before he spoke, but when he did, his voice was calm and commanding. "I'm Lucian, the dorm monitor. I wanted to introduce myself to all the new students."

A part of me felt bad for being rude, but after what I'd gone through with that crazy jerk, I wasn't in the mood to be nice. Especially to gorgeous boys who had the nerve to stand there and be . . . gorgeous.

"Nice to meet you," I replied flatly. "I'm Shea, but this isn't my room. I'm in 225. This is Aidan O'Connell's room." Being the dorm monitor, he should already know that, but I thought I'd make his job easier. "Did you want to meet him, too?" I asked, and was surprised at how much attitude I had.

He had done exactly nothing to deserve my wrath. It must have been residual feelings from my experience with Bite-Boy.

No matter how hard I tried to put on a nice smile, a scowl would instantly replace it.

Lucian appeared to sense this as well because he suddenly leaned down close to me. "Nice to meet you, Shea."

23

Then his eyes constricted.

Like Frank's.

I stepped back in fear.

"Are you on drugs?" Was this some kind of new campus drug that messed with people's eyes? Maybe this guy would think he was Dracula, too. "Get the hell away from me. I'm going to report you to . . . to someone . . . I don't know who yet, but you shouldn't be in charge of anything if you're doing drugs!" That even sounded lame to me.

Lucian was more surprised than before. He looked like Frank had when I'd refused to obey his "no screaming" order.

"I'm not on drugs," he stated simply.

"Yeah, right." I crossed my arms defiantly. "Well, you did your job. You introduced yourself, now go introduce yourself to everyone else." I slammed the door in his face.

I knew I had completely overreacted, but I didn't care. Cute or not, there was something about him I didn't trust.

I turned around and jumped slightly when I saw Aidan standing in the bedroom doorway with a huge grin on his face.

"What are you smiling about?" I found his amusement contagious.

"You certainly told him," he beamed.

The boy looked positively proud of me. I suddenly needed a hug. I ran up to him and felt relieved when his arms wrapped around me. "Can we just have a first-day do-over please?" I mumbled into his chest.

"How's breakfast sound?" He pulled away with a grin.

"Perfect." I sighed in relief. "I'll meet you in the lobby in a half hour. I'm going to complain to somebody, damn it." I wasn't sure if I was actually going to make a formal complaint, but I hated making empty threats.

I hurried to my room, successfully avoiding the "Lucian welcoming wagon." After showering quickly and slopping my hair into a wet ponytail, I hurried down to the lobby to wait for Aidan.

It was a small lobby with one main desk and four couches. Of course, no one was there, so I couldn't report anyone at the moment. That somehow made me feel better, and I was starting to rethink my whole complaint rant anyway. Maybe I had just been upset about what had happened to me with Frank, so I'd taken it out on Lucian. I felt the bandages on my neck. The injury barely hurt, but the whole experience had been pretty terrifying.

Whoa.

My stomach dropped.

I whirled around, expecting to see Frank, but there was no one there, just a door to the supply closet.

For no reason that I could explain, I knew something horrible was behind that door.

And like every idiot in a horror movie, I walked over to it. Before I could chicken out, I grabbed the knob and turned.

Locked.

Of course it was.

My feeling didn't go away though. Something felt wrong.

"Shea? You ready?" Aidan's voice interrupted my crazy obsession with the closet. I really was going nuts.

"Yeah." I turned around and walked over to Aidan. "But I think I'm going for a nice chamomile tea instead of coffee this morning."

"Good plan." Aidan nudged me affectionately.

CHAPTER 2
LUCIAN

I stared into his brown eyes. So many humans in America had brown eyes now. Maybe it was being in Arizona again, but I hated this place. I hated the dry, dusty air of the desert, the artificial plants and plastic breasts, the bleached-blond hair and the smell of slathered cocoa butter.

It was a den for lizards. The sun made their skin leathery, and the more insane among them fried and cooked it in tanning beds. I'd never been one for beef jerky. Human flesh should be kept tender, juicy.

I knew he couldn't pick where he'd been born, but it was a good move for Adnachiel to stay here. Keep Shea in the desert . . . the middle of the desert, where the sun was high and night was short. After all these years of losing, maybe that little beasty wanted to win. It didn't matter. He could even hide her in the arctic land of the midnight sun, and I would burn in the gray light of her shadow and still take her.

The putrid heat rolled a long line of sweat down my back, and I smiled at the distasteful sensation. It wasn't pleasant like the heat of Egypt. There were no turning sands, and the people didn't smell of frankincense and myrrh, like the Babylonians and Assyrians. Now those were a people. They used to bring boatloads of resins from the Phoenicians. Queen Hatshepsut had reeked of the stuff.

These paper dolls had no depth and no weight. They couldn't fathom such a rich fragrance. The women in this generation smelled of rotten flowers and alcohol. Nothing of the earth, the soil. No, it was nothing like Egypt . . . nothing like Nefertiti.

Shea Harper wouldn't be any different. She'd be cheap and easily controlled. This round would be easier than the last; she'd make number seven. Poor Adnachiel. With Shea being a woman, she didn't stand a chance against me. The men were harder, but my skill and age won over every time. They were just playthings for this immortal game. Still, a female. That was new.

Women in this generation didn't have willpower like they used to centuries ago. My pupils barely had to constrict and I was inside their minds. Puppets; that was all the human race had amounted to. They were even controlled by their own devices and creations. Larger puppets sat in big buildings, making advertisements to brainwash the smaller masses. It was a joke. The whole "class system," I'd seen it before.

I touched my shoulder, feeling the deep scars underneath. I wondered if any of them would fight back. I laughed to myself condescendingly. Of course they wouldn't. They'd have to acknowledge that they were modern slaves. Working, fighting, just for food on the table and a roof over their heads, all the while their small fragile lives consumed in work and believing the lies of the invention of "retirement."

In a way, I pitied them. It made humans easier to feed on. I was putting the poor bunnies down before the factories and offices slowly squeezed the life out of them. I laughed again at the thought of my own mercy.

Lucian the Merciful. Now that brought a smile to my face as I stared at the mangled body shoved into the supply closet, his brown eyes still open wide in frozen horror.

I wondered about his life, if I had taken something too carelessly, but one glance at him and I knew what he'd become. He'd been a young man, enthralled with the power of being Dorm Monitor. A small power for a slave. I shook my head. He would have lorded himself over the "lessers" the rest of his life. Even his blood had a sour tint to it . . . but that hadn't stopped me from drinking him dry.

Have not, waste not.

I yawned, throwing his body over my shoulder. It was a shame Shea had been so curious about this closet, and a good thing I'd locked it behind me. She'd almost pried it open, strong for a small-framed woman. I needed to take her before she understood what she really was.

Although, knowing hadn't helped the others.

I wondered what the next one would be like. Was this female thing a trend, or a different tactic? I would have to wait another five hundred years to find out. At least this was a change, unlike Adnachiel trying this old middle-of-the-desert move. Honestly, I'd already looked up their files. They'd both been born and raised in Phoenix. By now, Adnachiel should have convinced them to move to some secluded valley where they could live out their days in hiding.

Did he really think I wouldn't find her? It didn't matter. Even with the sun and heat, I'd still beaten him last time. I'd played this chess game before. He thought he could castle and move his king safely behind these plastic Arizona pawns, using the daylight to his advantage.

To me, unfiltered light was a curse. What good was the sun, that raging orb fueling all life, surrounded by the blackness of space? It's only saving grace was the reflected light it cast on the moon, that soft controller of all the oceans.

I swallowed, thinking about the correlation throughout history between women and the moon I so adored.

I resolved that it didn't matter that Shea was a woman. She may have slammed the door in my face, but that was just a fluke. She would succumb to me like all the rest. Still, she had noticed my eyes. Most humans weren't quick enough to see the millisecond they constricted before they were under my control.

Her powers protected her from my mind. I laughed, unable to fight the surge pulsing through my dead veins. This might be a fun challenge.

It had been centuries since I'd felt . . . anything, watching time pass and ages shift from glory to decay. If she were a man, I'd just take her, force her. I was so much more powerful than their greatest of strengths. Adnachiel, he always stopped me, if you could call what he did to them *stopping* me.

It was losing, any way you looked at it. His face sickened me, even after all these years. That would-be loyal dog. Shea didn't know that he'd slit her throat just as readily as I would. She'd

30

die oblivious in his arms after he'd lanced her. That last look of betrayal on their faces . . . like Moses . . . how could he stand it? Every time.

I breathed in the air and coughed it out, so much dirt in every inhalation. Seducing her the old-fashioned way wouldn't be a problem. I'd kissed my fair share of desert rats with sand in their teeth while waiting for the Vessel to reveal its location. I'd known it would be in the desert, I could feel it. I just hadn't known which one.

Now that I had found her, this might be entertaining. I always enjoyed the hunt, but adding seduction to the fire could be enough to satiate my growing distemper with eternity.

At least for a while.

A small drop of the dorm monitor's blood dripped down my back. My nostrils flared at the scent. I should top up before talking to Shea again. I walked candidly through shadows until I was outside. I had to wait until nightfall to ditch the body.

I moved quickly past a few meat-bags. I nodded graciously, explaining that the boy was a friend of mine who'd passed out from drinking. They didn't notice the dried blood down his mangled arms. They laughed, agreed, and went inside; no mind control needed.

Oh Adnachiel, was this really the safest place for her, to stay where she'd been born, never leaving the desert? It didn't make sense. Unless he thought she'd never use her powers.

If that was the case, then he was a fool. No matter how careful he was, every Vessel eventually did.

***

I sighed. Normally, the fresh night air was a relief, but it was still ninety degrees. The only benefit to my brief stay in this sweltering hell was the cactuses. Desert plants bloomed at night. Their biggest pollinators weren't butterflies or hummingbirds; they were bats. I breathed in deep. The scent was made to attract them. The fragrance was too pungent for most mortals, but for me it was the smell of bliss. If vampires were cursed, why did nature itself procure a gift for us, to bloom in the hours when we roam?

A yearning grew in my stomach. How long had it been since I had a garden and tilled the soil? I growled, hating the idea. That'd been over three thousand years ago. It was strange, how just being in the desert was stirring up old memories, feelings I had long since buried with my mortal flesh. The sooner I took her and left the desert, the more I'd feel like I always felt.

Calloused and powerful.

I jumped into the air, flying over the city lights. If I soared high enough, all of that noise, all of that movement below slowed. Above the cloud cover, it was silent. Except for planes. I wouldn't make that mistake again. However, when a passenger had screamed upon seeing me hovering outside his window, the noise had been worth the reaction. The stewardess restrained him as he continued to call out hysterically.

What a sight.

Now it was still. I glided slowly in the atmosphere, watching the small lights fade in the distance. I could be lazy and drop the dorm monitor's remains in some canyon, but I needed a break from the desert. I thought about taking him to the Pacific Ocean. It wasn't a far fly from here. Maybe I'd pick up a few snacks to refuel on the way.

No. No sense being careless now. She had awakened, and I needed to use every moment to my advantage. Why this nostalgia? It wasn't like me to delay a battle, even a pathetic one. I had waited five hundred years to stick it to Adnachiel again. Besides, Caelius grew restless in his cage. If he knew about my little ocean excursion, or any sort of misstep from the goal, he'd be furious. Furious, but helpless to do anything about it. Unless he sent my Second-Borns, in which case I was his, caged or not.

I sighed, letting the body slip from my hands and splat thousands of feet below in a deep, desolate canyon. The desert would bake his bones and rid me of the mess in a matter of days. I straightened my shoulders, brushing off the now dried blood from my black T-shirt.

Time to go do some dorm monitoring.

Even though her classes were now over, I landed close enough to the school to walk to where I'd last seen her in history class, a useless subject. A human had said it best: history was written by the victors. Then it was taught and force-fed to the masses. Besides, her history wasn't something she was going to find or learn about in books; it was in her blood. Her sweet, nourishing blood.

I felt my irises expand, covering my pupils. A little hint from my body. I definitely needed to eat something again before we met.

I scanned the treats walking by in their short-shorts, the strong smell of bleach still lingering in their platinum hair. One caught my eye as she bounced over.

"Hi! You must be new here, or I know I would have totally seen you by now. I'm Melissa." She giggled as the words spilled out of her mouth like warm honey. I smiled, pointing down to my dorm monitor badge as her cheeks burned red.

"Oh, I didn't know we had a new monitor. I was *very* close with the old one." Again, every word was pinned on seduction. Her breasts heaved in her paint-by-number shirt. One foot fidgeted with the other as she raked her manicured nails through her hair.

I let her continue. It was a child's game. A real woman could seduce any man, but not a vampire. Although, I'm sure Nefertiti could have. Living or dead, she could have moved the oceans. Her eyes had burned like the center of the sea in a storm. I missed those magnificent purple eyes.

I coughed, looking away and feigning embarrassment. I shouldn't toy with my food. Again, why was I so wrapped up in nostalgia and comparison? Meaningless comparisons about beauty and a life long dead. I should just eat her and find Shea.

Now, I'd done it. The whole swarm followed Melissa over: five more large-breasted, tan, flirtatious women. Another one stepped forward, her shorts just an inch above the curve of her cheeks, leaving little to the imagination. "Don't let Melissa embarrass you. I'm Audrey. If you didn't guess already, we're the main bitches in the cheerleading squad. You don't seem like the kind of nerd who would be a dorm monitor. You're too hot." She winked, unashamed of her brash nature.

My eyes constricted, and like the mindless bunnies they were, all their mouths dropped open. "Now Audrey, that's not a nice thing to say. I like being a dorm monitor." They all leaned in as I spoke. My mind was blank. I couldn't decide what to fill their fragile brains with.

I peered at all of them at once: father issues, competitive mothers, self-worth fed by false gods in Victoria's Secret catalogs, boob jobs at young ages before their bodies had fully grown.

The saddest case was Melissa. I looked deeper into her eyes. She was a copy of all the other girls. She'd end up just like her mother before her, and then she'd have two more daughters just like her. Over and over through her bloodline, the mindlessness would continue. Lucian the Merciful. I took her hand and spoke gently, compelling the other girls.

"You don't know where Melissa went. The last you saw her, she was getting drunk with some boy named Adnachiel . . . no . . . you'd know him by his mortal name: Aidan. You saw her with *Aidan* at a party. If anyone knows where she is, it's him. And you feel like he's a liar. At least, that's what you'll tell the police when they come looking. He's hiding something. You want to make his life hell while he's here in college. I'm the new dorm monitor and you want to help me, anytime I need it. You trust me without fear."

They nodded, and one of them drooled slightly. I jumped into the sky with Melissa. It was too quick for their human eyes to register the strong breeze that shook the trees beside them. And night could play tricks with the senses after all.

Melissa struggled for breath in the thinning atmosphere, but her eyes remained fixed on mine, full of lust and servitude. "Melissa, such a sad life. Do you want me to end it for you and give you bliss?" I let her regain control of her mind for a moment.

She saw the earth below and screamed, squirming from my grip. I watched her fall a thousand feet. When I caught her, I wrapped her in my arms. She cried into my chest and I felt a pang of guilt. Lucian the Merciful indeed. *It's not nice to play with your food. Just finish it.*

I clenched my jaw over her soft neck. She flinched for a moment, but I took the time to fill her body with a deep, aching sort of orgasmic pleasure. Her limbs trembled as she peed herself. Something turned my stomach. Was it boredom? The taste of silicone from a leaking bag in her breast? Whatever it was, I just couldn't finish. All I could think about was Shea. Why was the Vessel a woman this time?

In this generation, they were nothing more than household pets. If men were modern slaves, women were the slaves of slaves. There was a time when they'd fought for something. Not too long ago they'd burned bras and demanded to be astronauts and physicists . . . now they wanted to be mommies.

The anti–birth control propaganda had created another generation of slaves. It was a simple tactic I'd seen the ruling class use throughout centuries: keep the numbers at the bottom of the pyramid large. It was called a *working* class. And that's what they did, until they died. Such servitude and breeding was all done in the pursuit of wealth. It was the carrot held by those in power, driving the masses to their graves.

Wealth: a sickening disease that turned humans against themselves.

Melissa was just a plastic toy caught in the system. Marketing worked. Imperfections were now damnations that had to be paid for with blood and credit cards, anything to fill the void of real self-worth.

I laughed as she moaned in bliss, still alive.

Suddenly, I shook her hard. An unknown fury began to radiate from my bones, my inner thoughts boiling to the surface.

"Don't you see what they've done to you? To all of you? Are you that mindless? Imperfections are the beauty of life! And all life was made from a mutation in genes! Do you really want to remain an amoeba? Is that what women are now: replications, empty dolls? If your only desire is to be slaves to a ruling class, if that's what mankind has become, you deserve to be harvested and fed on like the cattle you are by Caelius himself!"

I let her body drop. This time she didn't scream, still wrapped in the pleasure of my mouth. When it thudded, dust encircled her like an iris. I shook my head. What had come over me? "Disappointing Lucian . . . and wasteful." I quickly landed in the mush that was Melissa and blood splattered everywhere.

It was too close to the campus. They would find this wreckage. I smiled, biting my own lip. "It's unwise to top up and use my powers. I'll just need to eat again." I kicked a piece of her pelvis bone. "But you have to do what you have to do. You made this mess . . . now clean it up." I gritted my teeth. I'd have sand coming out of every hole for days. I spat her lingering blood out as I felt my eyes burn.

My body rose, a sandstorm mounting behind me. "Remember this little move, Moses? Lock your windows, kiddies, and pray to your gods. It's going to be a dark night." There was nothing like a small plague of locusts to cover up a miss-feed.

Their buzzing was heard miles off. The ground shook as swarms of insects covered the night sky with the blackness of their large bodies. They hurtled mercilessly toward the campus, along with dust and anything else the tornado-like wind drew in by the flapping of their wings.

An inch. An inch of dirt and locusts would dissolve Melissa.

My little friends could carry the bones away and feast in the canyons.

It wasn't a smart move. Taking a pawn with a rook. I might be revealing my power too soon to Adnachiel. He didn't know how much I'd grown over the last five hundred years, but he'd seen this move before. I smiled, unable to filter the rage as the swarms crawled onto my body, taking over the school. He'd asked me to use this power once, and I had, out of sheer loyalty.

I heard all of their rushed footsteps as the meat-bags ran. I heard the screams. Now, I felt like I was in Egypt again. To think, in the end they'd blamed all those plagues on God and not Moses. The bible was not the most accurate form of history. They talked about Moses's power, but they missed the part about being helped by a vampire and a beast. And they missed the very greatness of the man himself. At that time, there'd been nothing Aidan, Moses and I couldn't accomplish for the betterment of all mankind.

His real name was Adnachiel, but during Moses's time, we'd called him Aidan. It had been brotherly-like affection. We'd been so bonded then. And now, after all these centuries, the family he'd been born into had actually given him that name. I hoped it pained him every time his mother stroked his hair and called him the same name Moses had gasped in his last breaths. I hoped it reminded him of his betrayal. I'd hate that name and that beast forever for what he'd done.

I refocused on the present as power surged through me, the pain in my chest stirring old wounds savagely patched by the passing of centuries. Things that went bump in the night had been more readily accepted and seen back then. Today's locust infestation would have to be scientifically explained. Global warming maybe?

Caelius wouldn't be pleased. This kind of exposure wasn't done anymore. I was tired of sitting on my hands, only using my gifts once or twice every five hundred years, all so that Caelius could have his numbers quietly increased from the shadows, preparing for his final release from the cage. Caelius only wanted the world to burn if he was the one ruling it.

I had only turned seven men into vampires. Still, those had been particular circumstances and unique humans I'd selected. But that had been a long time ago. I hadn't turned anyone in close to five hundred years. I hadn't been tempted. Only after I took the Vessel and battled with Aidan did I feel so compelled, hollowed out, and desperate for camaraderie. It was a pattern that repeated, despite my arrogant protests of needing no one.

Only one human could have broken the routine. It was a shame women didn't survive the transformation. There'd been a brilliant botanist a hundred years ago: Helena Madison. She'd deserved to have more time. The things she could have done for this planet—that might have been exciting to see, to stay alive for. Still, she would have seen the world become this.

Why a woman? This Shea Harper. I'd assumed the Vessels were only male, like us. But to come in this form, this fragile form . . . something was different. I could sense it. Let Caelius rage. If the game was different this round, I might as well dust off some of my old favorite tricks, show this Shea what she was in for.

I heard their voices, all of their mindless, fear-driven voices coddled inside buildings and cars, even over the beautiful storm of locust wings. I continued to let them crawl over my body like old friends, touching my skin. A girl nearby didn't make it inside in time. She was suffocating as the winged creatures crawled into her mouth.

I sighed. My arms dropped as I calmed the storm. The insects scattered, flying back into the night they'd been called from. I looked at the thick layer of dirt and bug carcasses covering the mess that was once Melissa.

Lucian the Merciful indeed.

I stepped on a large, juicy one and it crunched under my black eel-skin shoes. I breathed in the dirt and the fear. It had been so long since mass terror rippled in the air at my presence. It was like Pompeii. The panic alone was thick enough to feed from. The power sharpened my senses. I could smell her. I hadn't noticed before, but her sweat . . . it was almost sugared, like a foreign nectar I had never tasted.

Perhaps I would taste it now. When I was charged like this, humans melted at my very presence. I leapt quickly into the air, landing in an alley behind a small coffee shop. She was drinking water. I smelled him too: Adnachiel.

His scent changed every time. Now he reeked like all the other boys at college, no doubt covered in expensive cologne. He did his best to blend in. But I knew the beast that was underneath.

I walked casually to the front and stepped in. The noise was the first thing that hit me. All of the voices were frenzied about the storm and dead locusts outside. My presence calmed the atmosphere. I heightened my sexual energy. It was like a magnet in the room. Men and women stared at my form as I walked by.

I ordered a tall coffee, black. A perky boy with curly hair left the register and insisted on giving it to me himself, bypassing the other employees. A line formed behind me, but they didn't seem to mind the wait. I looked back, casting a small side smile. That was enough for them. They laughed uncomfortably, nodding, trying to mutter something about how good the coffee was here.

The curly-haired barista returned. His hand shook as he gave me an extra-large cup, on the house. The hot liquid sloshed and burned my hand, to his horror. I reached up and grabbed one of his curls, pulling his soft, newborn-like face to mine. The room quieted further. They were all holding their breath, hoping to see something more.

I patted his cheek, whispering in his ear. "Relax. You didn't hurt me. But later tonight, you'll wait for me in the alley. I'll need something else to drink then. You'll tell no one."

He nodded, smiling from ear to ear. I casually looked toward Shea and Adnachiel. Nothing. She didn't even turn. She'd missed the whole display. I laughed, letting my hold of the room go. The bustle begun again, everyone asking about the bugs. I sneered, walking past the line. Turning the empty chair next to her backward, I plopped down, my legs spread casually open as I leaned forward.

Her eyes caught mine, but her mouth didn't unlock with desire. She was genuinely angry that I'd joined them. I straightened my back, coughing as I took a sip of the scalding liquid. I let my smile peel back farther, but it seemed to aggravate her even more. "I just popped in for a break. I've been running around campus, trying to make sure everyone's okay. Freak storm, right? How are you guys holding up?"

"We're fine," she spat, turning her body toward Adnachiel.

I took a moment, trying to figure out my next move. A tall woman with long legs invited herself to the table, sitting obnoxiously close to me. She laughed, using the same line I'd just used on Shea.

"Hey guys, whatcha talking about? I'm Kristy, number 150 in your dorm, and we are all super freaked about the bugs! Gross, right?" She shook her head, setting her hand on my thigh. Shea and I both eyed that hand.

I picked it up as if it were diseased and returned it to her. I could easily have compelled Kristy away from us, but Shea had noticed my eyes constrict before. It wasn't worth the risk.

I gritted my teeth. At least this paper doll had helped me realize how rusty my pickup line was. If I wanted to charm Shea and not have this be another smash-and-grab like in the past, I'd need another angle.

Kristy was undaunted by the rejected flirtation. "So, the word that's spread around campus is you're the new hot dorm monitor. All us cheerleaders are talking about it. There's this party tonight, I'd love you to come with me." There was that hand again. This time it reached deeper and squeezed, her long nails leaving marks in my thigh.

I eyed Adnachiel, who seemed bemused. I wondered how he tolerated this sort of mortal and if his tastes had changed along with mine over the centuries. To my knowledge, he hadn't loved anyone after I'd killed Mailid decades ago.

Kristy looked briefly at the other two. "Oh, you can totally invite your friends . . . just as long as you're there." She laced her other small talon through my dark brown hair, now more wildly tossed than usual.

She grabbed a handful tight. "Look at this shaggy scruff. Did you get caught in the storm?" She inched her way closer for a kiss. That was enough.

I stuck up my hand and her face landed in it. I slowly pushed her back. "Listen . . . Kristy, was it? I don't know you, or your little friends. If I liked you, you'd know. These bold advances of yours reek of how many men you've let take you. You have nothing for me that I want. You can take your plastic eyelashes and bat them somewhere else."

It was hard to stop myself. I was furious that she had interrupted my conversation with Shea. I used to not mind cheap women throwing themselves at me. But when it was all the time, when everyone could be so easily drawn in, it became shallow and empty. It added to the loneliness aching in my hollow bones.

I looked down, closing my eyes. I didn't open them again until I heard her retreat out the door, the small bell jingling as she passed. I couldn't let my eyes show their rage. I took a few deep breaths. When they opened, my gaze fell on Shea's soft face.

I sighed despite myself, my brow furrowed. She still looked angry. She leaned back in her chair and crossed her arms, looking at me squarely. "That was a bit harsh, don't you think? It takes a lot for a girl to approach a guy."

Before I could rationalize, the words came rolling out like hot lava. "Do you *think* it takes a lot for a girl like that to approach a guy? Really, Shea? I don't think it does." I leaned closer to her, my anger boiling over. She winced slightly, but I couldn't stop myself, just to breathe her in a little deeper.

"I've been stalked, chased, and had trash like that throw itself at me for as long as I can remember. They don't want *me*,

Shea. Not what I really am. They're just addicts, addicted to the pleasure they think I can give them. They want this body, and their fake beliefs in what I am, and that's fine.

"Sometimes I want to play, but it's nothing. It means nothing. Girls like Kristy will breed, and with each generation, there'll be more of them. Soon they'll swarm just like the locusts outside. Then, the last beautiful, unique spark of humanity will die out along with the inventors, freethinkers, and radicals. Perfection is a diseased idea that has infected mankind." I wanted to spit out my own disgust for what humanity had become . . . for what I had become.

She leaned so far back in her chair, I was sure there were groove marks on her spine. I sat, truly embarrassed for the first time in ages. What was I saying? I was always in control. It couldn't be the desert alone that was making me act this way.

Something was off.

"I'm sorry. I don't know what came over me. Just . . . people like that, that's all I've encountered for so long. I mean, since I started working here. It got to me, but that was no reason to . . . I . . . I apologize," I stuttered.

This had gone horribly wrong. Was I that out of practice with having a real conversation with someone? It had been a while, at least a hundred years since I'd found anyone worth talking to. Still, this was humiliating. I didn't know if her face was more shocked by my venomous words about humans, or my apology after. What was worse was the smirk that hadn't left Adnachiel's face since I'd sat down. I should address that and put the pup in his place.

"So, Adnachiel, what did you think about that storm of

locusts? Remind you of anything . . . or anyone?" Now my smile returned as his faded.

He literally growled, scraping the table with his nails as he spoke. "My name is . . . Aidan. Just as familiar and easy to say as the word *locust*."

I scoffed. "Is it *easy* to say? After what you did to him?"

If it had been a cold day, I'd have seen a stream of hot air blowing out of his flaring nostrils as his eyes bulged. "Listen, this table is for two *friends*. Not for some freak with obvious daddy issues. Why don't you draw some black eyeliner under your eyes and go tell your sad story somewhere else?"

Good move.

Should I play the wounded guest, or should I just grab her now and forget my plan and see what strength Adnachiel had in this new form? I paused, letting the anticipation build. "Just trying to make conversation. You and Shea don't seem as mindless as the other kids on campus. I thought we might have something in common . . . *Aidan*." He almost winced, hearing me spit his endearing nickname out like a curse. I had to admit, I winced as well. I hadn't called him by that name since Moses.

I swallowed hard and continued my ruse. "And Shea, about my eyes this morning, I'd like to apologize for that as well. When you asked if I'd been drugged, I was shocked. I actually went to Rapid Care. It turns out there's been a new drug around campus. One of the cheerleaders gave me a drink when I first arrived. I think she slipped it in, like a roofie. I'm new to the school and wasn't expecting that kind of welcome. That's also why I came off a little harsh to Kristy. Although, I do stick by everything I said."

I casually stood, surveying the air outside, taking a long sip of coffee. "I hope we don't have any more strange weather. There's blood in the water after all." I eyed Adnachiel one last time, whose hands were still frozen in claws on the table. He'd love to rip my skin off . . . just as much as I'd love to see him try.

"Shea, be careful. There are enough male Kristys out there, too. Don't take any drinks from anyone you don't know." My cold stare stayed on Adnachiel. "Or from anyone *you think you know* for that matter." I coughed, wiping dust from my black shirt. "Better get cleaned up and continue checking on everyone."

Without giving her another glance, I walked to the door, tossing my coffee in the trash on the way out.

I casually made my way to the back of the shop, my thirst burning. I remembered how food used to taste. Now it tasted like water. Everything did. It all had no flavor. Candies, drinks, meats . . . all of it was nothing. The only thing my taste buds picked up was blood. Again, why was I reminiscing about things dead, like my old senses? I was so much more than all of that now.

I leaned heavily against the brick wall before turning the corner. I could smell the shampoo the young curly-haired boy had used this morning. I could feel his perspiration covering his milky skin as if it was my own. Would I really trade these sensations, the power, all for one sip of coffee? No.

But what about sugars, salts, and spices? My only variation was the different blood types. But at most, that ranged from sixteen groups. With food, you could make a thousand dishes, and they'd all taste intrinsically different.

I licked my lips and my body surged with anticipation as my fangs grew. I knew his blood would be sweet enough for

46

me: B-positive if I wasn't mistaken. The air was still, the perfect moment to strike. But I didn't move. I froze.

I should take him. Now that I'd pushed, who knew what Adnachiel would do? I doubted he'd pull out his queen or his bishop yet . . . but he might. In the next few days, I should feed as often as possible.

The curly boy was wringing his hands. His body language was wide-open and easy to read. He looked about seventeen. His accent gave away that he wasn't from the city but the South. The sweetness in his voice was undercut by the small traces of pain, a fractured life that he couldn't hide. I could imagine. It must have been hard, being homosexual in what was no doubt a small town. The scars on his hand and upper arms were old. He had received the blows in childhood, no doubt.

Still, he had freed himself and moved away. His earlier experiences hadn't broken him. Even a cold monster like me could feel the warmth of his radiating open heart.

My stomach turned. I knew better than to use my heightened perception before I fed. It was easier to let myself assume that he was like everyone else here. Now I had soured the meal. My palms sweated, but I controlled the sensation. I had gone hungry before. I was not like these new vampires who had to scratch every time that itch made their skin crawl.

It was painful resisting a feed, more painful than anything I'd experienced in human form . . . but not impossible. At this point, I was more controlled by my own desires than the blood that churned in my ancient veins.

My lips moved slowly as I spoke to the boy's mind. "Leave. Go to your dorm. Never again listen to any voice that says to meet you in a dark, secluded location. You're smarter than that. You will live in the light. You'll move as soon as possible out of this hick-area to a more progressive city where you'll meet a good-hearted man like you . . . and you'll find happiness. You'll have a good life. You'll stay away from shadows and anything or anyone that smells, feels, or looks like the man who came in earlier and told you to meet him here."

Quickly, the boy shook his head. As if coming out of a fog, he turned the corner, passing me without a second look, and headed toward the dorm. Another embarrassment. What was this, Lucian the Merciful again? I knew what I really was. No sense changing. That ship had sailed thousands of years ago . . . with Moses, and before that, with Nefertiti.

I should have just taken him. I bit my own tongue, letting my body slouch to the ground as I rested my palms on my eyes. Why couldn't I get my head in the game? I was acting like it was another century passing, waiting for Adnachiel. What was it about Shea that threw me?

A college kid with a large letterman jacket walked by and tossed some quarters at my face. "Buy yourself a new life, you homeless trash," he muttered, laughing to himself.

I lunged and buried my hands through his chest, cracking his rib cage open. I ripped out his heart and swallowed it whole. He fell to the ground, lifeless. I leaned toward his face, wiping the blood from my mouth. "Who's trash now?" With one hand, I pulled his body over my head and threw it into the open dumpster as I lumbered toward the football field behind the café.

I compelled a handful of maimed, grounded locusts, forcing them to crawl their way toward his body. It would no doubt be their last meal.

 CHAPTER 3
SHEA

The ego on that guy! What did he say? *They're just addicts . . . They want this body . . .* Dude! What a narcissist! Lucian was hot, but not that hot! I wanted to high-five Aidan when he told him to draw on some black eyeliner. Lucian was definitely a bit on the emo side. His apology had seemed sincere though. I still felt a burning hatred for Frank biting me on my first day. So, if he was telling the truth and he really had been drugged, maybe I should cut him some slack.

Ugh!

No. He was a dick and I needed to stick to that! This was how *bad boys* did it. They were total a-holes to everyone except their prey. Then once they had their prize, they'd treat them just as crappy as they did everyone else. What on earth would make me think he wouldn't treat me exactly the way he'd treated Kristy? Granted, the girl was coming on strong, but holy cow! Lucian was so cruel. And he had made a point to say he stood by *everything* he had said. *Everything.* That included his mean-boy remarks to Kristy.

Nope. Still on my shit-list.

Aidan and I were walking to our dorm. We didn't take our usual way back because he insisted that we stick to the lighted path. He said it was safer and made some comment about people lurking in the shadows or something. I guessed my encounter with Frank had freaked him out, too. I didn't argue. I just wrapped my arm around his and let him lead the way. It took a bit longer than it should have, but we arrived at our dorm unscathed.

Walking me to my door, Aidan leaned down and lifted my chin with his hand. "You okay? That Lucian guy didn't scare you, did he?"

"Scare me? No. Annoy me? Yes," I said with a roll of my eyes.

This appeared to worry him because his forehead got all crinkly. "Annoy? That sounds like a girl fighting the urge to like someone."

Did it? I guessed if I used every romantic comedy ever written as a reference, the word *annoy* was usually followed twenty minutes later by true love. This was definitely not the case with Lucian. "You've been watching too many John Hughes movies." I reached up and hugged Aidan. "Good night."

His hug was a little tighter than normal, but I didn't mind. It was actually quite comforting after the last two days. He whispered in my ear, "Good night, Shea. If you need anything, I'm two doors down."

"Really? I had no idea." I pulled away with a smile and hit his chest playfully, but when I saw that his worry crinkles hadn't gone away, I looked at him seriously. "You're the first person I'd call for anything, dufus."

Aidan smiled at that. He walked down the hall and entered his abode with a small wave. I waved back and went inside my room.

Apparently, Gerta was still partying because she wasn't there. I took my second shower of the day. For some reason, my run-in with Lucian made me feel dirty. Like I had let him manipulate me, and now he thought he had gotten away with it. Things like that always bugged me.

I remembered when I was in high school and Paul Butters had talked me into drinking a beer. I had made it clear to everyone in our small class that I planned on never drinking. I'd felt pretty strongly about it. I didn't like losing control and alcohol epitomized *losing control*. But I'd wanted Paul to like me, so I drank it anyway. For weeks, Paul had bragged about the fact that he'd talked *the pure Shea Harper* into drinking. I'd felt so crappy. Like I had let myself down. Like I had let a boy manipulate me into doing something I genuinely didn't want to do.

Of course, it helped when Aidan threatened bodily harm to Paul unless he stopped talking about the incident. Don't get me wrong, everyone loved Aidan. How could you not? But when it came to messing with me, everyone was scared stiff. Needless to say, Paul never teased me again.

I was feeling like I had back then. Like Lucian had convinced me to do something I didn't want to do. He'd made me have an iota of sympathy for him. But he was an egomaniac liar who probably saw me as a challenge. The girl who wouldn't fall all over his every word. I had to keep reminding myself that I was no more than a conquest to him.

It depressed me for some reason.

I put on my most comfortable jammies and snuggled deep into my down comforter. Maybe a good night's rest would cheer me up.

***

Okay. I was definitely in dreamland. The forest was really green. It was too bright and colorful to be real. Even the bark of the trees was a light copper-red and the trunks were at least the size of my car.

"We're in the redwoods," a voice said behind me.

I turned around to see Lucian standing in the shadow of one of the giant trees.

Great. I was dreaming about a-hole-boy now. I tried to control the dream by making Aidan appear to kick this guy's butt, but dream-Aidan was a no-show.

"You can make him leave now," I said to my subconscious. "I love the place, just not him in it."

"Why? Can you sense what I am?" Lucian was in front of me in the blink of an eye.

"A jerk? Yes. And wake-up call: a rock could tell that." Maybe this was my brain's way of telling him off and relieving all that stress from earlier this evening.

Lucian tilted his head. From the look in his eyes, my words stung. "It's deeper than that." He brushed his hand against my cheek.

Even in a dream, I felt every cell in my body tingle. Stop it! I wouldn't let this guy win!

I smacked his hand away. "Keep your hands to yourself. And stay out of my dreams!"

***

I awoke drenched in sweat. What was that? I hated the fact that I'd dreamt about Lucian. It was Aidan's fault. If he hadn't planted the *romance* bomb in my head, I never would have given Lucian a second thought, except to avoid him like the plague. He seemed to bring those with him anyway: locusts heralding his entrance. I knew that was unfair, but it somehow felt fitting in the moment.

I looked over at my clock and hoped it was morning. There was nothing worse than thinking you'd slept the whole night through only to find you were asleep for an hour. I was both relieved and slightly annoyed to see it was five in the morning. Technically, I had been asleep for seven hours, which was just enough time to make me feel rested but too early to make me want to get up at five in the freaking morning!

I sat there staring at the ceiling for another twenty minutes until I finally decided to get up. Gerta was sleeping soundly on the bed next to mine. I tried to be as quiet as she must have been when she'd come in last night since she hadn't woken me. Grabbing my running clothes, I quickly dressed in sweat shorts and a tank, then laced up my tennies. I put my dorm key on a chain and placed it around my neck. I winced slightly when the metal hit my bandage, just a reminder of the crazies who roamed the planet.

Carefully, I exited my dorm room and walked out into the morning breeze. It was still dark. Sunrise wasn't for another half hour or so, but it felt good to breathe in the semi-cool air. I stuck to the lighted pathways since I could hear Aidan's lecture-voice scolding me: "*Stay where people can see you.*"

As I ran, I had a sudden burst of energy, as if I could take on the world. I knew it was just the endorphins from running, but either way, it was amazing.

Every muscle cried out in joy as I ran faster and faster through the campus. It was exhilarating. I felt alive.

"Shea?" I heard my name being called behind me.

I stopped, breathless from running, and turned to see Lucian standing near a tree. It was so close to my dream I almost thought I was dreaming all over again. But when he walked toward me, I knew I was completely awake.

And completely defensive.

"Still up from a night of partying, are we?" I was surprised to hear how much judgment was in my tone.

Lucian simply stared at me, as if he couldn't decide if it was worth pursuing any type of conversation. "I'm afraid we've gotten off on the wrong foot. It's my fault really."

"We can at least agree on something," I said. Wow. I was rivaling him in meanness at this point. But my instincts told me there was more to this guy. After the Frank debacle, I planned on listening to my instincts from now on.

"So much hostility. I'm not sure I deserve it," Lucian continued. "Can we start over?" He was a few feet away from me now. His eyes were filled with so many different emotions—insecurity, anger, confusion—I couldn't tell which one was real. The boy apparently didn't know what to think of me.

"Just stay where you are, thank you very much." I put my

hand up for emphasis. "I don't know what your obsession is with trying to be my friend, but reality check, there's something about you I don't trust." I crossed my arms. "Or like." Harsh, but true.

"And I want to know why. I admit, it fascinates me." Lucian looked at me with a quizzical expression. I could tell it really *did* puzzle him.

"Well, you're going to have to ponder that one on your own time. I'm in the middle of a run."

And I was off.

I couldn't believe how rude I had been. I was never like that, even to people I couldn't stand. The weird part was the fact that I really didn't hate Lucian. Sure, he was obnoxious. Sure, he'd been a jerk to Kristy. But he had been nice to me. I guessed I felt like I had to be the defender of everyone he had wronged, as if somehow treating him the way he treated others would be a good wake-up call.

I decided to head back to my dorm and cut my jog short. The Lucian confrontation had thrown off my whole Chi. The more I thought about it, the more it irritated me. What were the odds that I kept running into him? Was he following me? Maybe the guy who claimed *he'd been stalked his whole life* was actually a stalker himself. For some reason the thought didn't scare me as much as I thought it would, or *should*. It wasn't that he seemed harmless, it was that he seemed genuinely befuddled at the fact that I wasn't fawning all over him.

I shook Lucian from my head as I saw Aidan jogging straight toward me from our dorm.

"Out for a run?" he asked with a smile as he stopped in front of me. I could tell he was trying very hard to sound relaxed, but those darn worry crinkles on his forehead gave him away every time.

"Yes, *Dad*. I brought my mace and rape whistle with me." Now that I'd joked about it, that wasn't such a bad idea. The thought of spraying Lucian with mace gave me a perverse satisfaction.

"Did I say anything? I just asked if you went for a run," Aidan responded defensively.

"But I could see your worried-face."

"Can you blame me? You were *bitten* on the neck by some vampire wannabe. I can't help it. It's my job to protect you." The way he said that made me pause. He didn't sound like the boy I'd grown up with. He sounded like he was a guard on duty and I was the princess who needed protecting.

"Your *job*? I thought I was your friend." I was kidding, but something in my tone must have made him feel bad because he looked upset.

"Shea. You know I didn't mean it like that. You're my best friend—" Aidan began.

"I was joking. Geez, lighten up. And as much as I love having you as my personal guard dog, I *am* capable of taking care of myself. I know it didn't look like it, but that Frank guy was about to book before you got there."

I thought back to that moment: Frank was biting me and my eyes burned, then I saw a flash of light. The guy had been freaked. How could I have forgotten that? With Aidan coming in and throwing Frank into a tree, I had pushed it from my brain. What *had* happened? I was about to spill everything to Aidan when something held me back. I didn't know why, but some

57

inner voice was telling me to keep quiet. It went against every instinct, since he had been a part of my life since birth. But it was so powerful I listened. I kept my mouth shut.

"I don't know, Shea. That guy was strong." Aidan didn't sound convinced.

He was right, the guy had been like a steel wall, but I knew what I'd seen. After my eyes had burned, Frank had been afraid. As in terrified. What could he have seen in me that would scare a guy like that? A thought to consider on my own. In the meantime, I had to play it cool. "I'm telling you, Frank was about to leave. Now, can we drop it?"

Aidan took a moment to respond. I was surprised when he pulled me in for a tight hug. "Of course. I'm sorry," he mumbled in my ear.

"You know, for a bronzed Adonis like yourself, you certainly are a sap." I smiled as I pulled away.

He grinned back and shook his head. "Sun's up. Breakfast?"

I nodded. "This time I'm going for the good stuff: chai tea with a shot of espresso."

He raised an eyebrow. "I might have to try me one of those."

***

The next two weeks were a lot more mundane than I thought they would be. The only excitement was when the campus police came to question Aidan about some missing girl named Melissa. But when Gerta and I gave Aidan a solid alibi, they backed off.

My classes weren't as great as I had hoped. I was rudely awakened to the fact that everything felt just like high school. I guess I hadn't really known what to expect, but almost nodding off in Precalculus hadn't been it.

I met a couple of new people, but no one special. I pretty much hung out with Aidan most of my free time. We would take walks around campus when the sun was about to go down since the temperature was slightly cooler. He'd always want to get back to the dorm before nightfall though. I seriously thought the boy was getting a phobia of the dark.

Gerta was okay. She tried to rope me into a mani-pedi day, but I managed to squirm my way out of that one. Not that I didn't appreciate a good mani-pedi, I just didn't want to spend the day with Gerta gossiping about all the campus drama. Too many people sleeping around, breaking hearts, and at least one full-out girl-catfight every few days.

Nope. Not for me. I was as drama-free as you could get.

Aidan and I pretty much hung out in his dorm room every night watching movies. Gerta was convinced that we were an item no matter how many times I told her otherwise. I realized most people thought the same thing, looking at us like we were adorable puppies. I didn't mind. Even though I knew I didn't have those kinds of feelings for him, we were still pretty possessive as far as friendships went.

The one thing I couldn't confess to anyone was the fact that I was kind of upset I hadn't seen or heard from Lucian the entire two weeks. He must have finally gotten the hint. But now that I hadn't seen him, I felt a little guilty about my offensive behavior. I knew I shouldn't feel that way, but the people-pleaser-nice-girl part of me wanted to find him and apologize.

There was no way in hell I would tell Aidan that I even

remotely thought of Lucian in any way, shape, or form. He had made it quite clear how he felt about him. So I kept my crazy-guilt-obsession to myself.

I was walking back from art class where I'd had to sketch a naked dude. Not exactly a comfortable moment. I hated admitting how much of a prude I was, but I had never seen a boy naked before.

Pictures, yes, as in biology class, but never in person. The teacher had made him pose lying on the floor with his arms outstretched. From where I'd been sitting, I was staring at a full frontal. I didn't think my face would stop being red for at least two more days. I just hoped no one had noticed.

I was about to walk into my domicile when I decided to see if Aidan was home yet. Knocking on his door, I waited a few minutes before giving up. I went into my room and plopped my backpack on the desk.

Gerta walked out of the bathroom in a robe with a towel wrapped around her head. "You're not hanging with your boyfriend?"

"Aidan is not my boyfriend," I said for the millionth time.

Gerta gave me a knowing look. "Of course he isn't. You keep telling yourself that." She smiled.

There was a knock on the door.

"Speak of the devil . . . " Gerta laughed.

"You don't know that's Aidan," I replied more defensively than I'd intended.

"Who is it?" Gerta called at the door with a grin.

"Aidan," came the muffled sound of bad timing.

I didn't make eye contact with Gerta as I opened the door.

"Let's get out of here." I took his hand and left the room.

But I could hear Gerta's words as we walked down the hall. "Have fun, you two!"

He stopped me. "What was that all about?"

I kept pulling him outside toward the walkway. "Nothing. She's just giving me a hard time." I paused and then blurted, "Everyone thinks we're a couple."

Instead of shock or repulsion or any other reaction I had imagined, he simply shrugged. "Yeah, I've been getting that too."

I self-consciously let go of his hand and looked up at him. "Does it bother you?"

"Not really. We know how we feel about each other. I don't really care what other people think." He smiled down at me. "Does it bother you?"

Did it? It was too complicated for me to say. But I didn't want to leave him hanging or hurt his feelings, so I playfully slugged him in the arm. "Nah. I just didn't want other people to mess up what we have." Saying it out loud made me realize that was exactly why it bugged me. If anything (and that was a big if) were to happen between Aidan and me, I wanted it to be a natural progression, not shoved down our throats because everyone was pressuring us to date.

"Good," he said, then placed his hands on my arms, looking me in the eye. "Don't freak out, but I think we should be social tonight."

Social? That sounded horrible! "You mean hanging out with other people?"

Aidan laughed, and it made his whole face light up. He really was a cutie. "Yes, I know. What could I possibly be thinking? But

61

Shea, it'd be good for you. There's a party at the Pillar House."

"I'm still healing from the last party." I touched the small scabs from Frank's bite two weeks ago. It was almost completely healed, but the psychological wound had grown exponentially. The thought of a party made me feel physically ill.

"Come here." He brought me in for a hug. Even though his chest was as hard as a rock, it was still my soft spot to land. Aidan hugs were the best hugs.

"You really want me to go to this party, don't you?" I mumbled into his chest.

He pulled away slightly so we still had our arms around each other but he could see my face. "Don't let some jerk ruin your whole college experience. We're supposed to have fun, get drunk, and party at least . . . three times before we graduate."

I laughed. "Three times, huh? You just come up with that number randomly or is there scientific research involved?"

"Definitely scientific research." He grinned. "So, you coming?"

I pushed him away with a playful grunt. "Yes, you big doof. But I swear, if that Frank guy is there—"

"If Frank is there, I'll kill him."

He was smiling as if he were joking, but the way he said it made the hairs on my arms rise. I didn't think he was capable of killing anyone, but in that moment, I was actually scared for Frank.

"Or maybe just call the cops," I responded.

"Or that." He nudged me affectionately. "I'll be knocking at your door at nine."

I mock-saluted him and we walked back to the dorm.

Nine o'clock came a lot faster than I'd expected. Probably because I desperately didn't want to go to this party. Gerta had already gone to some other shindig she'd been invited to, so I only had Aidan as my security blanket for the evening's festivities.

He and I walked to the Pillar House, which was about a mile off campus, so it was quite a trek at this time of night. I felt completely safe with him, but I couldn't help looking over my shoulder every few minutes or so. I hated that the whole experience with Frank had sent me into paranoia-zone, but it had only been two weeks and I hadn't bounced back yet.

The party was certainly hopping by the time we arrived. It looked like a giant hand had taken a heaping scoop of people and stuffed them in the house.

Aidan carefully led me inside. He was being overly protective tonight, sweetly so. Once we were in the mayhem, I found that I wasn't as claustrophobic as I'd been at the other party. People stood around in tight groups as opposed to the shoulder-to-shoulder action like before.

"You want something to drink?" Aidan asked over the noise of the music and crowd.

"Maybe some water," I replied.

He rolled his eyes but didn't argue with me. We walked by a set of stairs going up to the second floor and he gently placed me on the fifth step. "Stay here where you can see everything. I'm getting those drinks."

Before he left, Aidan smiled at me. "You going to be okay?"

"I'm fine, geez. It's not like I'm socially inept."

"Inept? Isn't that an SAT word?" he joked.

"Just get me my water," I said as I moved all the way to the railing so that people could still use the stairs if they needed to.

He walked into the maw of the party and disappeared from view.

I loved that Aidan had scanned the whole house and picked the most strategic spot for me to sit. I really could see if anyone was coming toward me. He was doing his best to make me feel as safe as possible.

"Hey." A familiar voice came from behind.

My heart jumped into my throat.

Lucian.

My magic spy-spot didn't work as well as I thought it would because he seemed to come out of nowhere. He walked down the few steps that separated us and sat down next to me.

"Mind if I sit with you?" he asked.

I felt so horrible about the way I had treated him before, I instantly nodded my head. "You kind of disappeared," I admitted.

"I didn't think my company was welcome," Lucian confessed carefully. He looked neither arrogant nor mad, just confused.

"Yeah, sorry about that. I took out all my issues on you. You just rubbed me the wrong way, I guess." Was that mean too? I couldn't control my words with this guy, and for some reason my words *wanted* to bite.

"I'm not used to that." He looked like he was trying to look vulnerable but failing miserably.

"See? It's not what you're saying, it's the way you say it. Admitting that you're not used to rubbing people the wrong way is fine, but you say it like you're the Queen of Sheba or something. Like everyone has always worshiped the ground you've walked on, and now you can't handle the fact that some lowly plebe doesn't like you." Wow. This apology was going fantastic. And I couldn't seem to stop. "You said at the café that you've been stalked your whole life? What are you, like twenty? Did little Rosy in kindergarten follow you home after school?" I suppressed a laugh by covering my mouth with my hand. The visual image of a five-year-old Lucian all broody and egotistical thinking he was being stalked by a kindergartner was somehow amusing.

And what was that?

Lucian actually cracked a smile. Albeit a very small one, but it was there, I was sure of it.

It made me instantly feel better about him. Like he wasn't such an arrogant jerk. I stopped my tirade and smiled. "Have you ever been in love?" Where had that come from? All I could think of was Aidan shaking his head at me. But for some reason, I really wanted to know if a guy like Lucian was capable of love. Usually, condescending, self-important boys thought they were God's gift to women, but never really opened up to anyone.

"Once," he said, and his eyes suddenly looked ancient. I never knew what people meant when they said they could see an old soul, but if they saw what I just saw: I got it. It was strange. He looked at me as if he had lived a thousand lifetimes.

"What's that on your neck?" he suddenly asked.

I unconsciously touched the small scabs, the last remnants of my ordeal with Frank.

"This weirdo-guy Frank thought he was a vampire. He bit me." I didn't want to talk about it, but Lucian asked with such concern I didn't want to be rude either.

His face revealed a whole lot of anger. "He *bit* you?"

"Yeah, I got away before too much damage was done. It's

65

all right." I felt weirdly pleased at the way Lucian stared at me. He looked like he would smash Frank like a pea if he had been standing in front of us.

It made me want to know more about him. "What was the name of the girl you fell in love with?"

I didn't think he was going to answer me. He paused, as if wrestling with pursuing the Frank conversation or opening up to me about his ex. Then he said, "Nefertiti."

"Nefertiti? Wow, her parents went old-school. But that's kind of cool. From what I've read of the chick, she was pretty badass." Being a history nut, I gushed, "I guess she was so loyal and in love with her husband they ruled Egypt side by side. And that was over three thousand years ago when women weren't exactly on the top of the food chain." I could feel my face burn red. I didn't normally puke out history lessons to strangers, but Nefertiti was kind of a hero of mine.

In the awkward silence that followed, I muttered, "Romantic, huh?"

Lucian didn't speak.

His expression went dark in less than a second.

I was terrified.

Before I could think to move, Aidan had lifted Lucian off the stairs and thrown him clear across the room.

"Aidan!" I yelled in shock.

He whirled to me. "Lucian looked like he was going to hurt you, Shea."

I just nodded. I'd seen it, too. And now Aidan confirmed it.

Lucian was off his rocker. My instincts had been right the first time. The guy was dangerous.

Lucian practically flew at Aidan as he body-slammed into the railing of the staircase.

Everyone watched the show at this point. I went for my phone to call the cops.

No signal.

I'd never seen a fight like this, and I was scared Aidan would be crushed.

But to my surprise, he was holding his own. I couldn't say the same about the Pillar House though. Their body slams were smashing holes in the walls left and right.

I ran out of the house to get a signal. Others were following me, not wanting to accidentally get hurt from testosterone-boys in there.

One bar. I dialed 911.

My phone was snatched out of my hand before I could hit "Call." My eyes went round in terror when I looked up to see Frank.

"Looks like your bodyguard is busy," he sneered.

I tried to run, but he grabbed my arm.

"You're all I've been thinking about, the taste of you . . ." Frank looked at me like I was a Big Mac.

I tried screaming at the people passing by, but they ignored me completely.

Frank recognized the danger of being out in the open, so he pulled me toward the side of the house. I tried to get away, but the guy was like Superman. I couldn't even loosen his grip on my arm.

This was happening.

He was going to finish what he'd started.

Frank was going to kill me.

Seriously? Death by a guy who thought he was a vampire? It couldn't get any lamer than that!

When he had me pinned to the side of the house, he put his finger to my lips. His eyes constricted like before. "No more tricks. Keep quiet and this will be over before you know it."

"You know that eye thing doesn't do what you think it does, right?" I was amazed at how condescending I sounded considering I was about to pee my pants.

Frank was more than shocked. He was downright baffled. "Impossible," he muttered in astonishment.

I kicked him in the groin, but he didn't flinch. What the heck?

Frank gained his bearings and looking as if he knew he didn't have much time. He pried my neck to the side and bent down to take another bite.

I screamed. A guttural scream.

I didn't know who was more surprised, me or Frank.

Long, sinewy strands of wood grew out of the planks on the side of the house. They slithered their way past my body and wrapped around Frank's neck like wooden vines going in for the kill.

It was safe to say both of us were seriously freaked out. Houses coming to life to save me? Had I done that? I didn't want to admit it, but I knew somehow I had.

Frank was choking. He lost his hold on me.

And I ran.

Straight into the safety of Aidan's arms.

Aidan and Lucian were no longer fighting. Apparently, my

scream had stopped them and they had come running.

Aidan gave Lucian a nod, almost like they had come to some sort of understanding. And the way Lucian looked at Frank . . . I was actually scared for the boy. I was about to suggest we call the police when Aidan made me look him in the eyes.

"We're going back to the dorm," he said, leaving no room for argument.

I nodded.

We left without looking back to see what Lucian was about to do to Frank.

CHAPTER 4
LUCIAN

To those hungry eyes still looking for party drama, there was nothing left of Frank. Nothing but a small fleck of dust picked up by the scuff of his dress shoes as I snatched him from the grip of wood around his neck and flew into the air. He coughed when we landed, desperately grabbing his throat.

I watched, turning over a small metal trash can and sitting on it as he gathered himself. First appreciation filled his eyes, then confusion. "Where are we? I mean, thanks, man. I think that bitch almost staked me!" He walked over to a window. "Are we in Boston? Did you *fly* here? No vampire can fly . . . I mean, we can move really fast, but . . . and we're inside, that's—"

I was now inches from Frank's face as his words recoiled into his sick, small-minded mouth. His pupils constricted as his meager powers tried to sense what I was.

Quickly, he bowed. "I'm sorry. You must be a Second-Born. I've heard . . . there are only a few alive. I thought your kind was a myth, but . . . I can *feel* your power." Frank's eyes widened in amazement as a small bit of drool left his still-exposed incisors.

I laughed, keeping the volcanic rage just under the surface of my skin, all the while planning what to do with him. "I'm not a Second-Born, boy. I *made* the Second-Borns. I'm the *First!*"

It was too much. The vampire cowered, kneeling on the ground in full servitude. "To think you saved a lowly vampire like me, I can't thank you enough."

My eyes burned like hot coals inside my skull. "Save you? Is that what you think I've done? You are nothing but a smear, a stain on the tip of my heel. Which fool turned you? Who's your father?"

His lips trembled, his mind moved beyond fear. "Please, I'm nothing. I've only been alive two hundred years. I don't know anything. My father's a good man. His name is Raphael, from the Louisiana District."

I leaned down and grabbed the scruff of his neck, letting my menacing voice sharpen his terror. "I do not know this Raphael, or his line. Who is *his* maker?"

Tears streamed down Frank's cheeks. "Please, master, I-I don't know his maker. I'm very young—"

My fangs enlarged so drastically they split the gums. Blood filled my mouth and the taste of it enraged me further. It had been ages since I'd felt this much fury. The idea of him "drinking" the Vessel. He didn't even know his lineage.

He was no better than the mindless, classless slaves of humans who roamed this earth. His blood was diluted. He was no vampire. He wasn't worth the title. *I should show him what a* real *vampire is.*

71

"It matters not the name of your line. I will smite them. I will hunt Raphael, your blessed father, and I will drink him like the mule-rat he is. He will curse the name Frank as he writhes in an agony unknown to our kind.

"All those he's turned will tremble in fear at their own demise. I will devour *every* drop of lineage that brought you here, save the original elder I myself turned. I will wipe the earth clean of their stench simply because you, you worthless, spineless worm, even dared to touch . . . to think that you could taste Shea Harper. I should thank you. You'll be an example of what happens to anyone who tries to touch what's *mine!*"

I started slowly. I exposed him to filtered sunlight at a gentle, intimate pace, enough to drive him mad. He experienced all the things that could cause agony to my kind, but not death. I couldn't stop. Every time I thought about his teeth being where mine had not, his lips on her neck . . . I wanted him to live another day, if only just to watch him plead over and over for me to kill him. Eventually his end did come, when I repainted my entire Boston flat with his entrails.

I'd been foolish thinking I should seduce Shea. I needed to take her. If bottom-feeders like this could get close, then Adnachiel was failing more than usual. She was not safe with him. I had to be there before he turned on her.

Aidan. My blood boiled and I wished I hadn't ended Frank, just so I could kill him again in this moment. When that dog had nodded to me, we'd agreed Frank needed to die. It was almost like it had been with Moses, as if all the thousands of years hadn't changed what we were, what we had been to each other.

I watched the blood slide over the darkened window like

sludge covering a smooth surface. That was what killing Moses had done to our friendship. In one moment, I'd lost them both. I should have listened to Caelius. I hadn't known what Adnachiel was capable of then. But for years we'd been like brothers. The three of us had freed slaves and changed the world. He'd made us better, both of us. Yet *Aidan* had killed him, and the way he'd done it . . .

My thoughts turned black with the memory. Shea was not Moses. I wouldn't be fooled again. I'd had a judgment lapse, but I would never side with that beast. I was going to take her straight out of his weak, pathetic grasp. Forget seduction. With other Vessels, I'd force Adnachiel to choose and he'd always end them. He'd prove where his loyalty was, and where it wasn't. He'd never choose me, or the Vessel. Not now, not ever. Maybe it really was time to fulfill my promise to Caelius and free him.

That thought produced a strange feeling. The idea of anyone's hands on her sickened me. Shea was *mine*.

I licked the blood from my palm and made a fist.

First things first.

Retribution.

***

Weeks passed. They rose and fell like waves over the ocean. It had been a month since Frank. My ears rang from the desperate cries pried from the flesh of thousands of devoured vampires. Some I ate, some I just ripped apart with my hands, watching the marrow spill out of their bones.

It was like the Viking era all over again, but this time I didn't have Gunnhild by my side to relish in the torment. We'd ended the Vikings. They'd been a challenge, but we'd wiped them from the earth. All to add salt to Aidan's eyes. His people, *that round*.

A warrior class, but still he couldn't protect the Vessel. Even in front of his brother, in front of Gunnhild, he'd shown his true beast. Always a servant to the Light, his master.

Poor Gunnhild. I'd turned him just to increase Adnachiel's agony, but he'd grown on me over the centuries. Admittedly, he'd been one of my favorites.

Remembering the tenderness and fondness I'd had for my children in my youth faded as I ripped open a young vamp's chest and pulled his spine through. They were so few, my original seven, and the trash they'd made was unacceptable, even if Caelius wanted the numbers increased incrementally. With every thought of Frank touching Shea, barbarity seeped into my mind, and I relished having an outlet for my confusing emotions.

I hunted.

I stalked.

And I alone reaped vengeance on the lineage of my son, Gracuri. But before I could finish devouring his New Orleans branch, he came to me.

It was a hot summer night in Louisiana. He placed his hand on my shoulder as if greeting an old friend. In my bloodlust, I popped it from its socket.

Shocked, he reeled back and reset it. "Lucian, Father . . . I've heard that someone in my family has displeased you. I've come to make it right." He reached to hug me as he always had. Something inside shifted. He held me tight, resting his head on my shoulder like he had in Thebes when I'd been displeased with him then.

When he pulled back, his eyes were warm and his golden hair picked up the light of the moon. I'd taken him in Athens. He'd always looked like the sun, as if he belonged to daylight. I remembered likening him to the Roman god Helios, who drove a fiery chariot across the sky. Romans and their gods; it was nonsense, but at least it was inventive.

He pulled me in again, tenderly lengthening the embrace, bowing his large gladiator frame to mine. "It's been so long, Father. Please, tell me what I can do to appease you."

I smiled, pushing him back. "You've always had the tongue for philosophy. And flattery isn't lost on you, my son."

He touched my cheek with the back of his hand. "Why have you been killing my children?"

Only now, after nearly a month of slaughtering, did I feel the pang of guilt. "They didn't deserve your name. Some didn't even know it. They were unworthy."

He laced his arm through mine boyishly as he pulled me forward. He was quick, unlike his sluggish descendants. I hadn't noticed the sound of a lake nearby, but sure enough, within a few steps we were there.

Water. He loved to walk along the water. That was where I'd met him for the first time. That was where I'd befriended him. I'd been younger then, and so had he.

He laughed, looking at my bloodied face as he pulled me into the lake. He took his time, tenderly washing my crimson frame. The cold and his soft touch changed my temperament.

I again looked at him like he was the boy I'd known then, before the wasted city and his slaughtered family had colored my view of him forever. Was it my blood that had corrupted such a sweet soul? Did I ruin everything I touched?

He smiled. "Why Lucian, you're looking at me as if you've ripped the wings off a butterfly. Do you still regard me with such sentiment?"

My jaw hardened. He knew that I did. He was using that sentiment now.

He pouted at my callousness. "I didn't mean to provoke you. It's just . . . I've missed you. It's been so long. Will you ever see me like you did before Thebes? That was the last we spoke, and now this. I fear I'll never be in your favor."

I hated it, the way my heart melted toward him. I knew it was the curse. You were bonded to those you turned. A strange sort of familial, loving bond. That was why I'd turned so few. It was not like with Aidan, where I felt bonded despite our differences. This was instinctual.

I paused, taking in the night as my wet hair dripped in his warm hands. He should let the back of my head go and stop holding me as if I were his world. My chest swelled. This must have been why Caelius had only turned me. He had one child to break his heart. I had seven to break mine.

His smile widened, his large white teeth sharp as a lion's. "Caelius really broke the mold with you. There will never be a need to turn others. You're too perfect, Lucian."

I growled as I smacked his hand away and lunged at his throat. Gracuri knew me too well. He could read my body language, my scent, my words like he was reading an open book. As hard as it was to hide my true self from Caelius out of fear, it was harder to hide that vulnerability from someone I had trusted. Someone I had come to love.

His smile didn't fade. "What are you doing, Father? Honestly, I'm worried about you. I know the hunt is on. It's that five hundred year time where you go after the Vessel and do your dance . . . but I've heard things."

I tightened my grip on his neck, trying to push all that I felt for him deep inside. "What things?"

Now he scowled. He looked more like the thing I should have killed in Thebes and less like the boy by the river. I left my mind open so I could direct my thoughts to him loud and clear: *Gracuri, I'll never see you without looking twice—once at the boy, and once at the monster. Those innocent people you killed, the blood from your eyes . . . the madness of it.*

He coughed, shaking his head, feigning like he wasn't still hearing my telepathy. "The rumor is that . . . well, you're sending a message not to touch what's yours. And what's yours is Shea Harper." His eyes fell flat as he pushed the pressure point in my wrist, loosening my grip.

I sneered, taking in a deep breath. The tips of my fangs opened as they sucked in air like they would blood. His concern shifted to amazement, as it always did when I accomplished something he could not, simply because of the dilution from my blood to his.

"You can breathe through your fangs?" he asked in wonder.

I let my hand fall from his throat and ignored his childlike curiosity. "I'm glad, Gracuri. Your words please me. The message has reached the Second-Borns, and no doubt Caelius himself by now. This should stop any of them from *accidentally* interfering in my affairs. The rumors don't misspeak. Shea is mine." I looked at him with a strange feeling clawing underneath my skin, a feeling

I couldn't yet describe. Was it territorial passion? Something lit within when I mentioned her name. All I could think of was one word: *mine*. Over and over, and nothing else.

Tears welled in his eyes and rolled like rain as my mouth fell open in shock. What was this?

He grabbed me with all the fervor of an estranged child. "Father, I was misguided once. I was lost in Thebes. I know Caelius asked you to end me there. I overexposed our kind. I was supposed to build slowly, quietly like the others. You know why I did what I did. You alone came for me then. You pulled me out. You showed mercy and saved me from the madness that had infected my mind.

"Please, let me do the same for you now. Your hands are soaked in blood, *our* blood, vampire blood. It's lunacy. There's territory, but this has stretched far beyond that. Caelius will be furious if he finds out how emotionally involved you're becoming with this Vessel. It's dangerous for you. Please, stop now, Father. Kill this Shea Harper and play your games with the *next* Vessel. It's only five hundred years. This Vessel has gotten to you, or maybe the hunt has. Whatever it is, you need to end it and walk away."

Fury rose inside of me as I directed my thoughts to all the living creatures in the water at our feet. Then the whole lake. One thought emanated from my mind: *Cut yourself open.*

Within moments our legs were no longer soaking in water, but blood. Gracuri gasped and slowly stepped out of the wet. He shook his head as his eyes darkened, his favorite white suit dipped in red.

Snakes with fresh gashes bleeding down their sides lifted me out of the blood and set me by his side. He didn't move or flinch in fear as they slithered by his white shoes. "How dare you doubt my intentions. I don't need you to look after me. I am your father, not the other way around. So listen well because I will only tell you this once more: Shea Harper is *mine*!"

He closed his eyes and took a deep breath, his curls still bouncing in the soft summer breeze. "I'm sorry, Father. Then I can't save you as you did me. You always were stronger. Is it done then? Have you killed enough of my babies to satisfy your rage?"

I stared into the forest beyond him. Maybe he was right. I wasn't acting like myself. Did I look like he had then? What would he think now that he too could see the savage, unkempt madman before him?

I wanted to embrace Gracuri one last time. I didn't know why I was feeling all of this nostalgia. What was wrong with this Vessel, or with me?

Why was the entirety of my years only desiring to be reflected upon now? I grabbed the back of his neck, pulling his forehead to mine until they touched. We stood there in the silence of our long years and hardened hearts.

"Remember when we first met, Gracuri? Do you remember what you said to me?"

He nodded. Another tear followed the dried traces of the ones before. He was the only one I'd turned who could still cry. It endeared him to me further.

Gracuri half smiled. "I will always feel that way about you. Even if you soak your hands in the blood of my line, even if you were to gut me and soak your hands in the juice from my still-pumping heart, I will never stop believing in you, Lucian. Who you really are. Time may erode all that's in me, all that we are and were to each other, but what I said to you that night will never change. And I will hold dear the deal we made the night you turned me and wear it like a code of honor until my death."

If I could cry, I would have done it then. His words shook me further. I imagined the tears that should be flowing down my cheeks with his.

The last time I'd cried had been when Aidan had died—for the first time—with Moses, and taken my tears and heart with him in the desert. That had been so long ago. And now, a son I had all but forsaken because of his brutality had brought me back to what I'd been before: a young heart that still hoped it could be more than Caelius's servant.

But was it Gracuri alone? Why did I feel more alive now than I had before Caelius found me near death in a ditch under the light of Nefertiti's window?

For the first time in a thousand years, my voice trembled as I spoke, revealing a moment's vulnerability. "I will leave the children you have left in your line. I know they are the oldest and dearest to you." Without a word, he grabbed me tight, holding me, his head instantly on my shoulder.

When he pulled back, his eyes were fiery, no doubt ready to start a new line. I pitied the town he showed up in next. "Then I will do this for you, Father. I will spread the word that Shea Harper is your *mission*. That you will kill anyone who intercepts that mission out of fierce loyalty to Caelius."

I nodded, a curious sort of coldness sweeping over me. "You will not be spreading a lie. It *is* for Caelius that I cleared your line."

His face softened, as if he saw something that I did not. "I am always on your side, Lucian, no matter what you do as the centuries pass. I will defend your honor with my dying breath, even if I cannot protect you from yourself." He took one last look as he stroked my cheek with the back of his palm. Then, like a lightning bolt striking the surface of the water, he was gone.

I fell to my knees. My nails grew into the dry dirt as I clenched fistfuls of it and forced it into my mouth. *Swallow it, Lucian. That dirt, that dry dirt is all you are. You're nothing but ash. Smother this heart. Your heart is dead, remember. It died once in Egypt, then again with Moses. Bury what you're feeling now. The dirt is what you are.*

I choked on the grit as it filled my stomach. Vampires got nourishment from being underground because that was where Caelius was buried, but this was toxic. I'd done this after Nefertiti died. Every night for months, just to kill the pain, I'd swallowed the sands of Egypt.

I had forgotten the sensation, the agony of it. Damn Gracuri. Damn Shea, Adnachiel, all of them. They didn't know what it was like, what I was. They thought they could make me feel something. But I was dead.

"I'm *dead*!" I screamed to the stars, bellows of dust escaping my lungs into the shadows of clouds.

I gasped, choking on the pain.

Only one thought remained . . .

This ended tonight.

***

I pounded on the door of her dorm room before catching the idiocy of it. I didn't need to knock. Ripping off the handle, I peeled the wooden door back like a flimsy piece of paper. My eyes first met Aidan's. Of course he'd be inches from her. I scanned his body. At least he wasn't holding anything sharp to fillet her with.

I stretched my hand out to the Vessel, her face still reeling in horror from the damage to her room. "Shea, step away from Aidan and come with me. I'll keep you safe." What was I saying? Safe? I wasn't going to keep her safe. I had to stop these feelings from taking over. Dragging her to Caelius would kill what was left of my human weakness. Maybe it really was time to give up this game.

I firmed my gaze, resolute.

Instantly, Adnachiel was at my throat. I doubted Shea could hear the thunder of his giant wings furiously flapping just out of mortal sight. But there it was in all his glory: the dog revealed. "You're uglier than your four brothers, *Aidan*. All those eyes, a mangled mess between lion, ox, man, and eagle. Tell me, if Shea saw your *real* form, do you think she'd still call you friend? Or would she tremble in fear like all mortals?"

Without a word, he flung me through the large window just past her. Had I been a lesser vampire, his well-angled toss would have cut open my throat.

He'd revealed his hand.

Even after our mutual agreement about Frank, he wouldn't hold back. Good. I was in no mood to fight the pain that mounds of dirt couldn't vanquish. His blood would make it easier.

I laughed, stepping casually on the broken glass of the window frame. My mouth barely moved as I spoke. "I know you used Shea at the party last month to lure me out. I only killed Frank so you wouldn't hurt her. Is that all you know now, Beast? Betrayal? Once we were like brothers, now I will use *against* you what was once *for* you.

"The wrath of fire still burns in my veins. Let the earth tremble. Let the ground quake and swallow you whole like it swallowed me for a hundred years in Pompeii!"

I didn't care about overexposing our kind. If Caelius was finally freed, I was sure he would forgive the infraction. Even if he didn't, I couldn't control myself. The agonies of betrayal swallowed me whole.

I connected to every drop of insect and animal blood crawling and squirming inside and around the building. All their blood was now the same pulse, beating to my rhythm. Then it was beating too fast. It beat faster and faster, like the ache in my chest, until they exploded. The whole building trembled from the impact. Cracks formed along the walls, their gruesome deaths shaking its foundation.

Lucian the Merciful indeed.

In Aidan's confusion, I grabbed Shea. I wrapped her safely in my arms, covering her mouth as the building started to collapse around us. The other meat-bags were running from rooms like fleas on a drowning rat. Still, I had to bury him. First the ceiling caved in, then the floor. He was quick, but not quick enough. The rubble would be his tomb, even though it couldn't kill him. Only one thing could end that beast. Still, I could crush his bones to dust and leave his skin for worm food, alive and in agony, like he'd left me in Pompeii.

I had Shea. The rest of the earth, and him with it, could burn for what they had done to me . . . for what they had done to themselves.

Blinding white light filled every pore. I couldn't see, or feel my body. Shea was my only thought. Aidan's brothers . . . no, maybe I was too late. I couldn't feel her in my arms anymore.

They'd killed her.

I'd won the game.

My heart wrenched. All these years, I'd thought it was Adnachiel losing, but with the loss of Shea I realized that his failing and mine were the same. The Vessels always perished. They lost, every time.

This couldn't keep happening.

Not again.

Not to *her*.

In that moment, I felt my heart break. I'd rather die than feel what came next. Fresh tears rolled down my cheeks like they had with Moses. My voice cracked. "I couldn't save them." My mother, my people, Nefertiti, Moses, Aidan, and now Shea. Grief, held back by an eternity of denial, hit me all at once. No matter how powerful I was, they'd all slipped through my hands.

Slowly, my vision returned. All I could see at first was a palm, then the person behind it took shape. It wasn't Adnachiel. It was *her*. Shea had used her powers against me.

Her face looked as shocked as mine. I was flooded with emotions I hadn't felt since before I'd been turned. Deep feelings, just seeing her alive: hope.

I followed her gaze to the giant burned chunk of flesh that was melted off my rib cage, exposing bone. That would take some time to recover from.

Her eyes moved from the blood up to the tip of my chin. Her lips trembled as she stared at the fresh teardrops hanging there. When her gaze met mine, she was vulnerable for a moment, then she closed off, unsure.

I struggled to stand, but my legs were like water. How could she be this strong already? She had no practice or knowledge of her powers. I looked toward her other hand. It was outstretched to the rubble that was supposed to bury Aidan. She'd blasted it off. In one motion, she'd nearly ended me and saved him.

I coughed as blood rained out of my mouth. "Wait, Shea, you don't understand. He's not who you think he is. He'll kill you . . . I won't let anyone touch you. Just come with me. I know I'm a monster. I know what I've done . . ." I closed my eyes. Enough. I let the wet of my tears fall off my chin as I tilted my head upward. What was this? I pleaded to *no one*. She was not Nefertiti, and I was not some love-torn adolescent slave. She was just another Vessel. She was nothing.

When my eyes opened, I met her gaze. *Maybe I should provoke her, let her end me now.* Adnachiel would finally win and I'd be free of this weight I'd carried for so long. A powerful wind dried the blood on my lips as he ran next to her. His face was as angry as mine.

I laughed, gurgling on my singed tongue, my voice filled with sarcasm. "Do you miss it, Adnachiel? Being so close to the Light, hearing the biblical cries of 'holy, holy, holy, is the Lord Almighty; the whole earth is full of His glory?' Tell me, after all you've seen, is it? Is it full of His *glory*?"

He didn't answer. A sadness overtook his features. It was a look I hadn't seen since the first time we'd been reunited after

Moses. "Don't look at me like that, Dog. You haven't won. This isn't Pompeii. This isn't goodbye either. Our fight doesn't end like this. We will have our day. I'll tell you what I told Frank and two thousand slaughtered vampires in my wake, Shea Harper is *mine*!" I flew into the air before either of them had a chance to move.

CHAPTER 5
SHEA

"Shea, come on, we have to go!" Aidan screamed over the sound of the collapsing building that used to be my dorm. It looked like an earthquake had decided to target McClintock Hall and nothing else. Had Lucian done that? Had Aidan? Had I?

I remembered looking at the rubble and being terrified that Aidan was buried alive. With one thought, all the broken pieces that used to be my dorm room, had flown into the air, revealing Aidan crouched on the ground. When he saw me, he'd jumped to his feet and was by my side.

Now that he was safe, my mind was reeling. I couldn't think straight. I had no idea what was happening, and frankly, I just wanted to wake up from this nightmare.

Aidan touched my arm and I jumped back a few feet. Lucian's words had somehow stuck with me even though they were lies. *He's not who you think he is. He'll kill you.* Lucian, the dorm monitor, had a hole inside his chest where I could see his ribs. I'd made that hole! I had been so scared for Aidan I'd felt my eyes burn and suddenly I'd been seeing a close-up of Lucian's guts. Then he'd vanished. In a puff of smoke, fog, ash? What the hell was that? The absurdity of the moment made everything spin.

I was going to faint.

Aidan's arms were welcome this time. How could I have even considered a word that monster Lucian had said? Aidan had been my protector since we'd been kids. But he *knew* Lucian, they had a past.

And they hated each other.

Lucian had tried to kill him.

Kill him and take me all in one swoop.

Aidan's voice was calm now as he whispered in my ear, "Shea, we have to leave. It's not safe here."

My terror and shock turned to anger. I pulled away. "Safe from what? From whom? From . . ." It was too much. I was pretty sure I was short-circuiting.

I was about to collapse.

He lifted me up and cradled me in his arms. "I'm sorry, Shea, but Lucian heals fast. He'll be hunting us soon."

I didn't struggle. I let him carry me. The word "hunting" rang in my ears. It was paralyzing. "What happened? What just happened?"

"I'll explain everything to you." I felt his soft reassuring kiss on my cheek. "We have to get somewhere safe."

That was enough for me. My brain didn't want to process anymore. It was seizing from shock.

I laid my head on Aidan's shoulder and closed my eyes.

***

"Shea?" Lucian's voice called out to me.

I opened my eyes. I was in the middle of the desert. There were hills and hills of golden sand for miles in every direction. It wasn't hot, even though the sun was beaming down on my face.

A dream.

Another dream . . . with Lucian.

Ugh.

Maybe everything that had happened was all a horrible nightmare, and now I was finishing off the night with some kind of sexy desert dream. I tried to picture myself waking up in my dorm with Gerta snoring softly in the bed next to me. I would laugh and tell her all about how I'd dreamed that I demolished our room and seared a hole in the new dorm monitor's chest. Funny, huh?

I almost believed it.

Until Lucian was up against me. I could feel the heat from his body radiating off of him. We weren't touching, but standing this close made me ache to be held. Even just a small touch would be enough. I imagined his soft lips on mine, then I remembered his forceful hands grabbing me, the fury in his eyes as he tried to bury Aidan in the debris, his ribs staring back at me like a grotesque statue.

I pulled away. "What are you doing here?"

"I've never been able to Dream-Walk before. *You* pulled me in," Lucian said quietly. He was different somehow. Not the arrogant boy I thought I knew, but not the raging hunter I had seen before either.

"Well . . ." I was at a loss for words. Why *had* I brought him here? And how the heck could I bring anyone anywhere while I was asleep? Dream-Walking? That sounded like some kind of horror novel where the heroine gets trapped forever in Nightmare Land. Maybe that was what this was? I decided just to be honest.

"I don't know why I brought you here."

"I see." Lucian reached up and lightly touched my cheek, sending shivers through my whole body. "I meant what I said before. Aidan will kill you. You're not safe with him."

"Aidan would die for me," I uttered defensively.

That made Lucian pause. It was a few moments before he responded. He pulled his hand away, both to my relief and disappointment. "True enough."

Before I could think better of it, curiosity overtook me. I reached out and pulled up his T-shirt to examine his stomach. It was deep red, like a third-degree burn, but his flesh was no longer open and broken. "Was I the one who blew that hole in your chest?" I asked, not really wanting to hear the answer.

Lucian nodded slowly. He stared at me so intensely I wanted to look away, but couldn't. There was something intoxicating about keeping his gaze. I didn't know what was wrong with me. I'd pretty much hated this guy up until the Pillar House, where we'd had a decent conversation. But then Aidan had attacked him and I'd gone back to hating him.

Then Lucian had disappeared for a month and I'd found myself thinking about our conversation. The way he spoke of Nefertiti.

The way he spoke. The way he looked at me. The way he looked at Frank for hurting me. It had been intense, to say the least.

90

That was the problem with time. The more of it that passed, you either softened your feelings or turned them into raging hatred. I had done both.

But in this dream . . .

This Lucian standing before me felt different somehow.

I tried to shake myself out of it, to remember how I truly felt, how my hatred for him had made me burn a hole through his chest.

Instead, I traced his red, inflamed skin with my finger. He shuddered from my touch. His eyes closed in contentment. I didn't know what had come over me. Every part of me wanted Lucian to take me right there in the warm sand.

I yanked myself away from him. "How did I do that to you?"

I didn't expect him to know, but having the power to rip holes in people with my mind terrified me.

"Honestly? I don't know. You shouldn't be this powerful yet," Lucian admitted. His fingers brushed against my hand as if he had to be touching me. I cringed as it sent a thrill through my spine.

There was a connection between us.

I had denied it before when I thought he was a pompous dorm monitor. But now it was as if a veil had been lifted. Even though he acted like a vicious monster in life, in my dream I could see deep inside him. His soul was pure. And the way he looked at me . . .

"What are you?" I asked.

"I think you know what I am." Lucian parted his lips and suddenly he had fangs. *Real* fangs.

Um.

"A vampire? Seriously?" Then a thought occurred to me. "So Frank was . . . a real . . ." Even though I knew it was a dream, I touched my neck for the remnants of Frank's bite. He wasn't a crazy guy. He was actually a freaking vampire.

My head started to spin.

Lucian's hand steadied me as his fingers intertwined with mine. It only made my head spin more. "You'll never have to worry about him, or those like him, again. I'll keep you safe."

I had to pull away. "Don't. I shouldn't admit this, but when you touch me, it drives me a little nutty. So just keep your distance. I'm hoping this is just a weird dream thing."

Lucian ignored my "no touching" request and took a step closer, holding my face in his hands. Oh man. *I think my brain just froze.*

He leaned close so our foreheads were touching. I almost lost my breath from the power of it. He spoke gently, "You are mine, Shea Harper."

Danger.

The word hit me like a gale force wind. I practically fell on my rump from pushing Lucian away so fast. "No, I'm not. That sounds stalker-y. And no biting! And no hurting Aidan! And just *no!*"

***

"You awake?" Aidan's voice welcomed me from my weird-ass dream.

My heart sank as I realized I was in a hotel room and not my dorm. All of it had really happened. My life had just gone from normal to insane-o in fewer than sixty seconds.

I tried to shake myself out of the coma I wanted to retreat into.

I could still feel Lucian's touch. I didn't want to admit it, but I knew with certainty the dream had been real. Whatever Dream-Walking was, I could do it, and I had been with Lucian.

It excited and terrified me at the same time. I knew he was the enemy, but a part of me saw something in him—something kind, something yearning to come out, but his monster wouldn't let him.

I rubbed my face, trying to think of something else besides Lucian. I needed answers, and not from vampire-boy.

From Aidan.

The person I trusted most in this world had been lying to me, or at least hiding some kind of truth, which equated to the same thing in my book.

I pulled my hands away from my face and looked him in the eye. "What in the *hell* is going on?" I could hear the anger in my voice.

My heart faltered when I saw the genuine hurt and shame in his expression. No matter what had happened, he still loved me. I knew that because I loved him just as much. It may not be romantic, but sometimes familial love like ours was stronger, fiercer. As if it was a living thing coursing through my veins, knowing that we'd die for each other.

I took a deep, calming breath. "Just tell me."

Aidan ran his hand through his hair nervously and started to pace. The room was small, so he didn't have much space to work with. "Trust me, Shea. This wasn't supposed to happen. None of it was."

I could tell Aidan was seriously stressing. I'd never seen him so panicked. He had always been my rock. *I* was the panicky one in our relationship, never him. I glanced out the window and saw trees. Pine trees. "Where are we?"

"Colorado Springs." Aidan continued to pace.

"What?" I was shocked. "What about my parents? Did you call them? How long was I asleep? Why are we here?" I was babbling, but having my best friend kidnap me and bring me to Colorado was way out of my comfort zone.

"One thing at a time, Shea." Aidan stopped pacing and sat down next to me on the bed. He reached over and held my hand in his. I didn't pull away. Holding his hand kept me grounded, as if mere contact could prevent me from going cuckoo.

"You've been out cold for about twelve hours, and no, I didn't call your parents. You can call them later, but in order to keep them safe I had to get you out of town. Lucian might try and use them as leverage."

"He wouldn't do that," I said, not knowing why. I wished I hadn't.

Aidan's expression turned dark. "Did you forget he tried to kill me?"

"Don't get mad. I just know he wouldn't use my parents as leverage. And of course I didn't forget he tried to kill you. I blew a hole in his chest, didn't I?" The look on Aidan's face confirmed it was true.

He nodded slowly. "Yes, you did."

I was overwhelmed again. "And I lifted that rubble with my mind?" I couldn't believe I was asking that. What was my life turning into?

He read me like he always had and let go of my hand, wrapping his arms around me. I leaned into his chest.

The lump in my throat made it impossible to swallow, but I was too numb to cry. "Oh, Aidan. What am I?" Was I a monster like Lucian? *I must be if I can rip a hole in someone.*

He kissed the top of my head and I felt a moment of relief. It was surprising how much Aidan's presence comforted me. I knew that no matter how crazy my world was about to get, he would protect me from it all.

"I never wanted any of this for you. I've tried to keep you away from danger your whole life. If you had never activated your powers, Lucian would never have been able to find you."

Aidan's words made sense to him, but not to me.

"So it was my fault?" I asked. "When did I *activate* my powers? Because Lucian has been around for over a month now." Then it hit me. "Frank." The first time Frank had attacked me, I'd felt my eyes burn. The guy had looked terrified. The next day Lucian was knocking on the door, introducing himself as the dorm monitor. "Lucian wasn't the new monitor, was he? I wonder what happened to that guy."

"Dead," he answered definitively.

I pulled out of Aidan's embrace. "How do you know?"

"Because I know him. He's a killer, Shea." He left no room for argument. "This is going to sound ridiculous, but Lucian is a vampire."

I knew he wanted to see a more shocked expression on my face, but Lucian had showed me what he was in my dream. It only solidified my belief that the dream had been real. "I sensed that," I lied. Why was I lying to Aidan? I just couldn't tell him that I was dreaming about Vamp-Boy. I knew he'd freak out.

"That doesn't surprise me. You're the first Vessel who's gained control of their powers so quickly . . . and the first female." Aidan was talking gibberish again.

I stood up. I couldn't be next to him anymore. He knew too much about me that I didn't know myself, and it scared me. I leaned against the dresser and stretched out my hand toward him. "Just stay there. I need to process. What's a Vessel? That sounds really *Lord of the Rings*."

Aidan smiled, though there wasn't much humor in it. "This is serious, Shea."

"You don't think I know that?" I shouted. "I'm in Colorado for God's sake! I've never even left Arizona before! And my best friend in the whole world has been lying to me and cohorting with a vampire!"

"Cohorting?" Aidan smiled for real this time. He stood up and faced me, gently pulling me in for a hug.

It was so easy with Aidan. Despite all the chaos I had just experienced, falling into him felt right. Like home. His chin rested on top of my head. Sometimes I forgot how tall he was. His chest vibrated as he spoke. "Lucian is very old, Shea. Like, over three thousand years old."

I lifted my head off his chest to make eye contact. I'd somehow known that Lucian was ancient. It didn't surprise me like I knew it should have. I was more concerned about Aidan. "What about you? You two acted like you knew each other, like you had a past, but I grew up with you. I know you're my age because I've been in your life every second of every day. Spirit

96

twins, remember?" There was no way Lucian could know Aidan, unless they'd become enemies when Aidan was in diapers. The whole thing didn't sit right.

Aidan sighed deeply. He leaned down and kissed my forehead. It felt so natural. So comfy. "You should sit."

I didn't argue. I sat back down on the bed and he joined me.

"I'm going to tell you everything and it's going to sound insane, okay?" Aidan didn't continue until I nodded in agreement. "You're called a Vessel, Shea. The first Vessel was born over three thousand years ago, and it took almost eight hundred years before another was born. But after the second Vessel's death, a Vessel was born every five hundred years like clockwork, and your sole purpose is to break a seal. But that curse can never be broken, Shea. Ever."

"Okay," I interrupted, "so I promise not to break this curse or whatever. Done. Couldn't you have just told me, so none of this crap with Lucian would have happened?"

He gave me a look that said I should be quiet and listen.

"Lucian wants to *break* the seal. He'll do anything to get his hands on you and *make* you do it. The seal is a prison created by my brothers and me to trap a very evil being. His name is Caelius. He's Darkness trapped in human form, and he's Lucian's father."

The words coming out of Aidan's mouth made sense logically, but I felt separated from their meaning, as if I was in someone else's body looking in. Even the word "evil" was foreign to me. I had never met anyone evil. What did that really mean?

I was starting to become dizzy again. I would have sat down, but I was already sitting.

"So I won't do it, no matter what Lucian says or does to try and convince me. If his dad is truly that evil, then I would never let a guy like that loose. That would be like springing Jeffrey Dahmer from jail, right?" I was trying to put what I was hearing in real-life terms. It kept me from hyperventilating and passing out on the hotel room floor.

Then something else Aidan had said hit me. "You and your brothers? Three thousand years ago? No, Aidan, you're my age," I insisted, "the *exact* same age. We were born on the same day, the same second . . ." I stopped myself, understanding creeping into me like an unwanted flu virus. "That's the way it works, doesn't it? You're born with these *Vessels*. You protect all of us." I'd always known Aidan was my personal bodyguard, I just hadn't known how literal that actually was.

Aidan nodded and tucked a piece of hair behind my ear. "My brothers and I were given a job eons ago: to protect the Light, with our lives if need be. Caelius is Darkness itself, and he decided he wanted to take human form and live among you. But once he became human, he realized he wanted to feed off life. He was the first vampire, Shea, and he turned Lucian. My brothers and I wouldn't stand for it. We had to seal Caelius before he destroyed what the Light held most dear: humans. So we trapped him deep within the earth, protected by wards that no one can break. No one but you, Shea."

"If you're supposed to be protecting this *Light*, why aren't you?" I asked.

"I am," he said simply.

It took me a few seconds to understand what he was saying.

"Wait. *I'm* the Light? Um," was all that came out of my mouth.

"A piece of it, yes. My brothers protect the true Light. We disturbed the balance of good and evil, and you are nature's way of preserving it. No action comes without a cost. The prison we forged for Caelius was unnatural. It may have been made for the greater good, but it was made against the will of the natural order. That's why a Vessel is born. It's nature's way of trying to fix what we did. Darkness was not meant to be bound.

"The Vessel is the key to breaking Caelius's prison. When my brothers and I realized this, I volunteered to be the human guardian of each Vessel. There have been six Vessels before you and we've managed to keep Caelius in his prison every time. I'd just hoped you'd live your life without using your powers and Lucian would never find you." Aidan's eyes were full of pain and regret.

I could see that he was holding back emotion. It pained him to talk about his past . . . his past what? Lives? Six Vessels. That meant he had lived six other times in the last three thousand years.

"Do you have all the memories of your past experiences?"

"Shea, I'm born aware every time. I remember everything."

There it was. The pain. If he had been successful every time, then why so much pain?

"So what? Normally the Vessels live long, happy lives and then they just die? That's how you've succeeded every time? And I ruined it by using my powers?" If I hadn't alerted Lucian by scaring the crap out of Frank, Aidan and I could have had a normal life?

But then I never would have met Lucian . . .

Good! What was I thinking? My life would have been a whole

lot better if evil-vampire Lucian hadn't eaten the dorm monitor and pretended to be a college student. Killer. He was a killer. I needed to remember that.

But Aidan's expression made me pause. There was the sadness again, and something more: shame. I had a sinking feeling in the pit of my stomach. "What happened to the other Vessels?" I stood up, needing to be separate from him. He averted his eyes. That was never a good sign. "Aidan?" My shouting forced eye contact.

"Yes, they died," he admitted softly, then stood up and held my arms to steady me. "But they didn't die from old age. Lucian killed them all."

I shoved Aidan away. For some reason, his words felt wrong. Why was I surprised that Lucian had killed all the other Vessels? He was a vampire. He had tried to kill Aidan . . .

But he had never hurt me.

"If Lucian wanted me dead, why did he tell me he was protecting me? Why didn't he try and kill me at the dorm, or earlier? He had plenty of opportunities, and I wouldn't have known what hit me." I had no idea why I was defending Lucian. Aidan's accusation just felt off somehow. Maybe Aidan misunderstood.

He rolled his eyes, angry now. "You totally like him! I knew it!" His eyes met mine with a fury I had never seen before. "He's a predator, Shea. He likes playing with his food before he eats it."

That rang true.

I couldn't explain why, but it hurt.

"But you said I could break Caelius's prison open. Why would he kill the only thing that could free his father?"

"I can't explain what goes on in a monster's head! Lucian destroyed the Vessels for the sheer joy of it." Aidan turned away as he said it.

There it was again.

More proof that Lucian was evil.

Why did I want to defend him?

I'd known from the beginning he was bad news, from the first second I saw him. So why was I so conflicted? It made me feel like an idiot. And why was I attacking Aidan, the one true friend I had? He had brought me all the way to Colorado to protect me, to save me from a vampire who wanted me to break his daddy out of some kind of hell-prison.

I practically leapt into Aidan's arms. I needed to feel close to him. He was more than a willing participant. "I'm so sorry, Shea," he whispered in my ear.

"What now?" I mumbled into his chest. The tears were coming, but I held them back.

"We keep running. I teach you how to use your powers. And we live." Aidan's voice was soft and reassuring.

I pulled my head back to look up at him. "Forever?"

Aidan's eyes were sad, but determined. He nodded.

I nodded back. My heart ached. My body was numb.

Before I could say another word, he leaned down and kissed me gently on my lips. It was so unexpected I didn't respond at first. But then all the chaos and mayhem of the last twenty-four hours poured out into that one kiss. The moment grew in intensity as we lost ourselves. I had only a passing thought of Aidan in a romantic way, but feeling him pull me in and the power of his lips on mine made my head spin.

I forgot about everything: the last few days, Frank, the blood, the rubble. There was only Aidan in front of me. His strong hands lifted me off my feet and onto the bed.

He softly pressed up against me, then pulled his lips away from mine. He lightly touched my cheek with his hand, his eyes staring at me with . . . love.

When Aidan leaned in to kiss me once more, I pushed him away. "We can't," I said suddenly. I loved Aidan, but I didn't know if I *loved* Aidan. I cared about him too much to lead him on if I didn't really feel that way. I needed time to think.

He was immediately gentle and backed off. "I'm so sorry, Shea. I didn't mean—"

"Don't be sorry. I was a full participant. I just . . . I'm not sure how I feel. I need time."

Aidan genuinely didn't look hurt at all. He looked hopeful. "You have all the time in the world."

I nodded slowly, letting that sentiment sink in. I suddenly felt tired, even though I had just slept for hours. "I need to rest."

"Of course. We have to keep moving though, so don't freak if you wake up in another state." He smiled.

I smiled back. "I won't." I leaned on the pillow.

"Sweet dreams, Shea," I heard him whisper as I closed my eyes and fell asleep.

***

I was in the desert again. Uh oh. I didn't want to see Lucian right now, not after everything Aidan had confessed. A part of me wanted to know his side of the story, but the other part was afraid he'd fill my head with lies.

And why a desert? I'd never liked the desert. I lived in Arizona, it was desert enough. Sand dunes were pretty on TV, but in person, they were messy and . . . sandy. If I was controlling this whole thing, why didn't I create some kind of cool environment like a beautiful waterfall or hot springs?

Nope. Just hills and hills of sand. "Seriously?" I said aloud to my subconscious. "At least give me a pyramid or something."

Three pyramids grew out of the dunes in front of me like giant triangular fingers grabbing for the sky. I gawked at the spectacle. It was breathtaking.

"I was a slave here once."

I turned around to see Lucian standing in the sunlight.

"I thought you burned up in the sun," I said with as much attitude as I could muster. I didn't want to fall for his act. I had to stay strong.

Lucian looked hurt at the anger he sensed from me.

I really wished he wouldn't look at me like a wounded puppy.

I was a sucker for a guy with a butt-hurt face. Especially if I was the cause of it.

He responded, "In your dreams I can walk in the sun. Even though it's not warm and doesn't feel the same, it's the closest I've come for centuries. I forgot what it felt like. Thank you."

"Don't thank me for anything. I don't like it when you thank me. I don't like it when you're nice to me. I just don't like any of it!" I sounded like a four-year-old and I knew it, but I couldn't seem to control myself around Lucian. Even in dreamland.

He stepped closer. Our faces were within inches of each other.

He stood staring. I stared back, thinking I'd win this contest, but Lucian took the prize when he brushed his hand through my hair.

My knees almost buckled.

"Your hair is luminescent in the sun. I didn't know that. It's like the surface of the Nile under the moon." His hand gently rested on the nape of my neck.

I shivered from his soft touch. I should have pulled away from him, kicked him, punched him. Anything! But his agonizingly gentle caress made me want to reach up and kiss him. What was wrong with me?

I changed the subject instead. "You were a slave?"

"When I was human, yes." Lucian's other hand traced the edge of my jawbone as if I were some kind of porcelain doll he was admiring. My stomach did flip-flops in response. "I hate these deserts. It reminds me of a time when I was weak and vulnerable."

"I can't imagine you weak," I admitted.

Lucian gently reached down and took my hand in his. I could feel every nerve in my fingers tingle at his touch. "You make me weak." He leaned down, his lips almost touching mine.

I'd never wanted anything more, but . . .

Aidan.

I pushed away.

Instead of angry and annoyed like I thought he would be, he looked genuinely wounded.

I shook my head to gain my senses back. "Just stay away from me. I'm not your food!" I warned threateningly.

Lucian stared with an expression of confusion. "I would

never feed on you."

"Yeah right!" I was starting to get angry now. "Aidan told me everything!"

Lucian snarled, anger growing in his eyes. "And just what did Adnachiel tell you?"

"He told me how you killed all the other Vessels, how you want to kill me! And that you're just toying with me until I fall for your little act and then you'll take me to Caelius or eat me!" I started to back away from him.

I had never seen anyone look that mad.

"He said *I* killed the Vessels? *Me?*" Lucian was fuming.

"Don't bother trying to deny it!" I exclaimed.

Lucian was on me in less than a second. I was so startled I didn't know how to react. His face was millimeters from mine. His eyes were balls of rage. "Why don't you ask him about the first Vessel, Moses?"

I snapped out of my stupor.

Before Lucian could do anything to hurt me, I made myself wake up.

***

I jumped slightly when my eyes opened. I was in the passenger seat of my own car with Aidan in the driver's seat. We were heading down an empty highway with no other cars or lights anywhere in sight.

"You okay?" he asked.

"Yeah, fine," I said, though I didn't mean it.

I turned away and stared out the window. I wished I could

erase Lucian from my mind forever. I never wanted to see that guy again.

And even as I thought it, I knew it was a lie.

CHAPTER 6
LUCIAN

"Lucian, Lucian, Lucian . . . am I not your father? Do you have no love for your maker? No loyalty?"

I half knelt, refusing eye contact.

"Ur-Nammu found you in some cavern, surviving on bats, near death, chunks of your flesh burned to ash. You were muttering in a lucid dream: Shea, you are my weakness . . ."

Now my eyes raised, but they weren't full of gratitude as they should have been. It was hatred, raw and unkempt. "I'm sorry, Caelius."

He instantly coughed, grabbing his chest as if I'd struck a mortal blow. He paused, breathing in deep. "Caelius? Not even the least among my grandchildren call me this. Babies that you created, that have created hundreds of children, don't dare to speak my name, though close to none have seen my face. And you, you say it as if I weren't your *father*!"

Even caged, his power was magnificent. He tossed my large

frame through a stalagmite without so much as a twitch from his brow.

I lifted myself slowly from the rubble. This wasn't the first time I'd been covered in the dust of his cavern, half-alive, and I doubted it would be the last. He'd beaten me worse than any pompous master in Egypt.

I gritted my teeth and kept silent, readying myself for another lash.

He smiled, and for the first time in over three thousand years, he sat down. My mouth fell open at the sight of it. He leaned back casually, his auburn eyes fixed on my slumped frame. His white teeth gleamed as he used his mind to take off my shirt. Once off, he tore it to shreds with a quick snap of his fingers. "Come closer, my son. I want to look at that wound."

The cavern was vast. I looked around for a moment, a ridiculous gesture, but I had to think quickly. In this weakened state, he could do what he wanted with me and I'd have no defense. He'd done it before.

I let my feet drag on the loose dirt. With every step toward him I did what I could to harden, to gut anything that felt alive inside.

My eyes fell to a large bestial skeleton behind him. It was the size of a building, its skull alone the mass of a house. Its wingspan spread out for yards. Ashliel, one of Aidan's brothers.

His life was said to have been offered freely like Aidan's other brother, Herostel, the earthbound angel like Aidan was now. They were the final ingredients to seal Caelius, or so Aidan claimed.

But I'd been there.

Herostel may have resolved to give his life over for the cause, but I'd *seen* Caelius drag Ashliel unwillingly to the pit with him, alive and terrified.

Caelius had taken his time slowly devouring him, inch by inch. Now he was just bones perched like a mantle behind Caelius, adorning his enormous cage like a prize. But some nights when I was forced to visit, I swore I could still hear the ghost of Ashliel's agonizing screams echoing throughout the chamber.

I stepped closer and swallowed hard. In all of the archeological digs in Egypt, they'd never find Caelius. No mortal would be able to follow the caves down this deep—it was too much of a labyrinth. Besides, the angelic seal in the hollowed-out catacomb would prevent that from happening, making Caelius and his angel bones invisible.

He motioned his hand in an appealing manner. "Sit with me, my son. We have much to discuss."

I was hesitant.

I knew my head wasn't right from my encounters with Shea, and if anyone could tell, it would be Caelius.

Of course he would send Ur-Nammu to retrieve me. We hadn't spoken since he'd tried to take Moses to Caelius. Only he would have the power to track me, break my protective seals, and lug my unconscious body back to Egypt.

I watched as Caelius's eyebrow raised and he motioned one last time. A final warning.

I closed my eyes, and for a moment I was back in the dream with Shea, feeling the soft texture of her pale blond hair. It had no place in Egypt, and yet it was as if she'd always been there, standing with me in the misery of that life I'd left behind with

Nefertiti.

I swallowed hard. Enough. If I wasn't with Caelius, I'd shove more sand down my throat. Who was I to feel like this? I was a creature now. A monster. I shouldn't have still been alive. I shouldn't have existed.

There it was, I'd found it: that familiar numbness and pain. Now I could speak to him.

I casually walked inches from his cell, if one could call it a cell. It was simple enough in design: a vast empty space, except for Ashliel's corpse. But outside of his cage, the Enochian beauty took form. The entire cavern was covered in the seal keeping Caelius in place. The writing looked even stranger than Egyptian hieroglyphs.

They were immovable. No amount of water, destruction, or torrent could break their script. It was written in the very air, burned into the core of the earth.

I sat as close as I could to him. It was the way he liked it, so he could almost touch me with his long fingertips. "I've never seen you sit down in here before. All these thousands of years. Have I upset you this much?"

He reached his hand toward my face and motioned as if stroking my hair. "I'm worried about you, my son."

I instinctively flinched, not thinking about my words before they spilled out. "You have nothing to worry about. I will bring you the Vessel."

He squinted, tracing his tongue over his enlarged incisors. They reminded me of the saber-tooth tiger before it'd been hunted to extinction. They were small now, but they could grow thicker and fiercer than any nightmare. When he'd fought the beasts of Heaven, I'd seen them grow along with his body. He'd had spiderlike black limbs and had been the size of a mammoth then, unstoppable, with blood eyes and teeth that had made Aidan's body quake in terror. He'd always been the weakest of his brothers.

That last thought made me grin despite myself. This seemed to change Caelius's temperament slightly. "You've always had a beautiful smile."

My lips recoiled. I averted my eyes, biting the inside of my mouth, reminding myself to think of nothing but pain.

He laughed openly, again pretending to touch my face. "You think you can hide from me now! You may be the strongest because you are my only child, but you are *mine*! I will always see you, Lucian."

His invisible touch moved along the surface of my skin, curving around my muscles, slithering up my legs. He was making his point. Even like this, he could touch, he could *own* every part of me. He opened my mouth and I felt his invisible lips on mine. He smiled, sitting there candidly like a god watching some puppet.

I couldn't stand to look at him. I stopped myself from explaining, protesting, or playing his game. If he wanted to pry information from my lips, let him taste the dirt still lingering in my belly or the ash of Shea's burn. Let him feel my agony and not my pleasure.

Shea . . . I cursed myself for even thinking her name.

His pressure shifted from my mouth and weighed heavily on my hips. "Do you want to know how much I know about Shea?"

There was no escape. He had me. I had to shut it down, to

kill my heart. I squeezed my hands into fists until my knuckles were white, filling my mind with death and blood.

He dragged a hand carefully through his short, pitch-black hair, biting his bottom lip while unzipping my pants. "When Ur-Nammu brought you, you were half-asleep, as if in some dream. I remember you as a boy. I wanted you then. It's because of that heart of yours that I saw fit to turn you in the first place. Then there was your undying love and devotion to Nefertiti, even as you lay dying by her window, beaten to death because of your passion. You know, the sculptures you made of her are everywhere. Most museums use it as her likeness."

It was good that he'd mentioned her. I snapped, letting my fury mount. "And what would you know of the outside world, or of passion? You've been sitting in rot for—"

Long nail marks moved down my chest. I watched his hand as he grabbed the air and tore down; peels of my flesh curled in thick slabs under his invisible touch. I clenched my jaw and said nothing. I hated the desert. It was the place where I'd been a slave. And now . . . had anything really changed? In the world amongst mortals and cattle, I was like a god, but in here I was just the whipping post.

His eyes swelled. He stopped just before the seam of my pants, blood seeping into the fabric. "You always ruin such tender moments between us. You know I have ears all over the world that tell me what you find too taxing to explain. I've even seen a sunset on an iPhone."

The auburn in his eyes turned bloodred. His skin paled further as he tilted his perfectly sculpted face toward me. He crushed it against the barrier. It singed his cheek as he whispered

112

in a dark fury, "You were supposed to be my hands in the world, Lucian. Why do you always push me this way? You have sired children of your own; you know how you *love* them. Even when you don't want to think of them, they drift into your mind and you long to touch what is yours. That's only a fifth of the way I feel about you. You are my *only* son . . ."

His voice trailed off. I felt it. I could lie to myself for a thousand years, and still it would be there: the sickening connection I couldn't escape from. It was an unholy, unfathomable devotion to him, and to those cursed souls I had foolishly turned in my youth. The closest words in mortal tongue were father and son. But that wasn't right either. It was deeper, sometimes purer, sometimes intimate, but mostly it was like an inexplicable possession. To love as a vampire was to *own*.

I'd had a real father when I was human. Onack the Great had been an honorable man who'd died fighting in the wars with Egypt. He'd been a Gutian, like Nefertiti, before those left of our kind had been enslaved or slaughtered.

Onack had given his life fighting by our code. I had no such honor; he'd robbed me of it when he'd begged me to hide amongst the Elamites and become a tradesman. It had saved me the fate of becoming a slave like Ur-Nammu and the others, or worse: a concubine to the Pharaoh like *her*.

And how had I repaid him, my real father? With loving the one woman who would guarantee my slavery for all eternity. His name, I barely noticed as it passed, was a murmur between my lips.

"Do you think of him often? Your *mortal* father?" Caelius's eyes burned like molten lava, but his voice was soft, almost tender.

"Not often." I spoke, again trying to freeze my mind. In this proximity, even an inaudible whisper could be heard by Caelius. He was watching me intently, listening to every ragged breath, looking for an opening: a way inside.

The numbness I'd relied on all these years always helped me in these encounters. It kept him from seeing, from really knowing me. Still, in the end he'd always win, breaking me down one way or another until I obeyed and acknowledged that I was *his*.

Even though the blood inside me longed for Caelius, I would *never* come to him willingly. But now, these past few months I'd been cracked open by strange feelings. I was *raw*. It was a dangerous time for me to be this close. If Caelius could twist me in his grasp when I was strong . . .

He sighed heavily. "I know you serve me. My blood inside you will guarantee that. But me? I've always wanted you. I *chose* you for a reason. Do you think there's anyone else I'd rather spend eternity with?

"My love, the love of our kind, is so much greater than what any other life-form can offer; you know that. You're my *only* son. If you were to free me tomorrow, I would not turn another. And yet, that same heart that I cherish within you has caused me nothing but misery.

"I'd hoped you'd placed childish notions of romantic love behind you in Egypt. Now I hear that you've been killing our own kind because this Shea Harper *belongs* to you?"

My stomach churned and my esophagus was flooded with a burning sensation. If I were mortal there would be acid eating away at my insides. "You misunderstand," I began. "These young vampires know nothing. One almost killed the Vessel. I made an example of him in order to send a message to the lesser amongst our kind not to interfere. I did this for *you*, so I can bring her here."

He cocked his head, pleasure overtaking his immaculate features. "I heard you smote the entire line of Gracuri. Did you finish him as well?"

I moved to speak, but he snatched the words from my lips.

"Don't lie to me, boy. I know you left him alive! I ordered you to kill him in Thebes! If you'd wanted my blessing to do it now, you didn't need it."

I rose. I knew it was because he'd mentioned Gracuri. The thought of him dead with his head skewered on a post and presented to Caelius, like he'd requested all those years ago, sickened me.

He was my son, but more than that, he was a friend.

Caelius closed his hand into a fist and my body crinkled like a crushed tin can. I was forced to kneel before him in a heap.

"You'll spend the rest of our conversation this way until you learn some manners. Since you are such a fan of eating dirt, you can speak to me from it. Oh, Lucian, when will you stop tormenting yourself like a worthless slave?"

I spat on the ground, my saliva mixing with the sweat rolling off my body as I tried to resist his brute force. *When you stop treating me like one.*

I directed the thought toward him, but he ignored it like a fly buzzing around his ears. "I'm pleased the Vessel is a woman. This means change, and change means opportunity. The Light is wanting to right the wrong of my imprisonment. Shea was

115

destined to be the key that frees me.

"I want to give you aid. You have been unsuccessful all of these years. Whether Adnachiel was involved or not, it is still *your* failing. This time you will not fail because you will not touch Shea Harper.

"I will send *all* of our kind with instructions to bring her to me. You are the eldest, the most feared, but this task is not fit for you. You will stand down and our armies will drag her to my depths."

"And what will happen to the girl once you're done with her? Will she survive this *dragging to the depths*?" The words rushed out. It was unwise, but I could think of nothing else.

He leered in silence. With my face pressed against the rocks, I could still feel the heat of his glare as a large shadow stood over me. Even if he'd released my body so that I could look in horror at his true form, I wouldn't have. I'd seen it once, and that was enough for all eternity. His shadow form extended past the seal, holding me down. His breath grated on my skin like sandpaper and shook the cavern like a trapped tornado.

I felt the tips of teeth hold my neck. They punctured either side. I winced momentarily but relaxed my muscles. Why did I always speak? It had been the same in Egypt. If I'd kept silent, I could have lived a long life. But I'd had to reach for the moon just to touch Nefertiti, and now I'd spoken on Shea's behalf. Maybe Caelius was right to break me every time I came to him. Maybe eventually that fire inside me would die. It would save me from this at least.

"You could beg me to stop and I would," he laughed, knowing my response.

116

"I have agreed to serve masters, but I have *never* begged. Not since my mother died. You know that. And you know I never will. Not even to you."

"Fair enough." He grinned.

His phantom teeth pushed in deeper as he held me in place, having his way with my small immortal form in every bestial way possible. He dragged out his pleasure to the brink of my sanity, bringing me to the edges of both ecstasy and pain until I moaned in madness what he longed to hear. "I will do as you say, Caelius. I will obey."

When he was done with my body, if you could call what was left a body, I was in a pile and his shadow was back inside his mortal form, looking satisfied and bored. It was always that mixture of looks, of conquest and new desire. That was what Caelius called love.

What sickened me was that I believed him. The way he worked over my body confused all of my senses, until I'd believe that his version of love was all there was in the universe and that I was powerless to stand against it . . . but I'd had real love before. I'd *felt* it. It had been long ago, but it still lived, even if I had died. It was out there in the world somewhere, for those who were lucky enough to find it, and it was not this. It was not an immortal kiss of servitude, a compassionless void of ownership. This wasn't love: it was breaking a wild horse.

He moved his mouth as close as he could to the lump of my frame. "In answer to your question, now that you've agreed to obey, I am not a murderer like the children you have chosen and their children. I don't need constant blood to survive. I fed once, on you! Once in Egypt before I was imprisoned! I've gone three

117

millennia without food. That's not what I want.

"I'm not looking to end this Shea or humankind. I merely wish to be free. I may sometimes seem cruel to you, Lucian, but understand that I've been trapped and restless for over three thousand years. Sometimes my temper boils. But I'm kind underneath, don't you think?"

My lips moved without provocation. "Of course you are."

He laced his hands through his hair, somewhat pleased with my obedient response. Still, it only caused the look of boredom to grow further. I knew it every time, and there it was again: he wanted to break me, but only as long as I kept getting up. His pleasure was in the conquest.

"When I turned you, it was to save your life, Lucian. You, having been a slave, should understand what it's like to be imprisoned. My power leashed like this is tormenting. I'm in agony."

His hold on my body loosened. I trembled as our gazes met. His face looked like it had on the night he'd turned me. I saw now that the only agony he was in was his own. "I had no idea that you were in pain."

His expression saddened. "And why tell you of my torment? For guilt? You carry enough of that around on your own. That's why I don't want you handling this Vessel." Now his invisible touch was soft, cupping my face.

After what he had done to me, I could think of nothing but obedience. That yes, I belonged to him. Yes to whatever he said, whatever he wanted.

He bit his full bottom lip, eyeing me with more obvious displeasure, knowing that he had full control. "I will send all

118

the others, but you . . . you she's already come close to killing. No Vessel has touched you before. And with my blood surging through you as my first and only born, I'm not surprised. But this Vessel is different. I'll send every vampire your sons have created, but not you. She might kill you, and for that I would not live, free or caged, to see the sunrise."

I nodded in acceptance. There was nothing else to do. Every thought was his. My own blood longed to please him. But it wasn't my blood. It was his blood in me. His blood keeping me trapped by a similar invisible cage.

Still, he could own this body, he could confuse my mind, but I knew deep inside why I was his favorite pet: because even now, completely subservient, my soul was starting to burn. Burn against every word in his mouth.

I couldn't kill that growing fire, even with a body beaten and trembling from his pleasures. "Ur-Nammu brought me here, but he said nothing. Is he still close? May I speak with him?"

Caelius shook his head tentatively. "You know he will not. It's because of you that his daughter is dead. He may be the first son you turned, but you will always be the vampire who killed his Nefertiti."

The words themselves ripped a larger hole in my soul than Shea ever could. "So . . . he still hasn't forgiven me then."

Caelius took a deep breath, his eyes full of fake empathy. "Will you forgive yourself?"

"No." The words were flat and moved out of my lips before I had a chance to stop them.

"Then you have your answer." I felt his phantom hand around my waist. It still sent chills up my spine. "Go now, Son.

119

Egypt is not good for you: too many memories here. When Shea is captured, and I am free, I will find you. If your children fail, come to me when you are rested and this Vessel is dead. Together we'll plan our strategy for the next Vessel, like we did once... before the first Vessel, Moses, came between us."

His last words stung, but I shook my head in acceptance and left. I didn't need to give him a reason to break me again. If it pleased him, he could make leaving grueling.

And it was.

When he wanted, his power snatched me from the entrance to the cave and dragged me back at such a fierce speed that my mind couldn't even register the movements. Then I would have to start climbing all over again.

It took an entire month to claw my way out of the catacombs. I cursed him with every breath for making it slow and forcing me to wander large periods of time lost.

I couldn't think about the Vessel . . . I couldn't think about anything but obedience and my loyalty to Caelius. Every broken bone in my body begged me to do as he said. Every sore muscle, every chunk of missing flesh. He was my creator, my savior. I had to obey.

I had to.

***

When I emerged, it was day. I hid under the surface of the sand for hours waiting for nightfall as the shadows moved inch by inch, ticking away the minutes with their slow stretching.

When the moon finally appeared, I tore through the sand,

120

leaving tunnels like a giant anaconda in my wake.

I headed toward Shea, sensing her location from the dream we'd shared before my encounter with Caelius.

I waited until I was in Colorado to think again, to feel anything that was mine.

I began what I called the "separating." It was the process of determining what was Caelius and what was real. It was always hard to distinguish at first, but I'd mastered it by now.

He could break me for a moment, a day, a year, but I would always come back to myself. Maybe that was the problem. If I could just stay broken, keep my head bowed and serve, if I could just be weak . . .

My thoughts found their way back to Shea. With her, I *wanted* to be weak.

I held the blanket that she must have been lying in at the Morning Star Hotel close to my face. Just breathing in her scent brought me a strange sort of peace. I recalled the way her fingertips had glided over my healing flesh when we'd Dream-Walked. I covered my eyes and felt her, the exposure cleansing me of Caelius's painful touch.

If Ur-Nammu hadn't come, I'd have sought her out that night in person, just to protect her from Aidan's lies. But Ur-Nammu's arrival had heralded bad news. Caelius wanted me to forfeit her to scum, to lesser immortals. All for whom? *Him?*

I laughed openly. I knew that trash wouldn't bring her in alive. Even if Ur-Nammu told every last vampire that only a *living* Vessel could break the curse, they wouldn't be able to succeed where I had failed.

And their idiocy could cost her life.

121

Caelius. It felt good to be free from his gaze. He should have listened more carefully to the message engraved in Frank's skin and the clan of Gracuri.

Shea was *mine*.

CHAPTER 7
SHEA

"What? No, seriously, say that again." I asked Aidan to repeat himself for the hundredth time.

"Just remember, you are a part of creation itself. Your blood has pure Light inside of it, and it allows you to connect to the earth, whereas Caelius is your opposite: Darkness. He can only consume and destroy.

"As a result, you can control any element: earth, wind, fire, water. You're an elemental, of sorts." Aidan sighed deeply. He may have been frowning in frustration, but his eyes were smiling.

"Of sorts? Elemental? So you're saying *I control the elements?*" I said that last part in a deep Gandalf-type voice because saying something like that was *crazy*. I couldn't decide if I had jumped into delusional-land or not.

We had been on the run for over a month now, and I was starting to wonder if any of the insane-o things that had happened to me had *really* happened to me. Maybe I had imagined everything and now I was giving myself superpowers.

Although, powers were easy compared to the conversation I'd had with Aidan a few weeks ago. I'd finally figured out how I felt about him. I loved him with all my soul, but I just didn't see him *that* way. He had taken it well and told me he'd always be there for me. I felt horrible, but he was like my brother. I had seen him in Spiderman Underoos for goodness sake! It wasn't that I didn't find him attractive—he was gorgeous—it was just . . . I didn't know how to explain it. I loved him and that was enough for me.

I could tell it hurt, but his mood had brightened considerably over the last couple of weeks. He seemed happy just to be with me, whether it was romantic or not. It made me love him all the more.

"Try again," Aidan instructed.

I had been trying for the last three hours to make a tree branch move. Aidan figured since I had connected with the wood in the Pillar House to fight Frank-the-vampire that it was a good place to start.

But so far?

Nothing.

Not even a twitch.

About an hour ago, I'd had a small surge of hope when the branch had moved slightly, until I'd realized it was the breeze.

Apparently, summoning strangling tendrils, ripping holes into vampires' chests, and lifting rubble with my mind were abilities only available when I was in extreme stress.

"Maybe you should attack me or something. Get me to activate my powers," I suggested, desperate for something to happen.

Aidan didn't like the sound of that because he reached out and touched my cheek, his eyes filled with determination. "I will never hurt you."

It was weird. It was almost as if he was convincing himself more than he was trying to convince me. I couldn't tell if I was just being paranoid or not.

Lucian's words always seemed to ring in my ears: *Aidan will kill you. You're not safe with him.*

Not that I should've given a crap what Lucian had to say. Aidan had given me the skinny on that particular monster. Caelius was his father for crying out loud! Aidan had told me about the many lifetimes he'd spent with Lucian, and that Pompeii had actually happened because of the fight between him and Aidan's brothers. Apparently, it had been the second Vessel, and when Lucian had decided to torture him by drinking his blood (ew), Lucian had gone too far and had started to drain the Vessel's soul. It had been enough for Aidan's brothers (though his name had been Atticus back then, weird!) to come down from wherever it was they came down from, and it had turned into a serious volcano-worthy smackdown.

But the worst was Moses. Freaking *Moses!* I was still reeling from that one. It sounded like Aidan and Lucian had actually been friends. Like brothers, really. And Moses had been their third musketeer. After years of living together as a family, Lucian had betrayed them both and taken Moses to free his father, Caelius. When confronted by Aidan, Lucian had chosen to kill the Vessel rather than let Aidan save him.

I'd managed to keep him out of my dreams. Well, that was a lie. I'd tried to connect with him, just to hear what he had to say for himself, but it was like he was gone, as if he wasn't on Earth anymore. I knew that couldn't be true. When Aidan had told me Lucian could fly, I'd imagined him floating in space or something ridiculous like that, but deep down I knew he was somewhere dark. Somewhere deep.

I only saw a flash of him once, like a tiny piece of a nightmare. He'd been in some kind of cavern, standing in front of a hideous monster, and behind him were the bones of another hideous monster. Then suddenly Lucian was thinking of my hair?

I'd woken up after that. It had been so strange, I hadn't known what to make of it. I still couldn't tell if it had been just an ordinary odd-bird dream, or an actual Dream-Walking experience. Either way, I hadn't been able to connect with him after that.

Telling Aidan definitely wasn't an option. The guy would kill me if he knew I was actively seeking out Lucian in my dreams. And besides, after the dreaded "talk," Aidan and I had grown much closer. I didn't want to do or say anything that would ruin it. I felt safe with Aidan, and safe felt pretty darn good at the moment.

"I'm not asking you to *hurt* me. I'm asking you to provoke me so I can get this juju going." I was getting pumped up. "Let's do this."

Aidan grinned. "All right, calm down. You need to control your power *without* provocation."

I sighed heavily, repeating the "rules" Aidan had drilled in my head. "Don't use your power out of the circle, and don't use too much of it. It will act as a beacon to any vampire, but especially the old ones."

I looked at the circle Aidan had created. Seared into the grass were strange symbols that apparently kept my powers hidden from all vampires as long as I stayed inside their border.

We were somewhere in the middle of the country, Missouri, off Highway D. It was all grass fields for miles with a smattering of trees here and there, and quite stunning in a peaceful kind of way. The tree in front of me broke up the monotonous rolls of green. My car was the unnatural sore thumb parked at the side of the highway.

I couldn't imagine Lucian or any other vampire finding us here in the middle of nowhere. They would've had to be randomly driving past or flying by. Of course, according to Aidan, Lucian was the only vampire he knew of who could fly. That didn't exactly calm my mind though. Vampires on Harleys could be just as scary. It was daylight anyway, so we didn't have to worry about any of them finding us at this particular moment, but I still didn't want to alert them to our general vicinity either.

Only one month and these thoughts were already becoming natural to me. I wished it were otherwise, but I had to accept that this was my life now. Unless Aidan planned on killing every vampire on Earth, we would always be on the run.

Aidan brought me back to our current task—getting that branch to move. "Good, you remember the rules. I can't shield your powers unless I prepare the ground with the Enochian symbols. Now concentrate on this little branch here." Aidan wiggled the branch.

"Oh, that branch? I'd been trying to move *that* one," I joked. Sometimes Aidan could be so teachery it drove me bonkers. But it was cute.

"Ha, ha," he said sarcastically. "We've been at this for hours. My feet hurt and I'm hungry. Make this branch move so I can eat a burger."

"You were eyeing that diner twenty miles back, weren't you?" I smiled. "You love the greasy-spoon diet. If I have one more patty melt I'm going to puke."

"Then stop ordering the patty melt," Aidan teased.

"I can't. It's a thing now. I have to find the best patty melt in the country. Hey, a girl has to have goals."

"Speaking of goals . . ." Aidan eyed the branch purposefully.

"Right," I groaned.

Here went nothing.

I focused on the branch with every iota of concentration I could conjure up.

Nothing.

Really?

So. Frustrated.

I decided to use that frustration, feed on it, make it breathe. I stared at that branch and thought only of connecting to it, to its core, to its essence.

Then I saw it—the inside of the tree.

Sap. Veins. Pulp.

Alive. Growing. Life.

It was as if I was inside it, a part of it. Its limbs were my limbs.

I opened my arms wide.

The two front branches opened with me, mimicking my every move. I made a branch wave at Aidan in a friendly hello.

"Holy crap, Shea! That's amazing!" Aidan's eyes were wide

with wonder.

"Watch this," I said.

I made all the branches twist and turn into beautiful braids of leaves and limbs.

As I did this, I started to feel light-headed. The power surged through me. I panicked and wanted to disconnect, but I couldn't. My own heartbeat pumped with sap. I felt my feet plant into the ground. I was becoming . . .

"Aidan," I cried out.

Then everything went black.

***

How had I gotten here?

Dreaming. I must have passed out.

At least I was standing in my own backyard in Phoenix. It was one of the few places I actually enjoyed when it wasn't a hundred thousand degrees out. It was magic hour, my favorite time of day. The sun was just getting ready to set and the clouds in the sky were a million different shades of purple and pink.

My backyard wasn't huge, but it wasn't tiny either. It didn't have any grass, only small lava rock like most Arizona homes. I walked over to the swinging bench my dad had built when I was four. It was made of wrought iron and wood. I thought it looked like it belonged in an East Coast brochure; it was out of place in Phoenix. But that was why my father had built it that way. He'd wanted to give us something different than what everybody else had. Thinking of my dad made me miss him terribly.

My heart almost leapt out of my chest when Lucian appeared

on the bench.

"Lucian," I exclaimed. Stating the obvious was a gift of mine.

He looked at me as if hearing me say his name was somehow painful. "It's been a while," he whispered.

I sat down next to him on the bench and my leg casually rocked the swing until we moved in a steady rhythm. "I thought I saw you once, but I think it was just a nightmare. The guy you were with looked like some kind of demon-monster-beast." I didn't mention the memory of him noticing my hair. It was too embarrassing.

Lucian stared at me. His eyes were full of so much emotion, I didn't know how to respond. "It wasn't a dream," he answered quietly. "I was visiting Caelius."

"Aidan said Caelius is your father." For some reason I needed Lucian to confirm it.

"He made me into a vampire, but I refuse to call him 'Father.' He wants me to stay away from you. He's commanded every vampire in existence to hunt you down. There are too many; I can't stop them all. If you stay with me, I'll keep you safe. The weaker children won't even try to stand against me. I sent a message to the lower class about what happens to any vamp who touches you through Frank's lineage."

I sat back, creating some distance between us. "Aidan will protect me, and I can protect myself. I controlled a tree today." I knew I shouldn't be sharing, but for some reason I wanted to. I needed Lucian not to be the monster Aidan painted him to be.

Lucian appeared disturbed by the news. "But you're so young."

"The younger the stronger?" I shrugged.

"That's never been the case. Moses didn't have full use of his powers until he was a grown man." Lucian leaned forward to be closer to me.

I leaned back until I felt the armrest dig into my back. "Well, I'm different, I guess. Probably because I'm a girl. Girls are better, you know." I cracked a smile.

Lucian paused, then the shadow of a smile ghosted his face. "*You* are better. Stronger."

"Thanks?" I wasn't sure how I was supposed to respond to that. The way he looked at me made me blush. "I shouldn't be here with you."

"Because of Aidan?" Lucian gracefully slid toward me until our knees were touching. I could barely focus on what he'd asked. My mind went numb from sensory overload.

"Aidan doesn't know about this." I closed my eyes. It helped keep me grounded.

When I opened them again, Lucian's face was an inch away, his lips almost touching mine. If I wasn't already unconscious, I would have lost consciousness right there. He was so close. I wanted to pull him in, kiss him, feel his chest pressed against mine, his hand caressing my thigh.

Whoa.

I stood up, leaving Lucian on the bench swing.

"Are you working some kind of vampire seduction magic on me? Stop it!" I reproached him breathlessly.

"Believe me, I tried. It didn't work, remember? You accused me of being on drugs." He stood up as well. I could feel the heat of his chest like a giant raging fireball of making-me-crazy.

"The eye thing. Right. Well, it seems to be working now." I

didn't want to believe I was having these feelings all on my own. I wanted something to blame. *Someone* to blame.

"Shea." When he said my name, it gave me shivers. "I *can't* compel you." Lucian reached down and cupped my cheek with his hand. I closed my eyes again, leaning into his palm. I was starting to enjoy this a little too much.

Then he asked, "Where are you?"

***

My eyes snapped open.

I was in the passenger seat of my car, parked in front of Lucy's Diner. It was dark outside, so I had no idea how long I'd been out. Aidan was next to me, stroking my hair worriedly. "You okay?" he asked.

"What happened?" I sat up, rubbing my eyes.

I could still feel Lucian's hand.

I shook my head to rid myself of my own foolishness. All Lucian wanted to know was where I was so he could take me and then feed me to his father. How could I have been so stupid? On TV shows or movies, I always hated when girls acted the way I had acted. I used to think no one would feel *anything* for a jerk. Just because a guy was hot wasn't reason enough to lose all reason! I hated that I was becoming a stereotype. It made me feel weak somehow, like I was an idiot.

Aidan nodded toward the diner. "I'll tell you over a patty melt."

I groaned, but didn't argue. Even though I'd devoured a patty melt every day for the last month, it somehow still managed to sound delicious.

In fewer than twenty minutes, I was sitting in a red vinyl booth with a patty melt placed before me on a Formica tabletop. Why did every diner look like it'd been built and decorated in the '50s? It was comforting somehow, an American staple that no one wanted to change. I took a large bite of my sloppy-cheesed, grilled-onion-filled burger.

And. Yum.

Once the protein entered my bloodstream, I started to feel more myself. "So, spill," I prodded Aidan.

Aidan finished a bite of a huge stacked burger. "I don't know how to explain it. You connected to the tree and your mind tried to make you . . . merge somehow. It was too much for your consciousness, so your body protected you by knocking you on your arse. You're lucky I was there to catch you." He smiled teasingly, then continued, "Only Moses was as strong as you. Remember the old parting of the red sea? That was him tapping into the water and separating it with his arms like you did with the branches."

Hearing Aidan talk about Moses only reminded me that my dream with Lucian had been real. Moses had been the only person the two of them had cared about mutually. It was strange to hear two enemies talk about a man who they'd both obviously loved. It made me wonder if Aidan and Lucian would ever *not* hate each other.

"Maybe I should take it easy for a while then." I felt weak, and the thought of connecting to another living thing like that scared me, almost as if I didn't have the right to feel that kind of power.

"Agreed." Aidan looked relieved. Even though he'd been keeping the conversation light, I could tell that my abilities scared him. Or at least how apparently fast I was learning them.

We sat in silence and quietly ate our cholesterol-filled delicious food. When the last fry was consumed, Aidan's eyes met mine. "Shall we?"

Before I could respond, a man slid into the booth next to me. With a quick flash of fangs, the vampire motioned to the crowded restaurant. "Hear me out before you decide to wreak havoc on me and possibly hurt some of these innocent people."

I glanced at the vampire to have a better view. He wasn't that attractive, which surprised me. I thought it was a prerequisite that all vampires be stunning. He had shaggy brown hair and a long, crooked nose. He wasn't exactly fit either. Kind of a general pudge all around.

"Speak," Aidan growled.

I was getting used to this growl of his. I knew he wanted to rip the guy's throat out, but the patrons of the diner were holding him back. The vampire was smart. He knew neither one of us would be willing to put anyone in harm's way.

"I'm the only one who knows you're here, so don't worry. I'm not calling in the big dogs," the man began. "I'm Chris, by the way."

"Chris, you'd better get to the point before I tear those fangs out of your mouth," Aidan snarled.

Damn, that boy was scary. But considering it was all about protecting me, it made me all warm and fuzzy inside. Was it weird that I wanted to give Aidan a big hug in the midst of Chris-the-vampire's spiel of why Aidan shouldn't kill him?

Chris put his hands up in a placating manner. "I was only turned thirty years ago, so I'm still young. I have no doubts you'd demolish me in two seconds. I used to be a detective in my human life, so I was able to track you two down the old-fashioned way: through witnesses. I admit, being a vampire makes it much easier to get people to tell you the truth, but that's not the point."

"What *is* the point?" Aidan was losing his patience.

"*This* is my point."

Before Aidan or I could react, Chris ripped the bolted-down table out from the floor and shoved it as hard as he could into Aidan's chest. The force was so great that Aidan, and his booth, were pulled up from the ground and flung back, destroying three booths behind him in his wake. The poor couple sitting in the next booth were pinned between their table and the other two booths.

Chris's iron grip grabbed me by the waist and the world whooshed past me at lightning speed. Faster than any car, Chris was running as if he were made of wind. It was nighttime, so it would have been difficult to see my surroundings anyway, but going as fast as we were going, all the lights looked like streaks of fluorescent markers written in the sky.

I tried to struggle out of his grasp, but these vampires were made of steel.

Louder than any lion, I heard a roar fill the air.

Aidan.

Even though I was helpless in Chris's grasp, my heart surged with hope and pride.

I almost felt sorry for the guy.

Almost.

Boom!

Aidan materialized in front of Chris as if he had teleported there.

Chris stopped and tried to run back the other way.

Not going to happen.

"Shea! Crash position!" Aidan called out, and I almost laughed from the absurdity of his statement, but I knew Chris was about to be bitch-slapped into next week, so I did as he said.

I curled into a ball in Chris's arms.

Bam!

I was free.

I was free because Aidan's fist hit Chris's jaw with such strength that it flew off his face—off his face! The guy had no bottom jaw!

He choked and coughed, shocked at the blood pouring from the open gape where the lower half of his mouth should've been.

It was pretty gross.

Chris's eyes were filled with panic.

And panicked people did stupid things.

Unfortunately, that included tackling me to the ground.

I couldn't fight him. He was too strong.

Aidan grabbed Chris's neck from behind and yanked him off.

Chris used the only weapon he had left on Aidan.

His fangs.

He bit down into Aidan's neck. It would have been comical if it weren't so terrifying. Without his lower jaw, his teeth sank easily into skin. Aidan grunted in pain, but couldn't get enough of a grip to pull Chris off of him.

I freaked.

I didn't know what biting meant. Did it mean he was turning Aidan into a vampire? Would it kill him?

I screamed.

I felt the wind around me, like nature was breathing. Breathing into me. Spinning. Building. Growing.

Until it was *mine*.

The tornado hit Chris full force.

He was off Aidan in the blink of an eye.

His body was torn into thousands of pieces as the tornado ripped him to shreds.

My mind spun. Rotating. Spinning into oblivion. The power flowed through me. I was made of air.

"*Shea!*"

Aidan's voice broke my connection with the wind.

The tornado evaporated instantly.

Then it rained.

I looked at my skin. The water was red.

It was raining Chris-the-vampire.

Ew.

"We have to leave. You shouldn't have used your powers. I could have taken care of him." Aidan helped me get to my feet.

"I couldn't let him bite you. He could have turned you or something." I was still dizzy.

"I can't be turned, Shea. We have to go." Aidan's voice was urgent. "You used your Light outside of my protective seals. Lucian knows where we are."

I tried to walk, but my knees wobbled. "I can't walk."

"I'll carry you back to the car." He lifted me in his arms. This was becoming our new thing. I couldn't really complain. Being carried by Aidan felt nice.

Initially Aidan had showed off his super speed, but after I'd almost vomited, he decided to walk like a *normal* person. In such a short time, Chris had taken me pretty far from the car. It made me realize the urgency of Aidan's warnings. If a newbie could move that fast, how fast could an ancient vampire move?

I really wished I hadn't thought that.

Two vampires suddenly appeared, one in front of us and one behind. If I hadn't known that they'd ran, I would have thought they'd materialized out of thin air.

Aidan set me down on my feet.

I wobbled, still light-headed.

The Nordic-looking vamp in front of us stepped forward. He had long, blond hair pulled back into a low ponytail. His skin was ivory and sculpted, his eyes bright blue even in the darkness.

"Hand her over, Beast." The blond man's voice was smooth yet powerful.

"Never going to happen, Gunnhild." Aidan kept me behind him, though it was futile since we were surrounded.

I tried to tap into my powers, but I could barely stay conscious. Aidan would have to get us out of this one.

"You're standing against two Second-Borns, Dog. You can't win. Even you know that." Gunnhild seemed so sure of himself as the other vamp moved closer from behind.

"We were brothers once, Gunnhild. Lucian turned you to hurt me. He never loved you. But *I* did." Aidan was genuinely hurt.

Brother? Lucian must have made this Gunnhild dude *because* he was Aidan's brother. It made my stomach wrench.

Gunnhild paused a moment. I could see Aidan's words affected him, but it turned to hatred in a flash. "Lucian is my father. You are the beast that betrayed me. You weren't even human, just a monster brought to Earth to kill *my* brother!"

"He was my brother too," Aidan said softly.

Why would Aidan kill his own brother? This conversation was confusing, but maybe it would buy me some time to re-juice.

Gunnhild spat. "My human life with you was fleeting. With Lucian it is eternal, and what he's done for me, he turned Ashgar—" He paused, catching himself.

I looked up at Aidan as he glanced behind him to who I could only guess was Ashgar. Unlike Gunnhild, the vamp had almost-black eyes. He was huge, and his black shaggy hair shadowed his face in an ominous way.

Aidan's eyes darted back and forth between them and I was horrified to see fear, doubt, and uncertainty. He didn't know if he could take them. Why couldn't I use my powers?

I had to try.

I concentrated on the wind around me. If I could create a hurricane, I could scatter these "Second-Borns" and we could run.

The more I concentrated, the more I stumbled.

My knees buckled.

Aidan caught me by the arm before I fell.

Everything wouldn't stop spinning.

I almost thought I had passed out completely because it took a few seconds to realize that Lucian had landed right in front of us.

"Give her up, Aidan," Lucian commanded.

"You know I can't." I could hear Aidan's voice crack.

Was he crying?

We must've really been about to lose.

"I'll go with them," I whispered to Aidan. "I promise I won't break the curse. I don't want you to die for me." The thought was unbearable. If Aidan died trying to protect me, as he had died protecting all the other Vessels, I could never live with myself. I loved him too much.

Lucian stepped forward carefully. "Aidan, I'm asking you just this once . . . to spare the Vessel."

"I can't." Aidan spoke so quietly I could barely hear him.

Then a chill went through my spine.

My blurred eyes peered up into Aidan's.

What I saw there scared me to the core.

I knew with every fiber of my soul that Aidan was going to kill me.

"Aidan, no," I said lamely.

Tears streamed down his cheeks. "I made an oath, Shea. Thousands of years ago. It's the world or you. You're the Light that frees the Dark."

"Aidan," I choked.

I felt the blade of Aidan's knife enter my stomach.

The pain was so intense I couldn't breathe.

The scream was so loud it was deafening, and then I realized it wasn't my own.

It was Lucian's.

I stumbled into Aidan's arms, this time because of the blood pouring out of my wound.

Aidan had stabbed me.

I dropped to my knees.

I looked into his eyes. They were full of anguish, but his pain was a slap in the face.

"I trusted you," I sputtered, blood trickling out of my mouth.

"I had to, Shea. I had to," Aidan kept repeating.

"I loved you," I choked, unable to hide my devastation.

Aidan grabbed his own stomach and his whole body twisted like it was in agony, like he'd been stabbed too.

I pushed away from him and crawled toward Lucian.

Lucian was on his knees, but when he saw me coming toward him, still alive, he rushed to hold me.

Everything Aidan had said was a lie.

He had killed them all.

Aidan had killed all the Vessels.

Aidan had killed me.

Suddenly a boulder came crashing down on Aidan's face. I screamed. As much betrayal as I felt, it was horrendous to see him crushed in front of me.

I looked up to see a smiling Gunnhild, proud that he had smashed Aidan to a pulp. "That's for Halfdan, Beast!"

Halfdan. Their brother. A Vessel. Aidan had killed his own brother.

Gunnhild turned to Lucian, his voice full of hate and contempt. "Take her, Father. Take her to Caelius. Or *we* will."

I didn't want to die like this.

Stabbed by my best friend.

My dead best friend.

I wanted to cry, but I was too terrified.

As I looked into Lucian's eyes, I could see the truth.

He'd never let anything happen to me.

"Lucian," I cried. "Help me."

CHAPTER 8
LUCIAN

"Help me."

Shea's words moved through my mind like jagged nails against the back of my skull. Everything inside my brain scrambled, leaving only one compelling thought: *mine*.

I had to think fast.

I had to save her.

"The Vessel must be alive to break the seal. If I take her now, she will die and be useless to Caelius. She's too weak. I need to help her heal, then I'll take her myself." My mind was moving the chess pieces. It was only a matter of time before Aidan lifted that boulder and tried to finish her off.

I squeezed her tighter in my arms.

"*Father*, she already has enough Light in her to break the seal, half-alive like this. We just need to drag her there." Gunnhild looked to Ashgar, confused.

I paused, then looked at them both. "If I take her now, she

won't *survive* Caelius."

"Why does that matter?" Ashgar squinted, his dark eyes assessing the situation. I had always enjoyed the fact that he was one of my brightest children, even though I hadn't turned him for my sake, but for Gunnhild's. Now, however, that same ruthless determination was working against me.

"It matters to *me*." That should've been enough for his tactical brain to figure out.

I moved my hand possessively to the small of her back, resting her head on my chest. The action sent both men reeling. I myself was at a loss for how it might look.

I'd only turned seven men total. Five weren't here, including Gracuri. I didn't believe in his gods, but I thanked someone for that. As much as Gracuri loved the theater, I couldn't face him or the others, not like this. Especially because this was beginning to look like a Greek tragedy.

Two of my own children waited for me to do what I knew I should: to honor Caelius and drag her to his cage. But these sons had been turned during dark times, and they were the most savage and cunning of my children. Gunnhild and I had ended the Viking era together before he'd met Ashgar. He had been crazed from the loss of his brother Halfdan then, and I'd ridden that madness with him.

He'd owned a century of my life, a time when I'd been something other than what I was now. They were both my living memories in that way, pieces of me that had scattered, but remained alive through their image.

It was unsettling to see them now, with my arms frozen, wrapped protectively around a Vessel. I let Shea go, propping

144

her up on the ground before I stood in front of her like a shield.

"We will not relent, Father. This Vessel has poisoned you somehow. She's dangerous; let us take her," Ashgar growled.

I scanned their faces. I'd shared so much with each of my sons, and they were hard like I was, savage and wild. It was part of what I loved about them, and what I hated in myself.

I felt their footsteps move, inching closer. They would dare to cross me if it meant pleasing the larger master: Caelius. They were hungry for power. They were so much like I'd been when I'd turned them.

These were my shadow children.

The side that was unseen, but living, breathing and demanding that I take her to Caelius.

Or *they* would.

That statement alone filled me with an unimaginable rage.

Again, one thought pulsed through my veins stronger than any bloodline: Shea Harper was mine.

"Lucian, *please*," she cried out again.

With the sweetness of her mouth, the word "mine" melted away. When Caelius had turned me and I'd died, my life hadn't flashed before my eyes. There hadn't been a holy experience, only a deep ache. Now, Shea's words were slow and all around me time shifted.

I saw Nefertiti, how the light had left her eyes when I'd tried to make her immortal. I saw Caelius explaining that we couldn't turn females, how there was nothing he could do to save her. Then there was Ur-Nammu's rage as he took her body to be buried, followed by endless wandering in the desert where that emptiness inside me grew larger than a black hole.

Then there was Aidan. When I'd met Moses, it had been the first time I'd felt alive again in centuries. That aliveness had ended when I'd held him, the knife in his heart still warm from Adnachiel's betrayal. That night I'd lost them both: Aidan, and what had been left of my soul.

Only the clenching of my fists returned me to normal time. I wouldn't lose Shea like I had lost everything and everyone before. I couldn't explain what she meant to me; I only felt it, deep and raw like the failures of my past. "Don't say another word. If you touch her, I'll rip out your throats and your bodies will be as lifeless as you were before *my* blood entered your mouth."

The two recoiled but did not flee.

Gunnhild ran quickly to Ashgar and stepped coyly behind him as Ashgar puffed his chest and widened his stance protectively.

It was a shame that Ashgar was even here. He was loyal and would never betray me, but I had seen them fall in love, and I knew that my words would never again reach him. If Gunnhild asked him to stay and fight to the death, Ashgar wouldn't hesitate if it meant protecting his beloved—vampire blood be damned.

Gunnhild addressed me from behind Ashgar's broad shoulders. "Father, just finish her and we'll leave this place *together*. We only hunted the Vessel because it was commanded by Caelius. All of these years you've failed him, but I know you. You never fail. I understand. I'm more than happy to hunt and kill every Vessel from here to eternity if it means you being in charge.

"You would have saved Halfdan. You would have let him live through the ages *with* us. After he was killed by that dog Adnachiel, you gave me vengeance, this new life, and a chance to

146

love again." His hand wrapped tenderly around Ashgar's bicep. "I owe you everything." His voice was flat, but underneath his tone was a genuine plea.

I sighed, looking at his stony blue eyes. "I wish you hadn't come."

I had already crossed a line by killing Frank, but killing my own children, no matter what they had become, was a crime. I could feel the pangs of connection twisting in my body, screaming in agony at the fear of loss. Still, as much as we were bound together, I couldn't lose Shea.

I tried again, knowing that Ashgar was already calculating his next move to support Gunnhild. If he didn't accept this final offer of peace, I would have no choice.

"If you are both truly loyal to me, I *command* you to leave. Back down from this battle. You are connected to me with more than just blood. Gunnhild, you are one of my favorite beings. This world would be less for me without you in it. When you asked me about Ashgar, I was the one who turned him so that he could be strong for you. I made him a Second-Born for *you*. Ashgar is loyal, a warrior, and a *good* man. I've enjoyed watching from afar as your affections bloomed through the ages. Leave now, and it can continue to grow. Your lives don't have to end here.

"If you have any regard for me as your father, get as far away from me as possible. It's true what I wrote in blood through all of those worthless children of Gracuri's. Shea is *mine*."

Gunnhild stepped forward, incensed, but Ashgar pulled him back. "I care not what you've done to his line," Gunnhild spat. "Gracuri was never a warrior like us. We've fought side by side.

147

I know you, Father. And this, this isn't you. Gracuri is soft. He came to all the Second-Borns asking them to stay out of this for your sake. The *weaker* among us agreed. His way of helping you may be to withdraw those you care about so that you don't have to fight them. But I never thought you'd raise a hand to your own children. And I believe that if you've crossed that line, then forcing you to face us *is* helping you.

"We have our ways, Father. You know mine. So I'm asking *you* one last time: give up this woman, this worthless Vessel. She makes you weak. We can all see it. Kill her or take her to Caelius and end the madness that's taken hold of you. Come with *us*. It's been so long since we've all traveled together. We can claim a town or two on the way to Caelius if you'd like. We can bathe in blood, relishing death in the moonlight. Please, Lucian, choose *us*, like you chose us once before."

I didn't move. I could hear every gasp as Shea fought for breath as if they were my own. Even if I saved her, would she survive? Was this madness, or was it the thing I feared most?

What was this all-consuming emotion?

Fear and shame filled my gaze as it met Gunnhild's. This feeling . . .

Nefertiti.

Moses.

Aidan.

After all this time, I felt it again . . .

Love.

I closed my eyes for a moment.

I would mourn them, but if I walked away from Shea now, no amount of mourning would stop the anguish of Aidan's

148

twisted blade.

When my eyes opened, they were hard, resolute. Gunnhild only nodded, reconciling his own thoughts to my actions. He drew out a long broadsword from behind Ashgar, the one I had given him when we'd taken the Walled City.

The sight of it only increased my pain, but I knew them. They would try and take her to Caelius, and if it meant going through me to do it, as much as it pained them, they wouldn't hesitate. They were warriors, and that was our creed and armor: to kill anything that made us weak. It was what they were asking me to do to Shea. It was what they were willing to do to me, because just as she was my weakness, I was theirs.

They'd decided and sealed their fate before they'd gotten here. Nothing I had said or could say would convince them otherwise.

But they were wrong. Inside my dead, cold, hollowed-out carcass, I knew that it was stronger to fight for that tender spot. Fight to keep it alive, to keep the weakness breathing. But it was more than that. My heart, my soul . . . *needed* her.

I had to mend Shea quickly. I didn't have time to draw this out, even if I should, to honor them. It was not in me to elongate their pain. Even the pain of trying to kill me.

Lucian the Merciful. I laughed at the mockery of my own thoughts. What I was about to do to them would be no mercy.

I stepped forward, letting the tip of Gunnhild's blade press against my neck. "Last chance. Betray me now, and I will kill you both. You will lose him, Gunnhild. Are you willing to pay that price?"

Gunnhild hesitated, but Ashgar cleared his throat. "Do not

149

fear for my life. I am yours, Gun. Whatever you decide, we do it together."

I winced as Gunnhild thrust the sword forward and lunged, his voice whispering under the ferocity of his movements, "I'm sorry, Father. This is for your own good." Ashgar leapt forward as well, trying to pin me down as the blade grazed the side of my neck.

It didn't matter.

As the only First-Born, I was faster than the both of them combined.

I twisted Gunnhild's wrist behind him just as Ashgar leapt full force. The turned blade plummeted deep inside his throat. I pulled it through and across as quickly as possible, but I saw it: the millisecond of horror and grief on Gunnhild's face as he realized that I had used his own hand to behead his world.

The sight made his arms instantly go limp. I took the blade easily from his hand, like taking a plastic sword from the grip of a small child, as Ashgar's head rolled away from his body.

"I warned you." The words weren't enough to conceal my exposed guilt.

His eyes were wide as he stared at Ashgar's dead, headless body. His voice became hoarse, squeezed, like the air escaping the lungs of someone punched in the gut. "No. I played this through in my mind a thousand times. We convince you, if not with words, with actions. We don't back down if you want to fight, and in fighting you remember . . . remember how much we mean to you. You're grateful. We save you, like you saved us once. You come with us. We live . . . forever together, Ashgar and I, we live . . ." His voice trailed off as he knelt by Ashgar's head, pulling it into his lap.

I reached a hand toward him. To soothe him? To apologize? I wasn't sure. His reasons seemed genuine, mistaken as they were.

His eyes finally met mine as he clutched Ashgar's head to his chest. I couldn't stand it. He looked just as lost and betrayed as he had when Aidan had gutted his brother.

But this time, it'd been me.

I had made promises then, to comfort him. Promises I had just broken.

"Gunnhild, I . . . if you would have just listened," I stuttered.

"Do it." He spoke his words into Ashgar's hair like whispering a prayer. "I won't forgive you for this. I'll hunt you to the ends of the earth," he choked. "Do it."

I lifted the blade from the ground, aiming it at his throat. My hands were shaking as I stared at them both.

It had to be done.

"I had to kill Ashgar. You wouldn't stop."

He shook his head, drawing deeper into his shell. "We would have followed you forever."

I raised the blade. "You were loyal to Caelius."

"We were only loyal to you, *Father*." His voice was mournful, and the tone cut me deeper still.

I dropped the blade.

I was weak. He was right.

"I'm sorry." I spoke the words, but they felt as pathetic as they sounded.

"Coward." He lifted the blade against his own throat. "You dishonor me, even in death."

"Wait—"

He plunged the blade through his own neck, yanking it across bone and flesh, falling limp, his own head rolling down to meet Ashgar's.

I looked in horror at what falling for the Vessel had cost.

"Lucian," Shea called, this time her voice a whisper.

I choked down my grief.

I had no time to mourn.

If I didn't save her, their deaths would be for nothing.

I wrapped my arms around Shea, cradling her face in my hands. "It's going to be all right." She barely nodded, her skin paler than before.

I pulled the knife out of her stomach, covering her wound quickly with my hand. "Stay with me, Shea. Don't pass out. I need you, I love . . ."

My lips parted hers. I wanted to breathe life back into her. I had given the kiss of death to all I'd cared for, and now I longed, just this once, to give life.

Her lips warmed beneath mine. My eyes closed as I fell into the feeling of her: her essence, her Light. I wanted to lose myself in that moment, to forget that I had just killed two of my most precious children.

Then something moved.

My eyes flashed open as I pulled her against my chest. I looked toward the headless bodies of my children, then to the boulder; Aidan was stirring. That stone wouldn't stop him for long. Even unconscious, there was only one way to kill that beast.

I leapt into the night air and flew.

I tore through city after city, ransacking jewelers for supplies while clutching her small body. As long as I felt her heart beating,

I was able to push on.

Finally, I took her home.

It was the place I went to when I had nowhere else to go. As far as amenities, it had the bare essentials: a bed and a shower, no need for a kitchen. Mainly, it was the place where I kept my keepsakes.

They were all around, like trophies of the life I'd lived, proof that I'd seen decades pass. It was my secret treasure trove. Even Caelius didn't know of its location. I couldn't think of anywhere else to bring someone so valuable.

I laid her gently on my large four-poster bed, the blood from her stomach inking the white fur blankets bright red. Her eyes were closed, but she was conscious.

I had to be quick.

In all my years home, I'd never seen out the windows. I savagely peeled off the black tint. Dawn was coming and every moment could be the difference between life or death for Shea.

I placed all the crystals and diamonds I'd collected along the window. When the last jewel was in place, I kissed her forehead and whispered into her golden hair. "Rest. You're safe now. Let the Light in. Feel its life. I'll bury myself in the dirt under this bed. I'll be right under you, still able to hear your heartbeat. Know that I'm with you. I won't leave you, Shea. But you need what I can't give. You *need* the sun."

I saw the first few rays as they hit the window and reflected in the crystals I'd placed there. It burned my eyes and a piece of my neck instantly turned to ash. Good. None of my kind could touch her here.

I quickly dug a shallow hole under the bed as the light hit the

153

jewels and reflected in every direction. I didn't want it too deep; if anything happened, even if my whole body turned to ash, I would leap out and save her with my last breath.

As I covered my face with the wet earth, I imagined what the room must look like. I had learned something like this with the sunshields in Egypt, but more so with the botanist, Helena, and her obsession with refraction.

I hoped it would be enough.

It had to be.

I needed her. I needed . . .

My thoughts paused as the black soil over me warmed slightly. My chest ached.

My longing for the sun was nothing compared to what I felt waiting in darkness . . . waiting for her heartbeat to gain strength.

And it did.

With every hour that passed, as she bathed in the heat and awe of thousands of reflected lights and colors, the sound of her beautiful heart solidified.

She would survive.

My children hadn't died for nothing.

"Aidan," she cried.

She repeated his name for hours. "Aidan, Aidan . . ."

It was torture, hearing both his name and her lamenting it. I hated feeling so helpless. I had to lie there and listen as she processed the betrayal of her best friend. I'd seen the betrayal of every Vessel by that dog. But they'd always *died*. They'd only felt the sting and surge of pain for a moment. They'd never lived to feel the full extent of heartbreak.

Only I had.

When he'd taken Moses and I alone had been left to grieve his death.

The bitterness of decades washed over me as I eventually heard her rise. I nearly jerked out of the dirt when she said my name.

I shifted in the soil as she walked around the room slowly. Then she knelt down and her hand gently traced the soft dirt covering my form. It sent a chill through my bones as all logic and reason left my mind. I wanted to embrace her, to pull her close to me.

"I need you." Her voice was cracked and raw from crying.

My mind connected with hers. I could use telepathy with any human, but Vessels were different. This connection was only possible, consciously or not, because Shea was letting me in. *Don't leave.* I spoke to her mind. *None of my kind know about this place, and the walls are engraved with Egyptian symbols that will ensure Adnachiel and his brothers can't find your Light. I am sorry, Shea. I will hold you. I'll give you whatever you need. Just wait for nightfall . . . and I am yours.*

"He's still alive?" Her voice was full of anguish and hope. Shea lay back down on the bed. "You were right about Aidan." She started crying again.

The very words made my blood boil. Of course I was right. That beast had killed them all. Caelius could wait to be freed, because after Moses, the Vessels hadn't mattered to me anymore. I just wanted to see Adnachiel in pain, to see if he really could do it every time. So I hunted, and sure enough, his blade would always find them.

This time had been different.

155

I didn't know why, but I'd actually thought he wouldn't do it.

When I'd killed Frank, I'd thought I'd seen the old Aidan. But when his knife had lanced her gut everything went white, and the pain of a thousand betrayals came rolling out of my tongue as I screamed with every broken thread of sanity. He'd gone through with it. He'd stabbed her like all the others.

He'd never be my brother again.

He'd always choose the Light.

I breathed slightly as dirt fell into my mouth. I was gutted and my mind was a jumbled mess, flipping back and forth from decades ago, to hours. Vampires didn't sleep, but being covered in earth like this gave rise to living dreams, like a film reel was playing across my irises, and I couldn't stop it.

I thought of Ashgar's severed head. I hadn't honored Gunnhild's last request, even though, in that moment, I'd understood perfectly how he'd felt. If Shea had died, I would have gladly lanced my own throat and lay clutching her in my arms. You could only lose love like that so many times in one lifetime before living itself became worthless.

In truth, I should have died with the other Vessels, or at least with Moses. Either way, I knew I couldn't go through it again in another five hundred years. Not with the loss of Shea. She was different. I *needed* her: my skin touching hers for her last breaths, for every breath.

If I wasn't buried, I'd scratch my nails down my face.

Gracuri was right.

Something was *wrong* with me.

I was thankful that he'd saved the rest of my Second-Borns, my most faithful, beloved children who would never face me like that in battle. But my Gunnhild, his Ashgar . . .

My warriors . . . were dead now.

By my hand.

How could I have done this?

It was only now, as Shea grieved her loss, her sobs cutting open my soul, that I felt the full severity of my own. I'd spent hundreds of years with each of them. Their faces and names were tattooed in my blood. They didn't make men like that anymore. Each had been unique. I was completely gutted by their loss.

Still, I hadn't been surprised to see them there. They'd wanted me to take her to Caelius, had needed me to. It was as if they'd known before I had, that I loved—

I choked down the word, trying to harden myself.

Was I a fool?

How could I have let something like that blind me?

I had told them that she needed to be strong when Caelius used her to break the seal. I knew what he did to things that were weak. He'd said he wouldn't kill her, but if she was vulnerable, he might, despite himself. That didn't matter anyway, because in truth, from the moment I'd held her in my arms, I'd had no intention of letting her go.

My stomach rolled in agony at the idea of Caelius's hands on her. How exactly would he "use" the Vessel to break the seal anyway? He had never spoken of the action, only the need for a *living* Vessel. But what did he *need* her for? I swallowed hard, still feeling his large jowls around the nape of my neck. Would he have bent Shea to his will in the same manner?

I growled in fury at the idea as my mind flashed again, moving to three thousand years in the past, to a time when I'd been as innocent and heartbroken as she was now. And like a maddened fever, I heard my own cries anew, remembering how Caelius had turned me under the light of Nefertiti's window.

It had been painful.

Savage.

He'd taken me and made me his, body and soul.

I'd all but forgotten that night, how I'd longed for death. His words, "But then you'll never see her again," had convinced me, and I'd let him continue on until the light of morning. We'd been able to walk in the daylight then. It was the seal that kept his blood and ours bound to shadow.

I cringed with the memory.

I'd *never* let him touch Shea.

I had never turned a son in that way. It had been by accident that I'd killed Ur-Nammu. It was only when I'd brought his bleeding carcass to Caelius's cell, asking him to tell me what to do, that he'd instructed me on the simple art of turning. It was easy enough, and it didn't have to be painful.

Even then, he hadn't told me that I couldn't turn females. He should have known that Ur-Nammu and I would go back for his daughter, that I would have wanted Nefertiti to be mine forever.

My lips around her neck had been soft. I'd taken great lengths to make it pleasurable . . . but as the light left her eyes and she slipped into death, I'd been struck with a sense of horror, which only increased as my blood didn't revive her.

Nothing ever would.

I'd brought her to Caelius.

It was *then* that he'd told me I could only turn males.

I'd killed her.

158

The woman I had sold my soul for.

I thought of Shea's warm lips, the way they curved when she said my name. Would knowing me turn those same lips cold? Would I fail her like I had failed Nefertiti? My insides twisted further.

After that night, Caelius had sent me away. Ur-Nammu hadn't spoken, but the hate I'd seen reflected in his eyes when he took his daughter's ashen body away from me still haunted my vision when the moon was high and full like it had been that night.

Only when Caelius discovered there was a Vessel had he summoned me back. He'd called me son again and said that I could make it up to him, that my foolishness with Nefertiti was shameful, but time had passed and she was gone. He'd hoped I'd buried all notion of being anything but his with the bones of her memory.

And in a way, I had.

I'd sworn without hesitation that I'd find the Vessel and bring it to him, that indeed I belonged to him alone. But I hadn't been expecting Moses.

My mind shifted back and forth, from Nefertiti to Shea to Moses. In their own way, they were all alike.

Moses had been charismatic and brave, an irresistible force of life, and I'd been wandering the desert for so long, eating death and sand, mourning Nefertiti.

At first he'd reminded me enough of the Pharaoh to hate him, but then he'd changed. He'd given up his title, worked as a slave, and been hell-bent on knocking down the golden scepter of Egypt. He'd wanted every man, woman, and child to be free.

He'd reminded me of the Gutians, of my father before the

wars with Egypt, before I'd been a slave to the Pharaoh myself.

And then there'd been his devoted: Aidan. The last time I had seen him was when he and his brothers had sealed Caelius. This time, he'd been by Moses's side and earthbound.

He'd still had wings, but only immortals could see them. Back then he couldn't hide what he was as easily. He hadn't been the practiced, polished dog I knew now. Back then we'd had long conversations about the Light and how he missed home and his brothers.

Living bound to the Vessel in human form for a divine creature like himself . . . how had he described it then? Ah, yes, like a shadow was always over his heart. Just breathing was painful. Death and hopelessness saturated everything he saw. He marveled at how humans could live in such a state. I'd marveled at his ignorance.

It was Moses who had stopped us from initially ripping each other apart. He united us. He united everyone he talked to.

There was just something about the way he'd explained things . . . like hope moved in his every thought, and he passed it on to those who'd stay and listen.

Even now I could hear his words, "Light and Darkness are not so different from one another. If we unite, here and now, we have a chance to do something, to really change this world. Join me, *brothers*. Together, let the three of us show Egypt that nothing can break the spirit of man or beast. Let us show them what it means to be free."

I should've opened my eyes and let the dirt fall in. I should've let every small rock cut my irises. Anything to stop the memories. I hated being in soil; it always had this effect. I didn't want to remember what I'd done for Moses, what I'd done for *us*: the plagues, the bloody water, the glory of freeing an entire people.

The betrayal.

Nefertiti, Moses, Aidan . . . everyone I loved suffered.

"Lucian, it's night." Shea's voice was shaky.

Quickly, I ripped my hands out from under the dirt and lunged forward. She fell backward, startled by my sudden eruption. I caught her just before her soft, pale hair hit the corner of my desk.

"Careful." I stared at her open mouth as her swollen eyes gazed over my dirt-covered form.

Her arms wrapped around my chest, then she pulled away. "Do you sleep in the ground all the time?"

I shook my head, the dirt from my hair falling on her legs. "Not often. It's restorative to our kind, but I hate the soil—the feel, the taste of it, the memories it evokes. I'd rather not be tethered to the earth with Caelius. This . . . place really isn't meant for sleeping. Having a bed was more for nostalgia than function. It's just another trophy for my room." I motioned my head to the keepsakes littering the floor and walls.

She nodded as I released her slowly. I stood up, making my way to the shower. "Wait a moment longer and we'll talk."

I needed to clear my head from the effects of being buried.

"Okay," she mumbled as I entered the shower.

I wanted to stay in the hot water, to let it wash away all of my past, but I couldn't just leave her out there, suffering as she was. I rinsed off the dirt quickly, then walked out to join her.

Before she could stand, I rushed to help her up, a towel tucked around my waist. My hair dripped down her hand as she

161

raised it to my chest. I was ripped apart inside. Looking at her just increased the racket that had started the moment I'd seen her in the dorm all those months ago. More than the warm water, I needed her to wash away the grime of my life.

"Shea . . . I couldn't protect them. I want to protect you—if I'm strong enough, if you'll let me." I slowly pushed her down onto the bed, feeling the quickening of her heartbeat. "I want to check on your wound." Her heart continued to pound as loud as a Viking war cry.

Her skin was smooth to the touch and completely healed, save a small scar next to her belly button. I rested my hand there longer than I should have, brushing it over the soft hills of her hip bones.

"I would have died . . . if Adnachiel had killed you." I leaned my face close to hers, surprised by the gentleness in my own voice. Her lips trembled underneath my breath. "The whole world can burn, but not you, Shea. I would give anything . . ." I didn't have to lean in closer. She grabbed the back of my neck and kissed me hard. Without thinking, my arms pulled her up to the top of the bed and my heavy frame fell over hers.

I wanted her. I needed to taste her. Every inch. I pulled my hands over her leg and raised it to my hip. Her kisses were deep, rich, and I felt with them all the longing of a young man deprived of fruit in the desert. She was my Eden, an oasis in a forgotten land.

Stop.

Even as my hips sank into hers, I needed to stop. She was still healing and confused. I knew I couldn't take advantage of her exposed emotions like this. She moaned and I lost all clarity.

Pushing harder, I ripped her shirt off, pressing the purple of her bra against my heaving chest.

Stop.

I slipped my hands down her thigh, cutting open her jeans with an elongated nail.

Stop.

Her hands moved for my towel, and I moved my mouth over her ear. My hot breath spoke to her in my native language, things I'd never said to anyone before, as I kissed the exposed pink just behind her small earlobe.

Her neck arched as my hand pushed from under the small of her back. I pressed my lips against a throbbing vein and kissed her soft flesh. I had to taste her.

Stop. Stop!

I shoved myself mercilessly from her voluptuous frame and walked to the center of the room. "I'm sorry, Shea. Forgive me. I'm not myself. You need rest, not this. There are clothes in the cabinet by the shower. Clean up and dress yourself. I'll dress as well. Then we can . . . figure out what to do next. We'll plan and prepare. I'll keep you safe."

I didn't meet her gaze as she ran to the shower, slamming the door behind her. I heard the quick panting of her breath and sighed, ashamed. Why did I always ruin everything I touched?

No. It wouldn't be the same with her. I wasn't going to rush this just to fill that ache inside. That hole. The need for every ounce of her. It was better if she hated me. She needed to keep her distance.

The door slowly clicked open. Her face was downcast as she stared at my frame. "Lucian . . . your back . . ."

With a small motion of my hand, I pulled a shirt out of an antique cabinet and laced my arms through. I coughed as I buttoned the front.

"I told you, I was a slave in Egypt before I was turned. The scars you have in life follow you in death. But rest assured, nothing can scar me now. Nothing's permanent." Even as I said the words, I felt their falsehood. Internal scars, those could be new, and those would last until my dying breath.

CHAPTER 9
SHEA

I had been seething, ready to give *the vampire* the cold shoulder. How dare he tease me like that? I had wanted to do anything to forget about Aidan and how he'd *stabbed* me . . .

I still couldn't wrap my head around it.

Aidan.

It hurt so bad I could barely breathe.

I didn't think I would ever stop crying. I had never felt pain like that before. And it wasn't the knife wound. Healing had been easy compared to what he had done.

Aidan had crushed me.

He was my best friend. The man I loved and trusted. The man I had joked with, laughed with, shared my whole life with . . .

My whole life!

Our whole lives.

My brain squeezed with pain.

It was excruciating.

It hurt too much to think.

To feel.

To exist.

And Lucian had given me the perfect distraction. Even thinking about how he'd touched me, kissed me, held me . . . it gave me shivers. I had never felt that way about anyone before.

But then he'd stopped. He freaking stopped! I was so humiliated. Did he know how hard it was for me to give myself to *anyone* physically? How vulnerable I was? And I had pulled *him* in. *I* was the aggressor. And he'd given me everything I had ever dreamed. Then he'd ripped it away from me like I was an annoying *fan*. Like I was one of those girls he used to talk about when I thought he was ego-boy: one of his *stalkers*.

So, I did what any completely mature girl would do; I got up, ran to the bathroom, and slammed the door. Yeah, real classy.

After stewing in my own humiliated juices for a while, I decided I was going to go out to Lucian and refuse to let him touch me. Okay, I was still being a shining star of maturity, but I didn't care. I wanted him to be tortured like I was tortured.

When I stormed back out of the bathroom, I saw his scars. Long, thick striations all across his back as if he'd been whipped continuously for years.

My heart melted.

As in a big gooey puddle on the floor.

All I wanted to do was run up to Lucian's back and kiss every scar.

And the way he looked at me. It froze me where I stood. His turquoise eyes stared with such intensity, I couldn't speak. Even if I tried, I wouldn't have been able to play it cool. I wasn't a game player and I never would be. Some girls could make guys like Lucian eat out of their hands by playing hard to get. Whenever I tried that, I just ended up not saying anything and making the guy feel uncomfortable until he excused himself and flirted with someone else.

I decided honesty was the only way I could handle the situation. "Look . . ." I stopped, not sure of what I wanted to say. He stayed silent, as if anything I said was important. I was used to Aidan interrupting me with a quip or a joke.

Breathe. Tears threatened to overwhelm me. I had to block Aidan from my mind. Even thinking his name caused me anguish. I ran my fingers through my hair and refocused my attention on Lucian. "I realize that I'm probably just another one of your conquests, and I apologize for being so forward. I'm not normally like that."

Suddenly all the emotional craziness of the last ten hours made me angry. "So, congratulations, I'm just like every other girl on the planet. I fell all over you. You were right the first time. I guess you're just too irresistible for any human." I was so ashamed and embarrassed I couldn't continue. I hated being the girl who *gave in.*

Before I could run back into the bathroom and slam the door again, Lucian was in front of me. He brushed his hand against my cheek and stared into my eyes. "You are not a conquest." His voice was almost a whisper.

I wasn't going to let him *lure* me into his charming-sexy-gorgeous stare. "When I was Dream-Walking or whatever, you said I was *yours.* That sounds pretty 'conquest-ey' to me." I knew that wasn't a word, but he knew what I meant.

Aidan would have made fun of me for it.

I screamed inside and pushed Lucian away from me.

I didn't want to think of Aidan!

But I couldn't stop.

He was so much a part of who I was and where I came from, it was impossible not to. It was almost like if I concentrated hard enough, everything that had happened would just be a nightmare. I'd wake up, he would be a couple doors down, and we would grab breakfast together.

I made it as far as the bed, where I not so gracefully collapsed and started to cry *again*. I didn't want to look that weak in front of Lucian, but I had no control over myself anymore. He was over three thousand years old; I was sure he'd seen a crying girl or two in his lifetime. I just didn't care. Everything hurt too much.

Before I could react, I felt his arms lift me up and place me in his lap, my head on his chest. I didn't struggle. I didn't have the strength. And I didn't want to. His strong arms wrapping around me was the only thing that made me feel sane.

A thought hit me.

I didn't want to care about the answer, but I did. "He's really alive?" My voice was choked with tears. I knew logically he'd tried to kill me, but I still loved him.

I still love him.

I could feel Lucian tense up, but his voice was calm as he said, "Yes. There's only one way to kill him . . ." He paused. "Even if I wanted to, I couldn't. And I've wanted to, believe me."

"So when Gunnhild smashed him with a boulder?" I asked.

Watching Aidan get crunched like that had been terrifying! And now that I'd had time to process, I found myself worried about him. I knew I shouldn't be. But it was second nature. My brain didn't function any other way.

"He's still alive, and he'll be fine. He's no more human than I am. He's a beast. Other than harming himself, his kind can't be killed by anyone but Caelius. They can only be slowed down." There was anger and admiration in Lucian's voice.

I pushed away from him. "I heard the crunch! No one could survive that!"

Aidan was dead; I was sure of it.

I stood up and started to pace frantically. "I just wanted you to save me. I just wanted to escape. I didn't want him dead. What have I done?" I was rambling, but my mind wouldn't let go of any of my fears. I should've hated Aidan. I should've been glad he was dead.

I started to cry again. I was such a mess.

Lucian was off the bed and wrapping his arms around me in seconds. "Shea, he is very much alive. He's tracking us even as we speak. The only way he can die is if he *kills* you. Once the Vessel is dead, he dies . . . then is reborn with the next."

His words cut me to my core.

Aidan didn't just kill the Vessels; he killed himself . . . every time. My heart suddenly hurt for him, even though I knew it shouldn't.

Every time he was faced with an impossible situation: let Caelius out into the world or kill the one he loved and save it.

He chose the world.

A part of me understood, but the other part of me was devastated.

Lucian's hand reached down and softly touched my stomach.

It was electric. "After what he did to you, I'm surprised you care." Then anger flared in his eyes. "Maybe I killed my children for nothing."

It felt as if he had punched me in the gut. "I get it." I turned away from him, trying to hide the catch in my voice. "I wasn't worth saving."

Lucian pulled me back around and held my face in his hands. "You are worth *everything*, Shea Harper."

I shook my head in his hands, trying to hold back my tears. "You didn't have to kill them! We could have flown away or something! I would never expect . . . I would never ask you to do something like that! I'm sorry. I'm so sorry." Hearing Lucian admit that he had killed his children for me made me feel like dying. "Oh God, Lucian, I'm not worth it. I'm not worth any of this. How can you look at me?" I stared at him through blurred vision. "I didn't want you to . . . I'm so sorry." It was all I could say.

Lucian leaned down and kissed my lips softly. When he pulled away, he said, "It wasn't your choice, it was mine. If I hadn't killed them, they would have taken you to Caelius, or worse . . . killed you. And that's something I could not allow."

"Because you want to be the one to take me to your father." Everything was coming out before I could stop it.

I wasn't blind. I could see that Lucian cared for me on some vampire-possession level. But one truth I knew for certain: Lucian needed me alive to rescue his dad. I wished it was because he cared about me, but I knew I was fooling myself.

How could someone like Lucian love someone like me anyway?

He was Dark; I was Light.

Literally.

But it didn't stop the way I felt. It didn't matter if Lucian was using me to release his father from his prison. I knew with certainty that we were connected. I was crazy to feel this way, but I'd known from the moment I opened Aidan's dorm room door and saw Lucian's face that we belonged to each other. I'd never believed in destiny before. It was always some fantasy or something people made up to justify how strongly they felt about each other.

But in this moment, standing in front of him, regardless of his intentions or faults . . .

I love him.

As soon as I thought the words, a flood of warmth surged through me. It was as if admitting the truth set my soul free. With all the anguish I had experienced over the last few days, this very second I was filled with a joy I couldn't explain. It surprised me so much I almost stumbled.

All of this happened in seconds.

Lucian's face still looked broken from what I had said about him keeping me alive for his father. "Shea, Caelius will never have you. I swear on my life."

He was intense. My knees finally gave out and buckled.

He caught me in his arms.

"Lucian." My voice was small. I could barely even hear myself.

He brought me in tighter. "I'll prove it to you. Now that my two disobedient sons are gone, I can take you back to Aidan. He won't try to kill you if he's not cornered. And I swear, I will kill

171

any of my kind who even try to put you in that situation again. I'll spend all of my days protecting you from afar, until your final breath. You'll never see Caelius. Will you trust me then?" His eyes were desperate. He'd be willing to give me up just to show his intentions were pure.

I reached up and touched his beautiful face. "Lucian." The warmth still spread through me like wildfire. Being with him felt right. No. It didn't *feel* right—it *was* right. Like everything in the universe was in perfect alignment.

He saw it then. The spark in my eyes. The love that I had forced down and denied existed . . . It was real. It was as if he couldn't believe what he was seeing. As if I were some kind of illusion.

"Lucian," I repeated. "I love you."

Gone was the monster, the killing machine, the vampire.

Before me stood Lucian, the boy, the once slave, the human.

His bright turquoise eyes looked at me with the same fire that flowed inside my body.

I could tell that he could feel it too.

Something bigger than us.

The Vessel and the one sworn to take it.

We were meant to be.

Our fates the same.

Lucian lifted me in his arms and placed me on the bed. I could feel the heat of his body against mine as we came together in a kiss. His lips were soft yet forceful, making my head spin. At the small of my back, I felt Lucian's hand grip tightly and pull me close so our stomachs were touching.

Clothes felt like barriers between us. I couldn't pull my bra off fast enough, and in one fluid rip, Lucian's shirt lay on the floor next to mine. This time our skin touched and it felt like fire. My hands held on to his back. It was the only thing that kept my mind grounded. Every touch, every sensation was charged with electricity. I honestly didn't know if I'd survive this. My heart pounded in my chest, loud and fast. This seemed to draw Lucian even more.

His kisses grew in intensity as he moved over every inch of my body. I almost lost my breath. But being near him became my breath. No matter how close we were pressed together, it wasn't close enough.

His back muscles tightened as his hands explored my curves with fevered passion. I wasn't sure how much more I could survive. I desperately wanted to devour him.

I couldn't see straight, the power was so overwhelming.

The more I kissed, the more I wanted.

Nothing had ever felt so amazing. I didn't want this moment to end.

Lucian moved his way up my neck with toe-curling, mind-blowing kisses until he reached my ear and whispered, "I love you, Shea Harper."

After that, my body and mind were his.

I'd never wanted anything more.

"I love you," I answered back.

Lucian and I became one.

***

I awoke later. I could tell it was still nighttime from the moonlight pouring in through the windows. It was Lucian's absence that woke me up. I'd felt his arms wrapped around me, but a few minutes ago he had left my side. I wondered if it was almost daybreak. Maybe he had to go underground again.

"Lucian?" I called out.

But there was no answer.

I didn't panic like I thought I would. My *normal* neurotic self would have jumped to horrible conclusions like "Lucian left me" or "Lucian got what he wanted, now he's over it." Granted, those thoughts obviously flitted through my brain, but they held no truth. I knew with complete confidence how Lucian felt. And I felt the exact same way.

I lay back in bed and smiled in contentment.

It had been my first time. It wasn't as if I had been holding out for anyone in particular. I'd just never met anyone who I wanted to do it with. And let's face it, Aidan made dating a little difficult. He'd be so pissed if he knew about Lucian and me.

My heart squeezed.

I tried to ignore the gaping hole of pain that crept up every time I thought of Aidan. Thinking of him used to conjure up warm fuzzies, but now it just conjured up tears and bile.

Still, it would take a lot more than Aidan to ruin my mood.

I had no idea how a Vessel and a vampire could make a relationship work, but I felt completely safe with Lucian.

We had talked for hours after making love, and he'd told me all about his travels and life. He was the oldest vampire out there besides his dad, and I guessed that made him the most powerful. I was pretty sure he'd left out a bunch of killing and mayhem, and I was grateful for it.

174

I loved him for who he was now, not for who he'd been then. I knew the Lucian today wouldn't hurt anyone who didn't deserve it. He had changed. I'd physically seen it with my own eyes. Our connection had brought him back to his humanity. I had no doubt he would still do whatever was necessary to protect me, but he wouldn't kill innocents. He'd made me a promise and I believed him. Lucian admitted that he didn't have the stomach for it anymore. He had already let some barista-boy go that he had planned to eat. (Gross!) He knew he had been changing then, but he hadn't wanted to accept it yet.

I grabbed a shirt and jeans that looked like they would fit from the cabinet and put them on. Maybe Lucian went to get food. I was starving. I could've used a patty melt right now. Of course, that reminded me of Aidan again, and I suddenly lost my appetite.

When my feet hit the hardwood floor, I surveyed my surroundings. The place was like a museum. There were shelves on every wall filled with trinkets, artifacts, and objects I couldn't even recognize. Knowing Lucian's age, it made me wonder how old some of the relics were.

I walked over to the wall next to the front door and examined his stuff up close. One item stood out more than any of the others. It was a necklace enclosed in a glass box. It looked ancient. It was made of gold and had what looked like hieroglyphs carved around its round border. In the center of the medallion was a perfect green stone. I assumed it was an emerald. It was stunning. Probably worth millions. I wondered if Lucian even used money. He didn't really need to with his "compelling" thing, but still.

I heard something.

175

It sounded like voices coming from outside.

I pressed my ear against the front door and I definitely recognized Lucian's voice, but I couldn't tell what he was saying or who he was talking to.

Normally, I wasn't a snoop, but my situation made me suspicious.

I tiptoed over to the window and as slowly and as quietly as possible, I cracked it about a half inch.

It was enough.

I could hear Lucian perfectly.

He was talking to another man, and from the way they were arguing, I could tell they knew each other. Maybe another one of his children? I hoped not. I didn't want Lucian killing anyone else he cared about for me. My heart couldn't take it, and I didn't think his could either.

"You should go back to Caelius, Ur-Nammu." Lucian's voice was angry.

"Caelius has been trying to contact you, and you've been ignoring him." The man named Ur-Nammu sounded disgusted.

"I don't wish to speak with him at the present moment." Lucian's anger was rising.

"I didn't believe what he told me. I had to see for myself." Ur-Nammu didn't seemed pleased.

"How did you find me?" I could tell Lucian was annoyed. He had told me this was a secret to all other vampires. As far as he knew, no vampire had set foot anywhere near this place.

Ur-Nammu laughed. "You think you can hide anything from Caelius? You underestimate his power."

"I never underestimate his power," Lucian growled.

"Is that why you killed your sons? You want to stay top dog forever?" Ur-Nammu accused.

Ouch. I didn't like this Ur-Nammu guy. He was acting like a real dick. But apparently, Lucian wasn't as shaken by his comment as I was.

"They were going to kill Shea. I did what I had to," Lucian responded flatly.

"Don't lie, boy. You may have turned me, but I fought alongside your father and helped raise you as a child in Gutium. They weren't going to kill her, they were following *my* orders. They would have taken her straight to Caelius. And Shea? You haven't called a Vessel by name since Moses. You've grown too close to her," Ur-Nammu implicated.

"And if I have?" Lucian's voice was quiet.

"I worry about you. You must take her to Caelius's prison, Lucian." Ur-Nammu's tone was pleading.

Screw him. I waited to hear Lucian's answer.

"Know this, Ur-Nammu: as sure as the sun swept over the eastern mountain in Gutium every morning, and as sure as you and I will never see that sunrise again, I will *never* bring Shea Harper to Caelius." Lucian's voice was like ice.

I had a surge of love for Lucian. He'd never let me go. My heart felt like it was going to burst with affection.

"Lucian . . . reconsider. The last time I saw you like this, you were in love with my daughter. And remember how that ended." Ur-Nammu's voice was just as cold as Lucian's.

"You of all people should understand, Ur-Nammu!" Lucian snapped back. "I had to watch Nefertiti die in my arms! I won't let that happen with Shea."

Ur-Nammu was quiet for a long while. When he spoke, his tone was different, almost vulnerable. "After all this time, have you finally left Nefertiti buried in the sands of Egypt?"

Now Lucian was quiet.

I held my breath, waiting for him to respond.

When he did speak, his voice cracked in agony. "I would have moved heaven and earth for her. Ever since we were children, she held my heart. I was enslaved because I tried to free you both, whipped to death and killed by the Pharaoh because of my devotion to her. I was enslaved again by Caelius because he tempted me to take his *bargain of life*, if only so that I could see her again.

"I've been dead for thousands of years, and inside I've had nothing but the pain of her loss. I know I don't deserve forgiveness, but I feel the way I used to feel when I'd see Nefertiti. Even more so. And I know that makes me a fool like it did before. But my soul *needs* Shea in a way I can't explain. I think she could help me heal. Ur-Nammu . . . I love her."

The man sighed. "Then it's as I feared."

Again they were both silent.

Ur-Nammu spoke brashly, this time tempering his voice with passion. "So be it, Lucian. If this is what you want, I will not require you to bring this Vessel to Caelius. I won't tell him that I saw you here and in this state. This never happened. Enjoy tonight . . . and all the days after."

Lucian sighed and his voice turned lighter. "I have your word then?"

"Of course, Lucian. I will do as I've said."

"Thank you, Ur-Nammu. I know Caelius is my father, but

you were close to my *real* father. You were like brothers, and your home was a second one to mine all growing up. I've missed talking with you—"

"We have nothing more to speak of," Ur-Nammu interrupted.

Lucian's words came out gritty, crushed. "Then all I have left to say is thank you. I won't forget this."

"I'll handle Caelius," Ur-Nammu replied thoughtfully.

"Goodbye, Lucian."

"Goodbye, Ur-Nammu."

A gust of wind shook the whole house, and just like that, Ur-Nammu was gone.

***

In less than a second, the door opened and Lucian stepped inside. I didn't have time to move from my obvious spying spot. I tried to stand up as gracefully and innocently as possible.

"Hey," I said lamely. I smiled. "Sorry."

Lucian was next to me in a flash. He leaned down and kissed me.

I put my arms around his neck and stared up at his big beautiful eyes. "Another bullet dodged?" I asked.

"Looks like it. He was the last bullet I was worried about." Lucian was visibly relieved. "I hadn't spoken to Ur-Nammu for thousands of years." A far-off look crossed his face.

"You okay?" I could tell he was in pain.

Lucian's attention focused back on me. "I am now."

He lifted me off the ground and brought me back to the bed, his body instantly on top of mine. The force of his lips parted my

179

mouth and I was pretty sure I went cross-eyed. Dang, that boy could kiss!

He traced his fingers over my body. "Now why would you put clothes on? It just makes my job more difficult," Lucian teased.

"Nothing good is easy," I teased back.

"Oh really?" He kissed the hollow of my neck.

Oh man.

I was in serious trouble.

I could no longer speak as he performed his magic and my head entered the clouds.

***

"Come to me." I heard Lucian's voice calling me.

I was asleep.

I knew I was asleep, but I couldn't seem to wake up. I was in that weird state where you're half-awake but still dreaming.

I couldn't tell if I was imagining Lucian's voice. I was aware of his body resting next to mine. Why would he be asking me to come to him if he was next to me?

I tried to wake up. I wasn't thinking clearly.

"*Please*, Shea. I need you. Come outside," Lucian's voice pleaded.

You're right next to me, I rationalized. But it didn't come out of my mouth. I started to feel trapped in my own body. I tried shaking my hand, arm, leg, anything to wake up. It was so frustrating!

"Shea! I'm in trouble! I need you! Please!" Lucian's voice was urgent enough to make me move.

180

I was walking.

But I was still sleeping.

Was I really walking then?

It felt real.

It felt like I was opening the door.

It felt like the cold night air was on my face.

But I was still asleep.

Something was wrong.

I was losing control.

"There you are, child." Now that wasn't Lucian's voice.

It was Ur-Nammu's.

I woke up.

It was too late.

I felt Ur-Nammu's hand clamp over my mouth before I could scream.

The world spun around me as his lightning speed took me away from the safety of Lucian's arms.

CHAPTER 10
LUCIAN

The door was open. *Open*. She was gone. It didn't make sense. The glyphs I'd inscribed on the walls prevented any vampire or beast from entering this safe haven. Even Ur-Nammu, with all his powers, couldn't step inside.

There was only one person she would have opened that door for. Only one beast that could have convinced her to "talk to him."

Adnachiel.

My blood boiled like the fires of Pompeii. I'd track him and take Shea if he hadn't . . . if he hadn't already killed—

I flipped the bed and threw it into a wall, shattering artifacts from Beijing to Iceland. It didn't matter. It was all junk. Every memory, every artifact was empty. This room was nothing more than a relic to house my lonely passage through death. But Shea had been here, filled with Light. We'd made love, and for once in my very long existence, I'd felt alive.

I was going to pluck every feather covering Aidan's wings one by one. I couldn't kill him; the only thing that could was killing the Vessel he was sworn to protect. If he had killed Shea, then he was already dead.

When backed into a corner, that dog would do it to save what? The world? He may not have cared about his own life because he'd just be reincarnated with some new Vessel, but Shea was worth letting a million worlds die for.

It always came down to the fact that Aidan loved the Light and its creations more than the "drippings," the Vessels. Even if the dripping was in human form, a form that could love, live. A form that had become his *best friend*.

If he were dead, if he had killed Shea, I'd wait patiently for five hundred years.

I'd wait.

I'd never hunt the Vessel again.

I'd hunt *him*.

If he was reborn, I'd go to great lengths to make sure the Vessel lived as long as possible, so that I could torture Aidan in every way that hurt a beast. He'd curse his immortality as I had mine. He'd beg for me to kill the Vessel, just to end his torment.

I hoped that she was still alive . . . for his sake and for mine.

I walked to the end of the room and shoved my hand through the glass case around a golden necklace with a green emerald. This was my first time touching it since they'd excavated it out of the ruins of Pompeii.

I'd looked everywhere for it, digging around in the ash and waste to no avail. The museum had encased it for display, and after taking it back I'd left it like that. To gaze at and never touch—like *her*. I latched it around my neck and tucked it under my shirt.

I kicked into a floorboard. It flew up and I dug the earth beneath until my nails raked over the top of a fresh pine box.

I placed it under my arm and walked out into the night air. I took a few steps then looked back at my home.

My sanctuary.

I turned away from it. Stretching out, 1 reached my fingers into the cool breeze. I summoned all of the nearby insects and beasts, as I had done with the dorm building. This time they would not explode—I would spare the creatures' lives. I had promised Shea that no more innocent blood would be spilled on my behalf.

The command was simple: eat, dig, tear until there is nothing left.

I closed my eyes, hearing the walls cave in behind me. I heard every treasure breaking as I squeezed my outstretched hand into a fist. My home collapsed into itself like a supernova. Nothing was left but a writhing pile of beasts and insects. If this place couldn't protect Shea, then it and all it housed was *worthless*.

Now that Shea's power had been exposed, Aidan's beast form was easy for me to see. Unfortunately, he was clever enough to hide Shea and himself under Enochian seals. That had never stopped me from tracking him before. It just took patience and time. I didn't have that luxury now. Caelius would send everything after Adnachiel, and that dog would try and kill her again.

He may have taken my queen in this chess match, but I wasn't without options, and I was better at this game than he was.

I opened the box and stared at it: the blade Aidan had stabbed

Shea with. It couldn't be done with simple metals, she was already too powerful for that, so he'd lanced her gut with a blade forged from heaven. Normally, it would've disappeared after he'd killed the Vessel, but because Shea had survived, it remained.

I stared as it gleamed with a strange sort of light that the box and mud had concealed. Her blood was still lingering on the serrated edge, and because of the contact, it glowed brighter than the knife. It was radiant like the sun and colored like the film of soap on top of water.

This was going to be painful.

I held its ivory handle and let the box drop. The sooner I found him, the better chance I had of keeping Shea alive. If she wasn't already—

I couldn't think of that now.

I sank the knife between the bones of my forearm and dragged it to my elbow.

This was a trick I'd learned from the Book of the Dead while trying to rescue Nefertiti's children from the Pharaoh Akhenaten. I'd never done it with an angel blade, but the idea was the same.

"*Ingrata dosu betan. Eakta norat shenu.* I call upon the Light to seek what is its own. Light to Light, follow the blood and show me Shea Harper!"

I screamed with an intensity that Caelius had never been able to derive from my bones as the Light poured into my veins and devoured my flesh. My whole arm turned to mush then ash in a matter of moments.

Nothing.

The Light did not respond.

The way was blocked.

185

As it moved up my chest, melting my right leg, I gathered what was left of my sanity beyond the pain. I had one shot left before it exploded and shattered my body. "Then show me the dog! Show me Adnachiel! The Light must go back to its keeper! If not the Vessel, then the earthbound angel!"

It ripped out of my skin, shredding my veins as it torched through the black sky like a banshee in search of a virgin sacrifice. My body collapsed. There was no time. I knew that the heat trail of that small speck of Light wouldn't last long. I needed help.

I closed my eyes and whispered. Within moments, he was by my side, forcing something into my mouth. I couldn't think. I just kept drinking, my eyes fixed on that distant stream of Light.

When I finally stopped, I was mid-gulp, staring into the frightened eyes of a woman in her forties, still clutching her BMW car keys.

Her look of shock matched my own.

I shoved her away and tried to stand. My newly formed leg and arm were weak. The rips over my limbs and the pinprick holes out of every pore in my skin freckled my whole body with pink. I fell as Gracuri grabbed my frame and leaned it over his own.

He stroked the back of my hair. I felt his tears land on my neck, wetting my muddied white shirt. Every inch of my body burned. The fresh blood was combatting the liquid fire I'd poured down my veins by injecting her blood into mine through a holy blade.

The curse of Caelius being bound in darkness, forbidden from the sun, from all light, was raging through my body with every breath, reminding me of what I really was, and who I belonged to.

It had been a suicidal move.

But it was worth it if it meant finding her.

Gracuri pulled my sloppy frame back, his eyes swelling. "*Father*, who did this to you?"

I laughed, which only seemed to frighten him further. "I did."

Confusion filled his features as he motioned the half-alive woman to walk toward us. He feigned a half smile. "You're delirious. You've been mortally injured. You need more blood."

I turned to her. She hesitated and I noticed the dried mascara frozen on her lower jaw from tears.

I turned away. I couldn't look at her, at myself. My horror only mounted as my eyes rested on a pile. No. A small mountain of dead bodies lay heaped where I'd stood.

I staggered from Gracuri, pushing him back. "What have you done?"

He reached for my arm to steady my balance, but I bared my fangs and he stood back.

Looking even more confused than before, Gracuri shook his head. "But, you called me, and when I came, you were near *true* death! There was a town nearby. My only thought was of you, the thought of losing you . . ." Gracuri began crying again. "I'm sorry. I know you don't feed en masse like this. I know it's like when you found me in Thebes—the entire city dead at my feet—but please don't abandon me again. What I did then was for love, and that's what I did now! Father, I don't care if this exposes our kind! I don't care if you're morally against it! You were dying and I was so afraid of losing you forever, I—"

I grabbed his head and cradled it in my arms. He wrapped his gladiator frame around mine and trembled as he wept, "I can't lose you," over and over again.

I knew in that moment I could never blame or judge him. He wasn't thinking clearly because of me. Just like I wasn't thinking clearly because of Shea. I would do anything for her, even *this* if it meant saving her life.

I buried my head deeper into his back.

All this death.

I truly was a monster.

After we'd made love, I'd changed. I'd felt as if the killer in me had died. But now, with Shea gone and my only hope drifting into darkness, the monster had re-emerged without my consent.

I sighed, pulling him back. Gracuri was my responsibility. "Forgive me for blaming you. I called you here. This was my fault, not yours.

"Thank you, Gracuri. You saved my other children from slaughter, you saved my life, and because you exposed us again, Caelius will no doubt demand your head as he has before. But I promise, I will defend you with my last breath. He will never have you."

He smiled, pushing my hair away from my face, his eyes full of concern. I touched a curl in his hair and pulled it straight. "I have to go and find her, Son. I need you to clean this up and never speak of it, even to the others. And I need . . . I need to feed."

He nodded, quickly pulling back. "There was another town close by. I can have you a dozen more—"

"No." I gently placed my hand around the side of his neck. "It will take too long, and even though, in hunger, I broke my promise, I still intend on keeping it. I won't kill anyone else, but I need to be powerful when I face Aidan. Do you understand?"

He rested his palm over mine. "Then I will go with you. I'll call the other Second-Borns. We'll save her together if that's what you desire, Father."

I shook my head. "If Adnachiel's outnumbered, he'll kill her. I won't be forced to stand against them, or you. I can't do it. I'm not strong enough, not after Gunnhild and Ashgar. Just clean this up and keep the others safe, hidden from the eyes of Aidan and Caelius . . . and me. Without Shea's Light, no one should find you. I taught you the symbols once, when we were younger. Do you remember?"

He nodded slowly, his eyes filling with horror. "But I have to be there . . . if you need me. And the others, you know not one of us would stand against you, even the sons you've abandoned."

I pulled him closer, my lips resting on the small of his neck just before the muscle of his shoulder blade. "You can be here for me *now*, Gracuri."

His eyes widened, his fear and confusion melting away to sheer pleasure. "But you've never—you don't feed on your children like we all do. Even when asked . . . when *begged*."

I sighed heavily. There was a reason for that. It was bad enough turning them, linking their hearts to mine for eternity. But sharing blood, feeding on them, it was the part of possession that gave Caelius such pleasure when he consumed me in shadow form.

It was owning.

To feed on your children ensured their loyalty and love for you. They would think of nothing else for hundreds of years, depending on the power of their own free will and the power of their maker. It would be complete. An obsession. Caelius's version of love.

"I've never asked because I don't want to harm my children. I don't want to hurt you, Gracuri. I have cared for each and every one of you, and my heart is pleased that you have all been free and without my influence, or as free as you could be with my infected blood pumping through you, not to mention the drop of Caelius's foul blood that gives all vampires eternal life. But to do this—"

He grabbed the back of my head and pushed my lips onto his neck.

He sighed, relaxing his muscles. "I have longed for nothing else, Father. Please, if this will help you, to feed on a Second-Born, then take me. I'll clean this mess up after and hide your children. Take what you need. It's an honor to serve you in this way."

It was sweet, like it had been the night I'd turned him in Athens. I made it painless and pleasurable. His body sank into mine as I felt my limbs growing in strength. And there it was. The link. With every drop, more of me was inside him, our blood and hearts fusing.

Instantly, I jerked away, thinking only of Shea. I wiped my mouth as my muscles surged with the borrowed power of a Second-Born.

I stared at his soft features. He looked weak, pale. I grabbed him as he staggered forward. "Gracuri, are you all right? I've taken too much."

He only smiled. "You really do love her, don't you?" He

grabbed me fiercely and kissed my lips. Before I could respond, he was gone and the pile of human bodies set aflame. I shook my head, already feeling the pangs of guilt and regret.

Gracuri was loyal and wild of heart. I'd taken more than blood—my final acceptance of his body, my final rejection of his feelings toward me . . . I'd hurt him this time.

I took in a deep breath. If I survived this, I'd apologize, I'd make up for it somehow.

I looked at the already weakened trail of Light and hissed, "I'm coming for you, Beast." I leapt into the air and followed the path.

I tracked it all over the world.

Aidan had been everywhere I'd traveled in the last millennium. Places we had battled before. That winged dog hadn't been able to fly since killing Moses, but he was still fast.

As useless as those wings were to him now, they were still made of spirit, and a dark creature like me could grab hold. And I would. I'd break every bone, flightless as they were.

The thought of his suffering didn't calm my growing unease. His behavior didn't make sense. Why was he visiting every place he had chosen to kill a Vessel? Was he also nostalgic, or was this a part of his deception?

It had to be his leftover trail from following me while looking for Shea. It wasn't fresh; the Light was dim. I kept following the heat until it got brighter and I finally discovered a fresh track. It wouldn't be long now before I ripped him open.

And there he was. In a forest near Amsterdam. He was just waiting there by a cave. Thinking? Plotting?

Seeing him filled me with relief and rage.

If he was alive, then so was Shea.

But why here? Had he stopped in town to buy drugs? Was he keeping her comatose so she wouldn't escape and come looking for me?

I ripped through the night air like a comet hurtling toward the earth. The sound barrier snapped in my wake as I crashed into him. The force of our bodies created a crater that demolished the surrounding trees and sent them flying like toothpicks spilled on a dinner table.

Before he could recover, I held his bloodied face to mine. "Where is she?" I screamed. "Where is she, you worthless, blind, senseless, Light-suckling dog?" I threw his body into a mountain. His bones crushed as he propelled through the other side, landing somewhere in a small town.

I didn't have much time. I scavenged the area. She was nowhere. I couldn't feel, see, or smell her. What had he done?

I flew to the town square, where his body had fallen chest-first on the spike of a metal fence. I bared my fangs as he growled.

He pulled the skewer out of his chest and took a step forward; the ground quaked beneath his feet. His power was alive in the very air we were breathing.

My eyes burned as I gained control of the animals in the forest behind me. Two could play at this game.

Instantly, he stopped. "Let's end this, but not here. There's no reason for this town and the ones around it to go down like Pompeii."

I spat, and it landed on his cheek as I laughed. "That was your doing, not mine."

He growled again, a sound so deep and ravenous it shook all

the houses and broke the windows. "That may be, but there's no reason for *these* people to die."

I paused.

For a moment, I felt something. Something strange. Why did he care? Who were these meaningless people he would postpone our battle for? I thought about the pile of bodies next to Gracuri, and of my own guilt and promise.

I was not the same vampire I'd been in Pompeii, and he was right: there was no reason for innocent humans to die just because he was a treacherous dog. I could torture him and find Shea without their lives being lost.

"Fine. We'll fight over the water just to remind you of Halfdan, the seaman. You remember Halfdan, don't you? Gunnhild and your *brother*?"

He clenched his jaw and nodded bitterly. In a flash, he was racing toward the North Sea. He arrived moments before me, running on top of the water. His kind could stand on it without penetrating the barrier. It was something about the essence of the ocean being likened to the spirit.

He turned, a fraction of a second before I could stop, and pounded his clenched fists into my chest. I smacked the surface of the water. The waves rose up around my body like concrete skyscrapers.

I sank.

Every bone in my spine was broken, blood pouring out of every orifice. It drew the sharks.

Let them come.

I extended my power and attracted anything alive in the vicinity. With quick movements, I shredded them like a ravenous tornado of death. Blood rose up from the depths and I with it. If blood was in the water, I controlled that water.

Aidan looked shocked. He shouldn't have been. It was I who had frightened the Pharaoh for Moses, turning all the water into blood and using it to attack the city.

I wrapped the tides around his invisible wings, pinning him in midair. I plummeted my fists into every inch of his muscled frame. His bones broke under my knuckles.

Eventually, my knuckles broke too, but I still pounded them into his body until they were mush.

Our strength diminished until we were both barely hovering inches above the water, my hold on his wings as light as a child's, yet he still couldn't resist it.

I spat blood onto his face in disgust. "Just tell me where she is, Adnachiel. I'm not taking her to Caelius, but *you* can't have her. She chose *me*!"

That did it.

We both had a surge of strength, our eyes alight in joint fury. He broke my hold over him. I quickly called the locusts, which he easily drove away, his wings sending small tornadoes across the ocean. I was surprised. They were useless for flying, but they still had power. Maybe it was something internal that had stopped him from flying after Moses's death, not the physicality of it.

I stood firm and sneered, unmoved. Gust of wind or not, he'd have to do better than that.

And he would.

I had to think quickly. I had to find anything alive in the water that I could control.

I had an idea.

I'd done this once before on a pious man as a joke. Later it'd been put in the bible as God's will, but it would do.

A large whale leapt into the air and swallowed us both. It swam fast and hard through the deepest, darkest cave toward the center of the earth. Aidan didn't react fast enough. Odds were, even as a beast, he'd never been swallowed whole before, and rolling around in an acidic giant whale stomach threw his game.

I had been swallowed by Caelius's shadow enough times to know the routine. It would burn, in an unimaginable way. But it would pass.

I grabbed his invisible wings and snapped them backward. I broke every bone. I pushed a handful of stomach acid into his chest as he screamed in agony.

"Just give her to me, Adnachiel, and I'll keep her safe while you live a long, boorish dog life! Why are you so incessant on keeping her only to kill her later?" As the acid peeled back layers of muscle, I pushed my fist through his rib cage and ripped out his heart. It would grow back eventually, but it was still pleasing, feeling it warm and pumping in my hand.

I let the pleasure get the better of me. He rammed his palm through my sternum and ripped out my heart, then stood back.

There we were.

Once like brothers.

Now and forever enemies.

Holding each other's hearts.

I couldn't help but smile at the irony. For some reason, he did too. He looked at me. For the first time in centuries, he really looked at me. "Lucian, what would Moses think, seeing us now?"

I dropped his heart and crushed it with my heel. "I don't know, because he's dead. Because you cared more about this precious world than him, than our friendship. You're just mindless and obedient that way."

He lowered his hand, still holding my blackened organ. "I do. I do care about this world. All the people in it. And it kills me, literally, every time I end a Vessel. And whether you believe me or not, I *am* sorry, Lucian."

I gritted my teeth as my incisors ripped my gums. I'd tear him apart. "You're *sorry?*"

His eyes grew downcast as he took a deep breath. He tossed the heart and I caught it, confused. What tactic was this?

He spoke without wavering. "I think we've been played here. When you had this thing swallow us, it hit me: you don't know where she is either. You kept asking, but it didn't register. I thought you were toying with me. But you're not, are you? You genuinely don't know where she is."

My mouth opened. No. This couldn't be right. The heat trail, all the places Aidan had gone looking for me . . . it never doubled back. It should have at least passed by the rubble that'd been my home if he'd grabbed her then.

"Impossible . . ." I staggered as I shoved the heart back in its hole. It would heal faster that way.

I needed to think.

I needed to start building my strength again.

I needed to get the hell out of this whale.

Within moments, I had it vomiting us up on the closest shoreline. Aidan gasped and brushed his arms and legs, as if that would remove the smell from his memory. I grabbed him and shoved him into the sand. "If you and I don't have her, then where is she?"

He shrugged me off, still gasping. "I don't know, Lucian! I was tracking her scent when you found me."

I clenched my jaw and spoke through my teeth. "We hate each other. That's fine. I'll *never* forgive you for Moses, but that's not going to help either of us find Shea. We can find her faster together. United . . . Light and Dark." I stopped. I knew this speech.

Although Moses had been more elegant, Aidan still smiled at hearing it. It was an awkward thing. It always was. I doubted his kind used their mouths in that way. Still, I couldn't help but feel strange seeing it again.

He reached out and grabbed my forearm in a pact like we'd made all those centuries ago.

"This time, *Aidan*, save her. Promise me. If we do this together, no matter how bad the situation looks, promise you won't kill Shea."

He winced, withdrawing his hand. "I love her, Lucian," he admitted. He shook his head, averting his gaze. "I know she loves you. I saw it even before she did, so I won't get in your way."

When his eyes met mine, they were wet with tears. "When I sank the knife in, it was like with Moses, but *worse*. I wanted to die. I needed to, just so I wouldn't have to see the look on her face." Aidan took a deep breath, then stared at me with conviction. "I will never hurt her again. I promise on my soul, on my brothers, on the end of the world . . ." His eyes were heavy and full of a deep, unrelenting sorrow.

I didn't move. The wind was calm around us. My chest tightened. Despite the feverish pumping of my regrowing heart,

197

it was hard to breathe.

Never in all these centuries had he agreed to not kill a Vessel if the time came. He had his duty, his obligation to the Light, to his beastly brothers. His *real* brothers.

I didn't know what to say. My eyes were fixed on his, and I nodded. We looked so much the same in that moment. Younger than our ancient souls, young and in love with Shea Harper. That was what it was. We had both loved Moses, but this was different. This was more.

His mouth barely moved as he spoke. "And I will *always* regret what I did to Moses . . . and to you."

He didn't meet my gaze then.

"What you did to me," I growled, "changed me. You made me into the monster you feared I was."

His mouth opened, but nothing came out.

Words couldn't repair the distance his actions, and lifetimes of misunderstandings, had created.

"Lucian, I want us to be—"

"Enough sentiment." I brushed the sand off my chest as if brushing off his words.

He coughed, unlocking the broken bones in his wings and straightening out.

We didn't have time for this. We needed to buck up and hunt whatever had Shea.

I turned from him back toward the vast body of water. I called and feasted on the bloodied delicacies of the sea while he bathed in the bright light of the moon.

When we were ready, we were both eager, refreshed from blood and light. "What have you found so far, Adnachiel?" I began.

He shook his head. "It's all masked, her scent thrown in every direction. Her blood, drops of it splashed here and there. I thought it was from you feeding. Whoever did this, they were good. Maybe even better than you. And if it's not *you*, that tells me we're dealing with one of your initial children. Someone ancient."

I shook my head. "No. I killed the two that would have betrayed me. The other five are loyal. They'd die before dishonoring their father in that way."

He grimaced. "I've always found the father thing a little creepy."

I shrugged and half smiled. "Yeah, me too. But it's—"

"And what do you mean you *killed* two?" he interjected.

Now my smile faded. I did my best to quell the anger ready to mount and break his wings all over again. "When you *knifed* Shea, they wanted me to end her. I refused and chose instead to end their lives. Like I told you before you gutted her, there was no need."

He looked over the sea and sighed. "I couldn't have guessed that, Lucian."

My fangs grew impulsively. "I thought after I *tortured* Frank and killed his entire lineage, we had an understanding."

His eyes widened. "I didn't know any of this. I was obsessed with keeping her safe. I didn't want . . . I didn't think I could trust you. It doesn't matter. The important thing now is finding her. It had to be one of your children who took her. Did anyone know where you were?"

I shook my head. "No." Then the reality set in. "Wait . . . Ur-

199

Nammu, but he wouldn't—"

"Ur-Nammu?" He lunged, pinning me to a towering palm. "You idiot! He was the one who made me think you were going to take Moses! He's Caelius's right hand when you fall through!"

I shoved him violently into the sand. "Moses would have lived if you'd given me time to explain it to Ur-Nammu! Had he known our relationship, he wouldn't have come. When you saw me take Moses, you just assumed the worst! I was trying to protect him, not take him to Caelius!"

There was a long pause as we stared at each other with unkempt fury.

Then Aidan cooled, looking away, not meeting my gaze. "I know."

I ground my teeth, tilting my head. "What was that, Dog?"

His voice was low and soft. "I *know*, Lucian. It was my mistake. I thought . . . I thought maybe you'd turned on us. It was only after I stabbed him, when we were dying as we fell from the sky . . . the look on your face, the betrayal. I realized then that I'd been wrong."

I took a deep breath. It had been thousands of years, and now he'd admitted his error. "You and Moses died that day, and all the goodness and hope I had left died with you. At that time, I didn't even know that killing the Vessel was the only way to end your life. I would have never betrayed Moses, Aidan. I would have never betrayed *you*. And it's the same for Shea now."

He looked up, his sky-blue eyes wet with shame. "I'm sorry, Lucian. After Moses, when the next Vessel was born, I tried to find you. When you found us, you were so full of rage. You took the Vessel without question and attacked me. You'd changed. I wanted to explain, but you wouldn't listen. Then after Pompeii, all of that death . . . I just thought you were dead to me as well."

I stepped toward him. "Not dead. You buried me under that rubble. It took a hundred years to claw myself out. I had plenty of time to hate you as I ate ash and molten lava."

He took a step back, furrowing his brow. "And what was I supposed to do? You tapped into the Vessel's soul! My brothers thought you were freeing Caelius in Egypt, so when they realized you were in Pompeii and cracking open the Light of a Vessel, they showed up to stop you. The fight cost countless of innocent people their lives. I couldn't let you do that again. All those people died because of us. And burying you was foolish. I know that. But my brothers . . . they would have *killed* you."

I grabbed his wrist and jerked his face to mine. "Don't play innocent. You didn't bury me to save my life."

"Of course I did!" Aidan shouted. "You may have hated me then, but I hated myself more. I didn't blame you for it. I accepted your hate as my penance. All these years . . ."

I squeezed his wrist, my incisors cutting my tight lower lip. As the blood ran down my chin, I could hear the sincerity in his voice.

"Yes, we've done things to each other, fueled by hate and regret, but I know the first blow was mine. I've carried the blame for what you've become. I'll never be able to apologize enough. But after Moses, you kept taking the Vessel, forcing me to kill my friends, brothers, the Light. I knew you were doing it to punish me. And I deserved it. I deserved every moment of anguish it caused me.

"But as much as I deserved your torment, the Vessels didn't.

201

And I prayed you would never find Shea because she's different, like he was. A part of me thought . . . if anyone could unite us like Moses, it would be her. Granted, she's not an eloquent speaker, but her spirit is like his was. I know you see it too.

"I've wanted to ask for centuries, but I couldn't risk the fate of the world on a theory. So here it is: you're still my brother, you don't like Caelius any more than we do, and you're not interested in destroying the Light. And this time, despite my feelings about her, you've fallen for Shea. When you talk about her, it's like how you used to talk about Nefertiti when we first met."

I let his wrist fall from my hand. The shallow hole in my ripped-out heart was mending. I could feel the fibers as they welded themselves back together. A dead black thing, but now I felt it as if it were whole again.

Care, concern, hope—they were strange things to feel for a beast I'd sworn to torment for all eternity. "If you thought I wouldn't kill Shea, why did you try to take her life?"

Again, his face filled with shame. "It was a risk. I could have been wrong. I could have been seeing things that I wanted to see in you, that I *needed* to see, to believe. I've been away from home, from the Light for so long, I worried that . . . I just wasn't sure. And I couldn't risk the death of this world for a theory. No matter how I felt about you, or her."

"I understand." It was a short response, but I couldn't hear any more. It was easier to despise him, to be callous, than to face the truth that all of this time, all of this wasted pain and misery, had been for nothing.

I looked at my empty hands. He was right. In all of our battles, no matter how much we tore into each other, he had never actually *killed* me. This whole time he'd been waiting for me, hoping I'd change.

"I don't want to believe that Ur-Nammu would turn on me. After Moses, he never interfered with another Vessel. He's Nefertiti's *father*, Aidan. I trust him as much as I trust my own left hand." I clenched my hollow palms into fists. "But you're right. He's the only one who knew where she was, and he's the only one who can Dream-Walk like Shea. He could have convinced her to come outside." I nodded to Aidan and he crossed his arms, resolute.

I scanned my memories, the look on Ur-Nammu's face as I'd held Nefertiti's cold body in my arms. "I just don't know why he would do this. He was my father's . . . my *real* father's best friend. They fought side by side in the Gutian wars with Egypt. My father knew I wasn't a fighter and sent me off to be a tradesman, but he kept Nefertiti by his side to fight. I asked her to come with me then, but she wouldn't. She was a warrior, as was he. That's why they were captured.

"When I saw them again, we were older. She'd already been forced to birth children for the Pharaoh as his concubine. I risked everything to free her, but I was a boy, not a vampire.

"I ended up enslaved alongside her father. He took care of me and found ways for me to see her. They were *family*. And she was . . . could I have been blind? I know he can't forgive me, the fact that my kiss took her life. But neither of us knew then that we couldn't turn women. After I turned him, *he* asked me to turn her. How could he take Shea, just to punish me for Nefertiti?"

Aidan took a long breath as he watched what must have been obvious pain pour over my features. "Can you track him,

Lucian? I've been trying since you left with Shea, following trails I thought were yours all over the world. He's better than I am at hiding her."

My eyes cleared as I shifted my focus from Nefertiti to Shea. "I'll need to feed. Don't worry, I'll feed on animals . . . and I have Gracuri who I can feed on, one last time. It won't take long. Stay here, and when I get back, we'll go *together*." I looked into his eyes. Yes, it was a test. If we were about to do what I'd planned, we had to trust each other without question.

He nodded slowly. "I'll wait here for you. No matter how long it takes—"

I was halfway across the world before he could finish his sentence. I fed on anything and everything that moved, except humans. My pile of dead bodies before I'd encountered Adnachiel still troubled me.

I'd become a killer, a monster, but I hadn't always been that way. Shea had brought me back to the boy who wasn't a warrior. I was a craftsman. I loved to build things with my hands. I knew all of that was outdated now but just the memory that I wasn't *this* was enough for me to despise all of the life I'd drank to kill my own pain and guilt.

Gracuri was more than willing to let me drink from him. His passion had doubled since our last encounter. I hated it. I hated seeing him so maddened with loyalty and desire. It would fade and normalize, and eventually he'd go back to his own nature and remember himself.

I cherished his nature. It was so unique and childish, despite his gladiator frame. It pained me seeing him like this. This wasn't the secret love Gracuri had always believed I couldn't see. This was complete and utter possession without refrain.

***

It didn't take long before I was on the beach next to Aidan again. I would have made him wait a hundred years to test his loyalty if not for Shea. For her, I couldn't stand to have him wait longer than what was needed for me to be at full strength.

Aidan eyed my mouth and I slowly wiped the warm blood from my lips. He spoke clearly. "Are you ready then? Let's track Ur-Nammu and get our Shea back."

I laughed candidly and grabbed his shoulder. "Now that we know Ur-Nammu has her, I know exactly where she is. He's taken her to Caelius, and if you want to get her back, you'll have to face my father with me. I'll die, but if you're willing to do this, you should know, you'll probably die too."

His mouth fell open as he stared at my resolute face.

I spoke slowly, needing him to digest my words. "You think that nothing can kill you, unless they kill Shea. Caelius *can* kill you. He's killed your kind before."

He swallowed hard. His eyes widened like a child's at Sunday school upon hearing that the devil was *real*.

I sighed. "But if he kills you, you're dead forever—no more being born again with the next Vessel. Your spirit doesn't go to the Light. I'm sure you remember your brother who was dragged to the pit with him: Ashliel?"

He coughed as if all the air had been sucked out of his lungs, his tan features turning as pale as my own skin. He nodded. "He sacrificed himself to make sure Herostel could complete the seal."

My brow raised. "You don't really believe that. You just don't want to look Darkness in its twisted face. Caelius *ate* your brother out of spite. He devoured him and keeps his bones framed on the cut stone behind him like a mantel—"

Before I could finish, Aidan was on his knees vomiting in the sand. He lurched, grabbing his gut and shaking his head violently. It was only then that I realized how much these beasts must mean to each other. Aidan and I had called ourselves brothers with Moses, and it'd always felt that way. Brothers not by birth, but by choice. But his *real* brothers, they'd probably circled the throne of heaven for—how long is eternity? A loss like that . . . no wonder he was loyal to them.

"I didn't say that to hurt you, Adnachiel. I just want you to be prepared. He will use any angle against you. He should be easier to face because he's still sealed, but if you're thrown off by seeing your brother's bones, he'll use that advantage in battle." I stared at his back as he rose, firm and resolute.

"Thank you for telling me, Lucian. I know it must be hard for you to stand against Caelius, to give up what has become your new family. I'm aware that if you do this and live, you'll be hunted by your own kind. I'm also aware that you're right: we both won't make it out of this alive. But one of us can save Shea."

His eyes were strong and fierce, the warrior inside hardening like stone. He nodded, and I did the same, wrapping up my own raw feelings and emotions. I filled myself with ash and flame. Fighting side by side, we would use every ounce of our powers, every trick, every ruthless and cunning tool we'd sharpened on

206

each other over the years on Caelius.

Together, we could save her.

CHAPTER 11
SHEA

Where was I?

My eyes opened to darkness and I couldn't make out any familiar shapes. For a second I thought I had woken up in my dorm and that everything had been one long dream.

But then Ur-Nammu's face came into sharp focus when he lit a small oil lamp.

We were in a cave. I could tell we were farther back from the entrance because there was only a small pinprick of light in the distance. I was about to make a run for it, knowing Ur-Nammu couldn't chase me in the sun, but his iron grip held me down.

"You'd be dead before you went five feet," he warned casually.

"You won't kill me. You need me alive," I answered back a little more brazenly than I had intended.

Ur-Nammu's eyebrow rose slightly. "I'll rephrase: you'd be unconscious before you went five feet."

That I believed.

Maybe I could use my powers. I tried to concentrate on the cave itself, the earth—make it move, make it crumble.

Nothing.

Maybe I was too scared.

I took deep, calming breaths.

Then I tried to connect to anything. Air. Water. Rock. Anything!

Still nothing.

"Are you quite done?" Ur-Nammu asked.

How did he know what I was trying to do? But like a lame-ass, I nodded.

Why wasn't my power working? Sure, I was still a noob, but at this point I should have been able to shake a rock or something.

Then it hit me.

"I'm already unconscious, aren't I? You can't control me awake, so you're keeping me asleep." I knew I was right. It was the only thing that would explain my complete lack of power.

Ur-Nammu actually smiled. I'd impressed him. Good to know.

"Very good," Ur-Nammu responded. "I guess I can lighten up the scenery now that I don't have to deceive you."

With little more than a wave, the cave turned into a house with a wraparound porch surrounded by acres and acres of wheat fields. I was now sitting on a wooden bench swing with a glass of lemonade in my hand while Ur-Nammu sat across from me on an old-fashioned rocking chair. The house was quaint and right out of a Norman Rockwell painting. The breeze was soft and the sun was shining. If Ur-Nammu wasn't sitting across from me, I'd actually be relaxed and wishing I was there.

"This is what you Americans like, right?" Ur-Nammu's voice was flat, as if he didn't really care but wanted to placate me.

I suddenly didn't want to admit how nice it was. I didn't want to be "cliché girl." But I guess I was to a certain degree because sitting there on that porch with a cool glass of lemonade felt pretty darn good. Screw old vampire a-holes.

"I think most *humans* would appreciate this scenery, thank you very much. Not that you'd know, since you're stuck in the dark all the time." I sounded like a spoiled brat.

I could only imagine how I came across to an ancient vampire.

"Just drink your lemonade," Ur-Nammu replied dismissively.

I threw the lemonade in his face. "Why don't *you* drink it?"

To my surprise, Ur-Nammu laughed. Being a dream, the lemonade was gone in an instant, leaving him completely dry.

But he looked over at me and his eyes kept a bit of the amusement he'd felt at my outburst. "Would you like another?"

I couldn't help it. I reluctantly smiled back. "Yes, please."

Another lemonade was suddenly in my hand. I drank its cool deliciousness. Taking a deep breath, I realized fighting with Ur-Nammu would get me nowhere. The fact that I entertained him with my temper was something I could use to my advantage. He liked 'em feisty, I guessed.

I glanced down at the glass full of liquid. "Is this how you're keeping me asleep? Drugs or something?" For some reason it didn't freak me out as much as I thought it would, and the more information I had, the better off I'd be. Maybe I could find a way to wake up and get the heck back to Lucian.

Even thinking his name sent butterflies through my stomach.

He had been my first. And to be honest, the experience had

been mind-blowing. It was all that was keeping me sane at the moment. Feeling him against me, his mouth ravaging every inch of my body—I shuddered.

I didn't have much of a princess complex, but seeing as I was unconscious, I kind of hoped Lucian would swoop in and save me. It went against my feminist nature, but I'd always been a sucker for a good romantic rescue, so my two sides were fighting with each other.

And frankly, I could use all the help I could get.

Normally, Aidan was the first person I'd think of to protect me. Maybe he had come to his senses. I didn't want to hate him. I didn't want to lose him. I rubbed my belly where he had stabbed me. It wasn't really there, so I didn't feel much, but the wound was deeper than physical injury. Aidan might as well have stabbed my soul. It certainly felt the same.

Ur-Nammu broke me out of my reverie by answering my question. "No. I'm draining you to the point of unconsciousness."

"As in, my blood?" I asked in horror.

Ur-Nammu gave me a look that I could only describe as curious. "You're with Lucian. I'm sure he's fed from you before."

I stood up from the porch swing, smashing the lemonade on the ground. "No, he's never *fed* off me. Gross."

Ur-Nammu was taken aback. "Gross? What's *gross* about drinking life? It's more intimate than anything you can imagine."

The guy looked like he was going to orgasm in front of me.

I tried to hide my disgust, but I was pretty sure my expression was in a permanent grimace. "Do you even remember what it was like to be human?"

Ur-Nammu's face went still. "That time in my life is burned

211

into my memory forever."

"You know what? I don't think it's *burned* enough. If you really remembered being human, then feeding off people would revolt you. Infuriate you. Make you sick! Anything but *intimacy!*" I had a feeling I was projecting my own issues onto the vampire, but I couldn't fathom that he wouldn't remember that humans pretty much thought drinking blood was repulsive.

Ur-Nammu was silent for a moment. He was watching me closely. I couldn't tell what he was thinking. I felt stupid standing in front of him while he sat quietly in his rocking chair staring at me. It was like when a stand-up comedian told a joke that no one understood.

Awkward silence.

When he didn't respond, my anger faded. I plopped back down on the porch swing and made it rock with my foot. "Sorry," I apologized. "You've been a vampire a lot longer than you were human." I examined his face. "Although you are kind of old looking."

Ur-Nammu laughed again.

It was such a startling contrast to his silent stares I actually jumped back in my seat.

"You remind me of my daughter," Ur-Nammu suddenly admitted.

I sighed. At least he was talking. "What was she like?"

"She was the most beautiful creature in existence." Ur-Nammu's expression was far-off like he was reliving his past. "So much so, the Pharaoh stole her from me and made her his slave, though he called her his wife," he practically spat.

I suddenly remembered his conversation with Lucian.

"Nefertiti?"

Ur-Nammu's eyes went wide with surprise. "Did Lucian speak of her?"

"He said she was his first love." I couldn't tell if knowing that Ur-Nammu was Nefertiti's dad was good or bad for me. And another thing that was bugging me was the fact that Ur-Nammu said I reminded him of Nefertiti. Was that why Lucian liked me? Because I reminded him of Nefertiti? Kind of cool in a seriously geeky way, but also awful in a heart-crushingly insecure way.

"Never were there two people who belonged to each other more. Soul mates of the truest form. Lucian tried to turn her, but men can't turn females, and she died in his arms." Ur-Nammu was watching my every reaction. It must have been bad, because he smiled, savoring my pain. "Did you think *you* were Lucian's soul mate?" He laughed, but this time there was no humor in it. "You're just the Vessel. He's attracted to your Light, nothing more. Look how easily he let me take you. Lucian got what he wanted and let you go."

Ouch.

I thought I was going to puke.

Ur-Nammu was tapping into my worst fears: That Lucian had never really cared about me. That he only wanted me to save his evil father.

But I knew in my heart it wasn't true.

Lucian loved me.

The thought filled me with a surge of light.

It was true.

It was pure.

And no jealous father-in-law-turd-face was going to take it

away from me.

I gave Ur-Nammu the snarkiest expression I could when I said, "Is that supposed to upset me?" His face gave me what I needed: shock and anger. "The thing about love is, when you're in it, there are *no* doubts. None. So nothing you can say will convince me otherwise. Lucian is coming for me. That's a certainty. The question is: what do you think he's going to do to you when he finds us?"

Ur-Nammu showed a flash of fear, then he went back to his stoic demeanor. "We'll see."

"So are you taking me to Daddy, or what?" I crossed my arms, annoyed at the old-looking vampire.

"It's not just to free Caelius that I'm taking you to him." Ur-Nammu eyed me with his annoying observation-mode.

I tried to keep my lame poker face up, but I was curious. "So what else happens when the curse is broken?"

"All vampires will be able to walk in the light."

Whoa.

Lucian and I could be together in the daylight without fear of him turning into ash.

"Do I have to die?" I figured I'd ask.

Ur-Nammu's eyes met mine and there was almost affection there. "I don't know."

"It probably doesn't matter anyway." I stopped rocking the swing. "Aidan will try and kill me first. Either way, it looks like I'm dying. Maybe if I died for Caelius, at least Lucian could live a normal life." Ugh. I hated to be a Debbie Downer, but my chances weren't looking all that great. There was no way Aidan would let Caelius free, which meant he was probably tracking me . . . to kill me. And even if he didn't find me in time, Caelius would kill me anyway. My future wasn't looking too bright.

When I peered up at Ur-Nammu, he was staring again. I wasn't that tough of a nut to crack, seriously. The way he examined me was like I was an anomaly he'd never seen before.

His voice was soft when he asked, "You'd willingly die so Lucian could be what? Happy?"

"Yeah, so? What do you care anyway?" I had no patience for Ur-Nammu anymore. The fact that he was drinking my blood to keep me asleep made me want to strangle him. And if I was going to die, it might as well be for love.

But I wasn't ready to die yet. I fully planned on using whatever power I could muster to kick Caelius's butt.

"I'm bringing you to Caelius to make things right and restore the balance. It doesn't reflect my feelings," Ur-Nammu admitted cryptically.

"What's that supposed to mean?" I wanted to know any chinks in his armor.

"It means spending over three thousand years in the dark is a torture I can't explain. I find myself escaping by Dream-Walking for years at a time, just to feel the sunlight. When I saw that Lucian would never bring you to Caelius, the thought of waiting five hundred more years was unbearable. I'm sorry it has to be this way, but you were born for a purpose, and I'm allowing you to complete what you were destined for. I have others to think about as well. We all need the sun, and as long as Caelius is trapped in his cage, we will never be free." Ur-Nammu definitely believed what he was dishing.

"Gee, thanks." My voice was laced with sarcasm.

215

A thought hit me.

I was always in control when I Dream-Walked with Lucian.

Obviously, Ur-Nammu had about three thousand years of experience on me, but I was also the *Vessel*, so that had to come with some kind of power perks, didn't it? I was about to find out.

I closed my eyes and concentrated as hard as I could.

"What are you doing?" I heard Ur-Nammu's voice, but I didn't open my eyes.

It must've been working.

I focused on Lucian.

If I could just get him here in this space, he'd know where we were and then he could come for me.

"You can't break my protection spells. Stop trying." Ur-Nammu's voice was commanding, but there was a note of worry in there too.

I could hang on to that. If he was even slightly worried, it made me more confident that I might get a message out. I kept my concentration up, remembering our night together. The way Lucian had touched me. The way he'd kissed me. The way he'd looked at me.

"*Stop!*"

My eyes jolted open when Ur-Nammu shook me.

I was awake!

He was scared enough that I'd get a message through that he'd actually woken me up.

It wasn't what I'd intended to happen, but maybe this was even better.

Of course, that's when I realized I could barely move. I felt so weak that it was difficult to keep my eyes open. Blood loss.

Serious blood loss. I'd always wondered what that would feel like.

I was so sleepy I just wanted to drift back into dreamworld, but I had to stay alert.

What do you know? We *were* in a cave. That first vision he'd given me had actually been accurate. The sun was shining outside in the distant exit like before, but it was setting.

I needed to get to that light.

"You've created quite a conundrum. I can't let you sleep because you may get word to Lucian or the beast, but I can't let you be fully awake or you could use your powers against me. You leave me no choice," Ur-Nammu said as he leaned down, with his fangs out toward my neck.

No.

I couldn't let him drink any more of my blood. He needed me alive, so I knew I wouldn't die, but my instincts were to make him stop. His teeth sank into my neck, but it wasn't the sharp pain of breaking skin as it had been with Frank. I realized this was because Ur-Nammu had been drinking from the same spot the entire time he'd had me. He didn't need to puncture new wounds, there were premade straw holes.

Ew.

I thought about his fangs. His teeth. The violation I felt. I was exhausted, but my fury kept me awake.

There was pure wrath in my veins.

Ur-Nammu screamed and flew back against the rough cave wall. He was spitting up my blood like it was made of fire.

My fire.

I felt a surge of satisfaction. So much so, I wanted to rub it in his face. "My blood will be poison to you, and you will rot and die if you drink it."

Ur-Nammu's eyes were full of terror. He believed me.

That was the first successful bluff of my life. I was pretty proud of myself. Maybe it was true. I really didn't know the extent of my power, so it was possible I could make my blood kill him. I was the Vessel, after all, and made out of Light, whatever that meant. The plus side was Light killed vamps, so intensify the heat, and blood equals liquid sunlight.

Of course, I didn't know if I could repeat the trick. My anger had triggered it. But I needed to continue the bluff in order to get outside.

I stood up with every ounce of strength I had. I wanted to make it look like I wasn't weak, like I had full capacity of my body. It worked because Ur-Nammu stayed where he was.

Although his expression turned back to that of a hunter, which I didn't like, I kept my voice strong as I said, "You're going to let me leave right now." I tried not to show any fear.

Ur-Nammu stood up. He wasn't a tall man, but he was intimidating. "I don't have to drink from you to keep you weak. I can break your legs and Caelius would still have his sacrifice."

"I ripped a hole through Lucian's chest, so I'd be careful with threats if I were you." I was terrified, but I needed to convince him I was at full power. I really didn't want him to break my legs. Once I had broken my pinkie and cried for a week. I wasn't good with pain, especially my own.

Ur-Nammu smiled wickedly. "My daughter used to lie to me as well. She was better at it."

Okay.

Run.

I whirled around as fast as I could and ran for the pinpoint of light in the distance.

Snap!

Excruciating pain ripped through my body. He'd broken my right leg! I could see the jagged edge of bone piercing through my upper thigh. It was so surreal I froze in place. I didn't even scream, though my body was on fire. I was in such total shock that I was still standing.

Ur-Nammu's arms cradled me to keep me upright.

I snapped out of my stupor and felt the roaring pain as if a stick of dynamite had ripped open my leg.

I screamed.

Ur-Nammu whispered in my ear, "Give into the blackness. Let yourself pass out from the pain. I'll fix it when you sleep."

Rage.

Rage.

Rage.

I wanted to break every bone in Ur-Nammu's lame vampire body.

I wanted the pain to stop.

Stop! I screamed in my head.

Crunch!

The pain was gone.

I shrugged myself away from Ur-Nammu with ease. His face was full of astonishment and fear.

I looked down at my leg. No wound. No broken leg. Not even a scar. Just smooth skin and the remnants of blood from where the bone had shot through.

I'd fixed it.

I'd fixed my own freaking leg!

I wanted to celebrate, except I was still with the ancient vampire madman who'd broken it in the first place.

"What else you got?" I taunted.

I felt like a true badass.

My nature wasn't to hurt anyone, not even Crazy-Pants in front of me, but I would if I had to. Or I'd try to anyway. I backed away from him, heading steadily toward the cave entrance.

Ur-Nammu didn't move. He watched.

I could see he wasn't exactly scared, but he wasn't sure how to proceed either.

Just a few more feet and I could run into the safe sunlight.

When I was positive I should be at the exit, I turned around to make sure I had gone the right way.

I had gone the right way, all right.

It was simply that the sun had gone down.

I was screwed.

Before I could think, Ur-Nammu's teeth dug into my neck.

Damn it.

Everything went black.

***

The next thing I knew, I was waking up again. I hadn't had any dreams. It felt instantaneous. One moment I was being bitten by Ur-Nammu, the next I was in some kind of chamber. I was definitely underground. The walls, ceiling, and floor were all stalagmites and stalactites, rough stone and dirt. I couldn't see any exits.

I could barely see anything it was so dark.

"Is this better?" a voice sounded in the blackness.

The cavern began to glow a dull blue.

It was huge.

Five football fields huge.

I skittered back when I saw the bones of a giant winged beast sitting in front of me. It filled the whole back of the cave, its wingspan too big to see. It looked like a dragon. A dragon! My mind couldn't seem to accept that as reality. It had barely accepted my current life as reality, but dragon bones? Serious overload.

The remains had been so distracting I hadn't noticed the man standing in front of me.

Caelius.

I knew it instantly.

I had expected to see pure evil incarnate, something like a black piece of coal with hands and legs like in the vision I'd had when Lucian had visited him. But Caelius was stunning. He had an ageless quality to him. If I saw him on the street, I'd think he was in his late twenties, but his eyes were prehistoric.

It was like when I first met Lucian, but about a million times more powerful. And speaking of those eyes. I thought Lucian's turquoise eyes were unique, but Caelius's were auburn. Was having crazy-colored eyes a prerequisite for turning?

I stood up and tried to appear more confident than I felt.

"Where's Ur-Nammu?" I wondered aloud. Had he just left me with the father of all vampires?

"He's standing right there." Caelius smiled with his pearly white fangs showing.

I turned my head to see him about ten feet behind me. His

face was stoic.

"Hey." I nodded in what I could only describe as a friendly manner. I had no idea why, but for some reason Ur-Nammu felt like dealing with a puppy compared to Caelius. I almost wanted to run up to him and beg him to protect me, but since he was the one who'd brought me here, I was pretty sure he'd veto that.

"You are an interesting girl." Caelius brought my attention back to him.

"Thanks?" I wasn't sure how to respond to that.

It was kind of annoying how all these ancient beings were somehow *fascinated* by me, like I was some kind of revolutionary science experiment.

I suddenly noticed that I was outside of Caelius's prison cell. The wall was invisible straight on, but I could see it out of the corner of my eye like a hologram. There were all kinds of symbols around it as well, which I could only assume were the seals that kept him in.

I was grateful that I wasn't inside with the monster, but it also made me wonder why Ur-Nammu hadn't delivered me straight to Caelius's feet. Why carry me thousands of miles only to drop me off five feet short of the intended target? I decided not to bring it up. I didn't want to give Ur-Nammu any ideas. Maybe I could escape as long as I stayed outside the angel barrier.

Caelius's face was amused, as if talking to me was like talking to a chimpanzee. He definitely thought I was beneath him. "You're the first female Vessel. Did you know that?"

"Um, cool?" I felt extremely weird having a conversation with the evilest of evil. It was so . . . *normal.*

"Females carry life, and you carry mine, Shea Harper. When

I feed off your soul, I will be made whole, and I will finally be free of this prison. You should consider yourself honored to be such a sacrifice." He had an air of arrogance that made me want to kick him. I didn't like the word "sacrifice" either. I really didn't want to die so this freak could wreak havoc on the planet. I had to come up with some sort of plan.

"Yeah, not so much honored as repulsed. You're kind of an a-hole," I said before I could think better of it.

I hated smugness more than anything, and Caelius had it in spades.

He was silent for a moment. When he spoke, his words were icy. "How could *my* Lucian love a vile thing like you?"

Thanks for confirming that Lucian loves me.

It was as if a huge weight had been lifted from my chest. If Caelius was upset that Lucian loved me, then I knew it was true. Not that I hadn't known it before, but hearing it from the father of all evil made it more real.

Caelius apparently didn't like the expression on my face, which was something akin to dreamy. "Your insecurities make you weak and pathetic. You are a flawed, unworthy Vessel."

"Sticks and stones, dude." Okay, "dude" was a little Valley girl, but the more casual and non-caring I was, the angrier Caelius became. Not that I should've been trying to provoke the most powerful vampire on Earth, but I really hated him.

Caelius threw his hand out and an invisible vise clasped around my neck. I choked instantly, clawing at my throat, trying to breathe.

He laughed at my terror. "Lucian loved only one woman in his lifetime. *One!* And for over three thousand years he pined over his loss. It made it *pure*. *True*. Then *you* come along and he falls in love with another! You ruined the perfect love story. You defiled it. I will enjoy killing you. I'll savor every drop of life from your body!"

"You'll have to kill *me* first."

Through sputtering coughs, I turned my head to see Lucian snarling at his father like an enraged lion. My eyes smiled at him even though my face couldn't. I told him through my thoughts, *I love you, Lucian.*

With a loud thud, Aidan dropped down next to him.

His expression said it all.

He was my Aidan.

He was sorry.

They were there to save me.

I blacked out.

CHAPTER 12
LUCIAN

Caelius dropped Shea to the ground like used newspaper. Her body thudded, and my heart with it. Even after my thoughtless trust of Ur-Nammu had dragged her here, she still loved me.

Everything inside ached and burned for her. Caelius smiled, reading my body language. "So it's true. You love this Shea Harper—*disgusting*. I had such plans for you, for us. I had my Adam and Eve. We would have ruled the world together . . . you were my chosen."

His jaw clenched as he took a casual step to the edge of his cage. "You are *still* my chosen. Once I release us into the daylight, I'll reveal everything to you—the plan, your place by my side. You'll have *real* love. And everything you've wanted. The only thing in our way is the Vessel. I had Ur-Nammu bring her just to the outside of my prison so you, my son, could deliver her to my arms. That's how much I trust you.

"She's the Vessel, so she'll slide right through the barrier.

Watch as I break the seal, and this world will be ours, my Lucian."

His hand stretched out as his shadow caressed my frame.

Aidan growled.

I was glad to have him by my side. "You know I can't let you have her, Caelius."

I lunged while he was still wrapped up in the pleasure of his fondness for a future I couldn't allow. I threw her body to Aidan. He instantly raced toward the opening.

A black and beastly shadow, one that had ravaged me for years, burst out of Caelius's chest as he screamed in fury.

It moved toward Aidan. Everything slowed. I couldn't let this happen. If I could keep Caelius back, Aidan could escape with Shea. He could hide her and keep her safe.

They could live.

The only thing it would take was my life, which meant nothing without her.

I sank my hands into the earth. A spark ignited inside me as Gutian words filled my lips, chants my father and Ur-Nammu had prayed to the gods before battle. It enlivened my blood with the heritage of a powerful people. I pushed my palms in deeper and called upon every ounce of ability I had. And then I called on the Darkness. The black itself.

I couldn't breathe. I felt a hole ripping in my mind, like a tear in space. My body shrunk and I fell inside. I watched as a puppet master—a shadow boiling red, filled with ash and smoke—rose from my body. My actual limbs remained still and frozen, but my soul was attached to the monster. My thoughts were its thoughts.

I grew its shape then surged toward Caelius's shadow just before he ripped out one of Aidan's wings.

226

Aidan shrieked in agony as the bone tore the skin down his back, but kept moving.

Caelius stood there, the true beast that lived inside him, staring at my own creation in *pleasure*.

He laughed.

The sound moved through the shadow in bursts and waves. He looked back at our frozen bodies, so small and insignificant now on the vast cave floor beneath us.

His words were thoughts and they penetrated mine. "So, my child, you've finally given in to the Darkness. Now it has your soul . . . now you are truly mine. Even if I release you, your shadow form will *always* belong to me."

I hissed, reedifying my words, keeping his control and the Darkness from overpowering me. "I am merely using the emptiness. I am not one with it. But I would give myself over to oblivion and worse for her. As my real father would say to me on the eve before battle: ours is a proud people."

I shoved my shadow talons through his chest and ripped as his form shifted around mine. "We are many, but united we beat with one heart."

No matter how I tore, he kept shifting. I couldn't fix my shadows around him, but our dance was blocking Shea well enough. He'd stretch and grab Adnachiel, dragging him back here and there, but Aidan was quick and making ground with Shea in his arms.

I shifted my form, absorbing rock and dirt, anything that his shadow couldn't seep through.

Now Caelius's anger boiled. His form grew ten times the size of mine. I'd never seen it so large. I felt myself being pulled into it.

I added more stalagmites and anything else I could consume. I kept my mind focused on my true father's words: "Though we may fall, we will never fail because we have given ourselves over to glory. To fight for those we love."

That was it. I knew what to do. It was simple, but the worst thing I could have imagined. I had to let go, to get sucked into him. This wasn't going to be like when he'd taken my body before. There was no coming back from this. I pushed the shadow of my spirit *into* his.

At first he howled as I burned his insides right through to the edges, then he squealed with delight as he began breaking apart my soul. Thoughts, memories, they all became fragmented. Feelings, cares, anything that I thought was mine was gone.

I couldn't remember the last words of my father's code. They were *important*. What I was doing was important. It was for someone, but for whom? What was I?

Nothing.

Everything slipped, and I began dissolving into him like paper into water.

Then something whispered. It was a hook, pulling me out.

"Ours is a proud people. We are many, but united we beat with one heart. Though we fall, we will never fail because we have given ourselves over to glory. To fight for those we love. Though our bones may brittle with time. Life may wear and kill the tenderness of affection, but the burning heart, the flame that is our people and what we stand for, cannot be stamped out of time. We are etched into the very existence of all things. We are, and forever will be, a people who fight for what we love. And love is the soul of all that's worth fighting for."

It was spoken in my own tongue, in Gutian. The words burst me through Caelius' shadow, forcing us both back into our small vampire frames. I stared into the wet eyes of Ur-Nammu as he held my flimsy limbs. He'd been whispering into my ear, bringing me back.

Tears welled in my own eyes upon seeing his face. "Why did you betray me? Why did you bring Shea here?"

He shook his head, replacing his vulnerable stare with a hardened mask as he stood me back on my feet. "I have my reasons. Believe it or not, I'm still fighting for the ones I love. Your father's words will never be forgotten by our people. We created that chant together as boys, and when we ruled side by side, we wore it like a code of honor."

Caelius coughed and our eyes found his, burning red like phosphorescent blood. "Am I interrupting this moment by wanting to get the *Vessel*?"

I was flung to the other side of the cavern wall, the impact crushing every bone in my body. I'd never actually walked that far in all my thousands of years. As I clawed my chest, trying to quickly shove my rib cage back into place, I saw the tip of the beast's outstretched wing. I hadn't realized how long it was. Aidan's brothers were a thousand times his mortal size.

I coughed blood. With all the speed I could force out of my soggy flesh, I propelled myself forward, only to find the worst. In that small moment, one fraction of a second out of Caelius's sight, he had dragged Aidan all the way back. He was pinned next to Shea's unconscious body on the dirt just outside the glyphs of Caelius's cage.

Before I could move, Caelius shoved me down next to Aidan.

Adnachiel's lips trembled as he spoke. "I was halfway across Egypt! I didn't think—I'm sorry. I wasn't fast enough." Blood spilled out of his mouth, matching mine. He was ravaged. I had no doubt that he'd fought harder and fiercer than he had when I'd faced him, but still, he was torn open, with only one wing left that hadn't been ripped from its socket.

Caelius laughed.

He slowly raised my body and Aidan's so that we could see him. He tilted Aidan's chin up toward the mounted skeleton of his beast brother, and mine toward Ur-Nammu, who was held up next to it, unconscious.

Caelius eyed Aidan's horrified face. "Do these bones look familiar to you, boy? I must say, I've eaten life for a long time, but nothing was as delicious, as *supple* as the heavenly skin of your brother, Ashliel."

Aidan tried not to respond as his eyes took in the full view of every meat-stripped bone. He gave into grief and unwillingly released a bestial howl that shook the cavern's foundations.

This pleased Caelius to no end. "You know," he continued, "I've taken Lucian in every way I've been able to imagine over the past centuries. It helps kill the time. But most of those methods I developed and refined by working on *your brother's* soft flesh.

"Oh, how he screamed and begged, pleaded for death. 'Mercy, Caelius,' he would cry. And he would call out for you, by name. For all of you, actually, hoping that you'd hear him, that you'd come and save him . . . his loyal brothers. But you didn't! You abandoned him to the Darkness! All too afraid to come down here and see for yourself what was becoming of his limbs.

He was still alive as I devoured each one.

"I guess there's no loyalty among dogs. You left him here, knowing full well what I'd do, didn't you, Adnachiel?"

Horror.

Sheer horror filled Aidan's eyes as he stared, fully taking in Caelius's words and the skeleton of his beloved brother.

He stared at the holes where his eyes must have been and gasped the words, "I'm sorry," before he began weeping in sobs, his broad chest shrinking in convulsions as he cried, speaking in an inaudible tongue that only his kind could understand.

I finally shouted, hoping to draw his attention away from Aidan. "Caelius, stop!"

He bared his fangs and spoke through clenched teeth, his grip re-collapsing my rib cage as I coughed blood in agony. "That's *Father* to you! Is it so hard to say? Watch . . ."

Caelius used his shadow form to pick up Shea's motionless body. He moved her lips like a puppet, forcing them to say "father."

Aidan's eyes shifted to mine, full of fear. I shook my head, then whispered, "He can't pull her in himself. Someone has to toss her in there. We still have time."

Aidan tried to rein himself in.

Caelius's grip tightened as he dropped her and pulled me inches from his face. "Time? What is this time that you have? I *am* time. I am the void. I am *everything*. When will you acknowledge that truth?"

His lips twitched as he spoke. He pulled Ur-Nammu's unconscious body next to mine and snapped his fingers. Ur-Nammu gasped, his eyes flying open. Caelius smiled. "Did you enjoy that little rest? Remember what I told you before. That nightmare is just a fraction of what I'll do to everything you love if you disobey me again."

Ur-Nammu didn't respond. He hardened, wearing the mask of a warrior. Caelius took a deep breath and sat down. "Now that you've been punished, I will allow you to speak. Just what do you think you were accomplishing, stopping me from devouring my Lucian?"

Caelius freed him from his hold. Ur-Nammu stuttered, gathering his strength as he forced his frame to stand tall and upright. "He would have died. I was saving him, Grandfather. He was like a son to me before we were turned, so . . . I . . ."

I could see the gears in his mind shifting, always the strategist. "I could only imagine, if that's how I felt, a lowly worm, how you would feel if, in your rage, you had accidentally killed him. I know how you adore him. You would have regretted it for all of time. He is, after all, the Adam to your Eve, isn't he? You have a plan that you've been waiting to exact for thousands of years. I merely wanted to honor that plan. I am, and forever will be, your loyal servant." He bowed.

I bit my tongue. I didn't want to believe it. When he'd pulled me out, I'd seen in him the same look my Gutian father had worn when he'd said his last goodbye. There was the code . . . there was love there. Loyalty. Trust.

Caelius sighed, his eyes shining with a mischievous look. "Ah. And after all, I do have claim to something very important to you. I suppose that's factoring into your whimpering now. But all in all, you're right. There is no replacing Lucian. I want my story, and I want it perfect. This world will begin again with me

232

as ruler. I have my Adam and Eve. I can break him. I've done it before. He'll be who I need him to be . . . and when he's not, I'll enjoy the process of convincing him.

"You are right, Ur-Nammu, there's nothing for me in daylight without my boy. Oh, and if you cross me like that again, that nightmare I spoke of will be nothing in comparison to the real thing."

Caelius motioned his head. "If Lucian won't throw the Vessel in, then you must do it." Ur-Nammu stepped toward Shea.

I rallied, and so did Aidan, but to no avail. Our bodies, inside and out, were hemorrhaging. He was too powerful for us.

I did the only thing left that I could do, which broke the last part of my dignity, something I'd managed to keep alive all these years. "Please."

The room fell silent. I'd never uttered the words after my mother, Anna-Steen, had died. Even when I was being beaten to death in Egypt, I'd never begged. I'd never said please.

Caelius leaned toward me, enthralled. "What was that?"

I didn't meet his gaze. I focused on Ur-Nammu alone. "I'm sorry, Ur-Nammu. I'm sorry for turning you and bringing you into this horrible existence where you've been enslaved by a creature more powerful than we can stand. I'm sorry that, in my ignorance and youth, I killed Nefertiti . . . my morning star. I'm sorry that I am who I am. I'm sorry that, on the eve of battle, my father sent me to be a tradesman with the Elamites because I was no warrior, but a sculptor and a poet. I should have trained. I should have been the warrior that you, he, and Nefertiti deserved, maybe if I had—"

Ur-Nammu turned, his eyes again soft. "Stop, Lucian. Your

father knew what you were and loved you for it. In our chant, you're the heart he died to keep alive. It was my failing. He kept you safe. And when I saw you trading in Egypt, I was a slave. I had failed to protect Nefertiti. I should have sent her away with you . . ."

I gurgled as blood moved through my punctured organs. "No, Ur-Nammu. She refused. And if you could turn back time, there are no words you could say to make her listen. She was always more of a warrior than any of us. She was strong, beautiful . . ."

He stepped toward me as Caelius's eyes and smile widened, as if we were performing some Greek tragedy for him. "I should have given her the medicine you'd created to make her sleep, Lucian. You'd wanted to escape with her then. I should have listened."

I sighed. He was wrong. "I've always hated myself for surviving, and she would have hated us both, Ur-Nammu. Had she awoken next to me, her people slaughtered and the remnants enslaved . . . she would have fought to get you back and been *killed*."

The air around him was silent, cold, as if he'd seen something I had not. "That might have been better. Instead she fought by my side, and we were all enslaved, but hers was the worst. The Pharaoh took her as a wife. She bore *him* children. He allowed her to see me in the slums. She brought me water as I worked in the mud on the statues of his likeness.

"I should have never reached out to you. You were a slave in Egypt because of me—because of what you felt for her. I betrayed your father's memory and risked your safety for hers. And now she . . ."

Tears ran down my eyes as I pleaded, "She's *gone*. But Shea is *alive*. I can't take back our past. I can't forgive myself for Nefertiti, but this isn't going to bring her back. Serving Caelius will only cause more pain and chaos.

"Whether I love Shea or not, she doesn't deserve to die at the hands of this monster! This planet isn't perfect, but it shouldn't have to suffer for *our* mistakes. Please, Ur-Nammu. If you've ever cared for me or my father, the code of our people, please protect her."

Ur-Nammu stepped back, then took a deep breath. Quickly he picked up Shea's body and threw it into Caelius' cage.

My jaw dropped in shock.

Ur-Nammu's eyes didn't meet mine as he said, "I *am* protecting our code by doing this. I am and will forever fight for the ones I love."

Caelius laughed as he held Shea's slumped body. He laughed and laughed, tears finally rolling from his eyes as he gasped for breath. "Lucian, you really thought *Ur-Nammu* would save her? You're so blind. And you begged! I never thought I'd see it!" He paused, the cavern falling silent. "Why not try your luck again?" His eyes were more terrifying than when he'd been a bestial shadow made of Darkness. "Go ahead, Lucian. Beg for her life."

I clenched my teeth, my insides shaking. It was too late. He had her. Aidan managed to get his arm free, Caelius's attention being solely focused on my agony.

He grabbed my wrist so tight his fingertips were clenching together. "*Don't*, Lucian. He's going to take her right now, no matter what you say. Don't give him the satisfaction."

Caelius scowled. "Oh, look at this. The two buddies back

235

together. I'm guessing you've resolved the whole Moses issue. Well, good for you. Lucian may have distracted me from explaining the heights of your brother's torture, but I haven't forgotten about you, Adnachiel.

"In fact, after I drink this whore dry, I'll show you firsthand what he experienced. I'll show you both, at the same time. You can bond in that as well. Although, you I'll kill and frame next to your brother. Lucian, however, is mine to keep and play with for *all of time*. He's like no other."

His eyes warmed as they traced over my haggard frame. Aidan growled and I bared my fangs. Caelius just shrugged as he moved the hair from Shea's neck. "I really would like to hear you beg, Lucian. How about this: if you beg, I'll start sucking her blood and breaking the seal."

Aidan scoffed. "That's what you're going to do anyway!"

Caelius shook his head. "Oh, you haven't been here long. But Lucian knows better. Drinking from her can be the *last* thing I do. My real flesh and bones haven't felt something alive and warm like this for a very long time. I've had to take pleasure in my shadow form, but with her body, there's so much I can do like this. I think I might just start—"

"Please, Caelius, just drink her."

The words came out, but not from my mouth. Ur-Nammu stood by my side, pleading so I wouldn't have to.

Caelius scoffed as he tossed Ur-Nammu's body carelessly into the black depths of the cave. "He'll wake up somewhere in Egypt. He's served his purpose and doesn't need to be here for the rest of this, not when there's so much fun to be had. A girl, a vampire, and a dog . . . all here for my pleasure."

236

He slid his hand along Shea's body, cutting a small gash down her side as he tore her shirt off.

Seeing him on top of her—

"Please." My voice cracked. My love for her meant more to me than all the pride I'd saved over three thousand years. Now, I finally understood my Gutian code of honor.

I continued, unashamed. "Whatever you want from me, I'll give it to you, just don't hurt her!"

He stopped, his face unamused. "You need to do better than that, *Son*. I've done things to you, unimaginable things, and never once did you do me the honor of begging me to stop. I've never heard the word 'please' uttered from your lips until tonight. Not once.

"Even when you were a mere mortal, hanging on to your last gasps of life as I pleasured myself, you didn't beg. This dog creature from heaven mounted behind me begged daily! Hourly! And I have done no worse to you! And *for her*! For her you beg to the likes of *Ur-Nammu*!"

I stuttered, my mind blank, flatlining in fear. This couldn't happen.

He took off his shirt and pressed his naked chest against hers, eyeing me with satisfaction as he rested his hips onto her frame. He ground his pelvis on top of her jeans as he grabbed her breast.

"Please, just drink her!" Aidan begged. "You miss your freedom, don't you? Why wait? Just end it!"

I stared at Aidan as his lips trembled with every breath. His face was ghost pale. He was as afraid as I was. Our love for her was that strong.

Caelius released his force over our bodies. We fell like puddles to the floor, both coughing and trying to unsnap the bones that were protruding out of our skin in every direction.

He licked the side of her face and feigned unzipping his pants.

Aidan and I shouted in unison, "No!"

He stopped for a moment, boyishly resting his body halfway on hers. "I want something that you two just aren't giving me. Let's make it sweet." He licked the space between her breasts as he peered back up into our desperate eyes. "Both of you are free from my hold. You can leave *now*. You won't get another opportunity like this.

"Adnachiel benefits because I don't kill and torture him in unfathomable, pleasurable, decadent ways. Lucian, you benefit because you don't get to sit and watch me suck the life from something you love more than yourself. Of course, I'll still have to break you once I'm out."

He looked at our hardened jaws and goaded, "However, if you both stay, bow and plead over and over into the dirt, calling yourself worthless worms, speaking my glory, and begging for me to drink her, then I will do just that. I'll start drinking until her body is lifeless. She won't experience any pain at the cost of my pleasure.

"Again, Adnachiel, you have much to gain by leaving, and more to lose by staying. If you stay, you'll be forsaking the Light by *praising* the Darkness. But you will save the Vessel from horrible things. And then I will *ravage* you.

"Lucian, it will be agony watching her die, and in all the years I've stripped you bare, you've never begged. I will require you to beg in the most *demeaning* way now. I'll want to hear it, loud and true from the both of you, or . . ." He again began grinding on Shea's motionless body. Though she was clothed from the waist down, it was still gruesome to watch. The pressure of his hips caused her to involuntarily gasp for breath as he moaned with delight.

Instantly there were two thuds: Aidan's body and mine kneeling to the ground. Caelius stopped as we both began pleading, loud and shamelessly in every tongue we could speak. He smiled, breathing in deep the torture his request had caused, ripping proud men apart from the inside by using what they loved the most. He smelled the soft spot between her jawbone and then sank his teeth deep into her neck.

CHAPTER 13
SHEA

Um. Ew.

I woke up *half-naked* with Caelius crunching into my neck.

I knew I should be terrified, but I was seriously repulsed.

He hadn't . . . ?

I did a quick mental check of my girl parts and thank God, the douche bag hadn't sank that low.

It pissed me off.

I concentrated as hard as I possibly could, focusing on my blood, turning it to liquefied sunshine like I had done with Ur-Nammu.

Caelius coughed and stumbled back a few feet, clawing at his neck.

"Choke on that, asshat." I couldn't resist.

I grabbed what was left of my clothes and put them on. It covered what needed to be covered, but I still felt vulnerable.

I turned at the sound of pounding on a window. In front of

me were Lucian and Aidan trying to claw their way through the invisible barrier that kept Caelius inside his prison.

I ran to them, but I couldn't touch them.

I was stuck inside the mystical jail.

The two of them looked like broken puppies, their eyes full of terror and concern.

Aidan spoke first. "Shea, you have to use your powers to get out of there! He can't use you if you're outside the barrier!"

I nodded worriedly. "Okay, let me concentrate."

Lucian's voice cracked as he placed his hand flat on the invisible wall. "Shea, I tried to save you, but he was too strong. I love you."

I placed my hand over his, though they didn't touch. "I love you too." Then I smiled. "And I can save myself." I nodded toward the sputtering Caelius. "See?"

Aidan cracked a very small smile, but it was Lucian who spoke. "It won't last. Get out of there."

"Right," I said and closed my eyes.

I thought about the wall and turning it to water. It was the only thing I could think of in that moment of insane distress.

That's when I felt it.

Like black ice seeping into my back.

I could barely hear Lucian and Aidan screaming at me as Caelius's shadow entered my body.

Caelius spoke to them, his voice full of what I could only describe as merriment. "You both begged me to drink, so I drank." He laughed. "Blood doesn't break this curse—it's just tasty. You humiliated yourselves for nothing." He was quite amused.

I tried to push out the Darkness growing inside of me. I

thought only of the Light and how it could defeat Caelius. His shadow was cold and instantly made my body shake, but still the Light grew bigger. I could do this.

Then I felt Caelius's mouth against my ear. "That's it. The more Light you generate, the sooner I can free myself."

"Caelius!" Lucian screamed. "What are you doing?" His face was wracked with panic.

Caelius turned to Lucian, furious. "Her blood is ecstasy, I'll give you that, when she's not tainting it with Heaven. But my prison was created by the beasts of the Light, and only the Light can break it." He licked the side of my cheek. "I need her *soul* to restore me. You should remember this, boy. You unknowingly tapped into the Vessel's soul in Pompeii."

Caelius's shadow pierced my heart. I could feel it wrap around my very being, like a boa constricting the life out of its prey.

I reached my hand out for Lucian and Aidan, but they were stuck on the other side of the prison.

Caelius had me.

He was killing me.

By devouring my soul.

Thump!

Thump!

Thump!

The ground shook as three giant men landed on the ground next to me. They were well over ten feet tall and all muscle. But as my consciousness started to drift off from Caelius's attack, I saw a flash of their true forms, beasts with wings the size of the bones in front of me. They weren't dragons; they were a mishmash of every animal imaginable all rolled up into one terrifying foe.

With the blink of an eye, they were in human form again. My mortal mind apparently couldn't comprehend what they really looked like. But even as giant human beings, they were horrifying.

Aidan's brothers were here.

The protectors of the Light.

I just hoped they didn't try and kill me first, as Aidan's original plan had been.

I had to be on my toes as much as Caelius at this point.

Caelius pulled back from me with a grin.

I wasn't happy in this situation, but Aidan's brothers evidently amused him.

"So the beasts have arrived. Sabrael, Harahel, and Gavreel, oh how I've missed you. Have you come to visit dear old Ashliel? You only had a few thousand years to save him," he laughed. "Or are you here for your baby brother, Adnachiel? He's doing a bang-up job keeping the Vessel from me."

"Adnachiel may have failed at his duty, but we will not," the one called Gavreel said.

"I'll devour you three quickly, unlike Ashliel," Caelius boasted.

Was he *that* powerful?

Everyone in the room was about to find out.

Gavreel seemed to be their leader, as he was the first to strike. *Whack!*

Caelius smashed into the invisible barrier like a rag doll.

That was my cue to get the heck out of the way.

If they meant Aidan had *failed* by not killing me, then they were *definitely* going to kill me.

Probably now-ish.

I need to get the ef out of there.

The angel named Sabrael whirled on me before I could move. His hand was the size of half my body as he wrapped his fingers around my waist. "Go to Adnachiel. He will protect you." His voice sounded like music as he lightly pushed me through the barrier and into Aidan.

Oh how I missed those arms.

I felt him kissing the top of my head and all my anger and worry and horror at what he had done to me vanished. I hugged him back fiercely, trying to drown out the epic battle now commencing behind us.

"Shea," Lucian's voice called out to me.

Aidan gently pulled away and let me fall into Lucian. Being with the two of them made me feel like we were going to survive this. I was with my love and my best friend. Nothing could stop us.

Except maybe the full-on supernatural battle exploding in front of our faces.

Aidan's eyes met Lucian's. "Get her out of here. I have to help my brothers fight."

Lucian nodded and took my hand, but I stopped him. "We can't leave Aidan to fight that *thing*."

Aidan looked at me pleadingly. "Please, Shea. Go with Lucian. I need to know that you're safe."

"Safe? Are you high? If you and your brothers lose, then Caelius is going to send every one of his minions to come after me again and again until the end of my days!" I said furiously.

"End of your days?" Aidan grinned.

I grinned back. Even in the mayhem of the epic battle taking place around us, Aidan still had to tease me. We'd grown up together. We had spent almost every moment of our lives together. He knew me better than anyone on the planet, and he still knew how to make me smile.

"Yes, the end of my days. Dork."

"Adnachiel!" Harahel called out.

Aidan was a warrior through and through. He turned to his brother. "I can't get past the barrier!"

Harahel reached his giant hand out and pulled Aidan through with ease. Aidan was a big guy, but he looked like a boy compared to his brothers.

Caelius was using the bones of Ashliel as a weapon against Sabrael and Gavreel, who had him pinned against the invisible barrier. Caelius stabbed Sabrael in the chest with a shard of bone. Sabrael yanked it out and stabbed it into Caelius's throat.

Caelius sputtered up blood and pulled the bone out just as easily as Sabrael had.

Trying to kill immortal beings was going to be harder than it looked.

Maybe Caelius couldn't be killed.

Maybe that was why they'd trapped him here in the first place.

Aidan, being roughly the same size as Caelius, ran at him full force. He looked like a linebacker taking down his opponent. It caught Caelius by surprise, so he wasn't able to protect himself. The two tumbled onto the ground, slashing and clawing at each other.

"I have to do something," I announced.

My heart jumped into my throat when Caelius pinned Aidan down. He was smaller and weaker than his brothers.

He was going to die.

"Shea, we have to go. Aidan wants you safe. Don't make his sacrifice for nothing," Lucian pleaded.

I looked into Lucian's turquoise eyes and saw nothing but worry there. "I'm not *sacrificing* him. That's not who I am."

Lucian held me back before I could pass through the invisible wall. "No, Shea. We have to go now."

Aidan cried out in pain as Caelius smashed his ribs with his hands.

I pulled free from Lucian, ran for the barrier, and passed through.

Lucian pounded his fists on the prison wall in fury. "I have to protect you! Let me in!"

"I don't know how."

"Just concentrate on my body! You passed through on instinct! You should be powerful enough to bring me in too!"

His unwavering confidence gave me the boost I needed. I thought of the barrier being made of liquid again. With a slight tug, Lucian was stuck half-in, half-out. I focused all my energy on getting him through to the other side. Within seconds, he stumbled inside the prison unscathed.

I had to get to Aidan.

His brothers couldn't pry him loose from Caelius's grasp.

Lucian's face was fierce. "Stay here and use what power you can." He leaned down and kissed me briefly. When he pulled away, I nodded.

Aidan's face was beet red from Caelius's grasp.

246

I shot out my hand and Caelius screamed in pain as I used wind to make his arm snap. He released his hold on Aidan.

Lucian bared his fangs and joined the beatdown of Caelius.

Not knowing which side Lucian was on, Gavreel shoved him aside like he was a blade of grass.

Aidan screamed at Gavreel, "He's on our side, Brother!"

Lucian held his hand out as if he was going to summon some kind of power.

Caelius laughed. "Your powers don't work inside this prison. Mine are limited and you are a dilution of me!"

Lucian recovered quickly. With lightning speed he wrapped his arm around Caelius's neck from behind and squeezed.

Caelius choked in pain and what looked like a little bit of pleasure. It was enough of a distraction for Harahel to rip off Caelius's legs and throw them clear across the prison.

It was gruesome.

But like a bad Frankenstein movie, Caelius's legs flew back to him and attached themselves instantly.

Caelius threw Lucian off with ease.

How on earth were they going to kill him? It seemed like a hopeless cause, and Caelius appeared to be enjoying the whole ordeal even though he was grossly outnumbered. I knew then that Caelius had been raring for a fight for quite some time. His visits with Lucian must have been few and far between.

Caelius was just bored.

I didn't blame him. I'd be batshit-crazy if I had to stay in a prison for thousands of years. And being that he was a creature of violence, this fight was like throwing him into the briar patch.

Home.

I was about to make his life suck.

I could feel my powers flow through me like a living being. The one thing Caelius had done when he'd tried to chow down on my soul was tune me into what made me tick. I knew I was something more than human, which was hard to wrap my head around. A few months ago, I'd been excited to get my dorm room. Now I was standing in an underground cavern watching angels fight with Darkness itself. To say my life had changed was a serious understatement.

But it had.

And I had power.

I closed my eyes and thought of daylight hitting Caelius's skin. I pictured the strength of the sun heating his skin, boiling his flesh like fire.

Caelius screamed in anguish.

I opened my eyes. His body was covered in boils and he no longer looked amused. His eyes met mine and there was burning hatred oozing out of them.

I kept up my concentration, though the sight terrified me, especially since I knew I was the one responsible for it. The blisters on his arms and legs were starting to burst and pop large amounts of puss.

I wanted to throw up.

I stopped my attack.

Sabrael turned to Aidan. "Remove the Vessel from here! Caelius cannot break the seal!"

Aidan's response was a resounding kick to Caelius's face. "She's done more damage than any of us. She can tip the balance!"

Gavreel chimed in, "Sabrael, listen to Adnachiel. Maybe we

can destroy Caelius, if it's possible."

"I'm right here!" Caelius mocked the angels, laughing. "And you know I cannot be killed, even in this humanlike form. We've known each other since the dawn of time. Three thousand years isn't even a blip for us. And you've forgotten one important detail."

The fight had stopped momentarily.

I wanted to roll my eyes. Angel-beast-thingies were such suckers. Caelius not only made them stop attacking him, but they were actually waiting to hear what he had to say.

Caelius's blisters continued to burst as he spoke. He looked like some kind of leprosy reject. "My dear beasts, if you're down here, who's protecting the Light?"

The fear that ran through that room was palpable.

Even Lucian had stopped to listen, as if the power of his father's voice kept him at bay.

"Don't listen to him!" I called out, feeling the need to step in. "He wants to even the playing field by forcing some of you to return to your Light or whatever. Caelius is imprisoned here; there is no way he can hurt the Light." I wasn't 100 percent positive, but my gut told me I was right.

And so did Caelius's face when he looked at me. I was ruining his plan and he loathed me for it.

"If I use the Vessel to break the seal, then return to my unbound form as Darkness, I will devour the Light without you protecting it. Do you really want to risk the Light on the word of a *girl*?" He was trying to gain back momentum.

I could see that Aidan's brothers were trying to figure out what to do. If they left, Caelius would win for sure. I had to do something.

"I'm the Vessel, moron. I'm the dripping of what they're sworn to protect. Don't you think I'd know if the Light was in danger? I can feel it in my bones, my blood, my *soul*. The Light isn't in danger, but *you*? It ends here," I said with as much confidence as I could.

Aidan and his brothers nodded and they repeated in unison, "It ends here."

It was frightening hearing them speak as one voice. I could feel the power race through my veins.

Caelius was scared.

Lucian looked over at me, pride beaming.

Caelius's voice practically squawked as he frantically turned to Lucian. "*Son*, help your father."

Lucian snarled. "Not even if you *begged*."

Caelius's eyes flashed betrayal and hurt. "You are my son, my only *true* son. How can you turn against me?"

"I was never a monster until you made me. I should have died in Egypt under the light of Nefertiti's window. Shea's finally brought me back from the edge of your madness—back to myself. Seeing you die will only bring me closure." Lucian leapt first, baring his fangs.

Aidan and his brothers quickly followed suit and ripped Caelius limb from limb, pieces of his flesh flying everywhere. His parts couldn't reattach themselves fast enough. The whole scene looked like a pack of dogs digging into Caelius's broken body.

It was horrifying.

I stood watching, not knowing what to do or how to react.

They clearly didn't need me.

I jumped suddenly.

It felt as if something had brushed up against my leg, but nothing was there. I was about to chalk it up to the wind from the slaughter I was witnessing when—

Boom!

The ground shook so violently everyone fell to the ground, including me.

It was instantly calm.

Everyone slowly rose to their feet.

My blood turned to ice as Harahel's voice broke the silence. "Where's Caelius?"

I searched the cavern with the others, but he was gone. Not even the tiny bits of torn flesh remained.

He'd disappeared.

Gavreel was by my side before I could think to move, but he wasn't focused on me. "The barrier is gone. With the power he absorbed from the Vessel, Caelius destroyed the seal."

"But the Vessel is still alive and her soul is intact." Sabrael tried to hide the confusion in his voice.

Gavreel shook his head. "Caelius used enough of the Vessel's Light to break out of his prison, but he is still weak. As soon as he feeds, he *will* try to finish draining the Vessel to regain his full strength."

Aidan walked over to me protectively. "I will never let that happen."

Harahel breathed in deep. "Caelius is vulnerable." He eyed Aidan knowingly. "Huntable."

Aidan nodded. "Killable?"

"We don't know," Sabrael admitted. "But you must try."

Sabrael placed his giant hand on Aidan's shoulder. "You are no longer tied to the Vessel. Your bond is broken, which means Caelius may not be able to be killed, but you can. Be careful and find him, Adnachiel. If he can't be killed, force him back to his true form."

"I will." I had never seen Aidan more determined.

Then Gavreel looked down at me. It was quite intimidating staring up at a giant angel beast. His voice was kind as he said, "Caelius no longer needs you to break free of his prison, but he still needs your soul to be at full strength in his mortal form." He nodded to Lucian. "This one will keep you safe while Aidan hunts Caelius down." Gavreel turned to Lucian. "All vampires can walk in the sunlight now, which makes the Vessel even more vulnerable. You have been an extension of Caelius's evil for over three thousand years, but the Light has made you whole again. We see inside your heart and know you will die for this Vessel. We are entrusting you with her safety. Are you willing?"

Lucian nodded. "I will protect her with my life."

This seemed to be good enough for Aidan's brothers. They all placed a hand on Aidan. They had a moment of silence and I was pretty sure they were communicating with each other. I was glad these guys were on my side because they were really scary.

"We must go back to protect the Light. It is our most sacred duty. If Caelius goes back to his true form and destroys the Light, the Universe will collapse. It's up to you to stop Caelius on Earth. Don't fail us again, Adnachiel."

"I won't fail you," Aidan vowed.

Before I could process what had just happened, Sabrael, Harahel, and Gavreel were gone.

Caelius free or not, I felt an overwhelming sense of relief. I knew the panic and mayhem would begin soon enough, but in an instant of zen, I just appreciated the moment.

It was over.

I was alive.

And I had my two boys.

CHAPTER 14
LUCIAN

I looked at her face. It was hopeful and somewhat elated. I guessed Caelius being gone and the fact that she was out of danger momentarily must have come as some sort of relief.

My only relief was that she was alive. For now. But Caelius being free meant the whole world was at risk. And the world could die for all I cared, but she was a part of it. If it burned to the ground, she'd be nothing but ash and smoke.

I pulled her close to my chest. She leaned in for a kiss, but I moved my head back. I just wanted to look at her, to feel the thudding of her heartbeat: alive. I stroked her hair. My Shea Harper.

A thought chilled my bones.

How long could I really protect her from all of this?

She leaned in again, and this time I didn't resist. I let my mouth melt into hers. The soft curve of her lower lip rested gently between my teeth as I moved deeper into the embrace.

I pulled the air from her lungs and it filled my own. I was hers, and she was mine.

Aidan placed his hand on my shoulder and coughed awkwardly. Shea instantly jerked back, blushing. His eyes didn't meet hers as he spoke. "I will definitely give you guys some alone time. I just need to be clear. My brothers are back protecting the Light. They can't track him, even if they stayed, but I can. I had enough practice through the centuries by tracking the scent of Caelius's blood in Lucian as we battled over the Vessels."

Shea shook her head and touched his arm. Now he looked at her. And for a moment, they were silent. I could see relief move through his body as his one remaining wing trembled with the loss of the other. In any other battle it would regrow, but it'd been severed by Caelius's shadow form, his touch of Darkness marring Aidan for the rest of his life. However long that was, for any of us.

She smiled. "Why can't your brothers track him? We're not leaving you alone. We'll hunt him together."

He shook his head no. "I can track him because he's Darkness willingly keeping itself in human form. I'm an angel in human form linked to the dripping of the Vessel, aka you. It's a similar energy exchange and should make it easier for me to find his influence.

"Lucian will keep you safe in the meantime, and he can train you . . . he trained Moses. You'll get stronger. You can Dream-Walk with me *every* night. He's weak right now. When I find him, you can meet me then, and we'll ground and pound him together and destroy his human form. All of us." Now he smiled. He and Shea had this "I get you" moment. I didn't interrupt as I could see the warmth of familiarity and kinship move between them as natural as breathing.

I sighed despite myself. It wouldn't be as easy as that. Caelius was clever and cruel. I could only guess as to what his next move would be. "You should start here in Egypt. It's obvious that he wouldn't be here, but that may be his game. He's sentimental, and injured or not, he'll want to lash back at me in any way he can for my disobedience."

Aidan growled. "He's weak from breaking the seal. I'll track him, and you and I will both have our revenge. He can't hurt you anymore."

I wanted to smile. I wanted to join this A-team mentality of happy endings. But I *knew* Caelius.

He shook my shoulders, seeing that I wasn't readily convinced. "I've tracked you and hidden from the likes of slime for centuries. I can do this, Brother."

I gave him a sly look. "Are you referring to the slime of my children?"

He grinned unabashedly.

I nodded. He'd roped me in with his use of the word "brother." He hadn't called me that since we'd been like brothers, before he'd killed Moses.

Aidan did have a way about him. With that small gesture, I was pulled into their illusion. The Darkness had its persuasions, but it was nothing to the small touch of the Light tugging on what you really were and what you needed.

"All right, *Brother*." It didn't feel right to say it back. But I had to try. "Keep your updates frequent, and I'll have Shea pull me into some of the dreams for counsel. I'm also pretty good at tracking myself, if you haven't forgotten. Found you every time—"

"Caelius is different. You know if you tried to track him he'd just mess with your head. You have his blood in you; he might use that. And it's easier for Light to find Darkness and vice versa. Your job is to keep Shea safe and *train* her. I'm sure you'll be better at it than I was. She . . . she lights up when she's around you."

We both looked at her and she stuttered. Aidan lunged in and wrapped his arms around her. She probably couldn't see it, but I saw his wing encase her entire body. That was the way his kind embraced. Rare as it was, it was beautiful, beast and all.

A tear rolled down his cheek as he whispered, "I'm so glad you're alive."

She nodded, a tear matching his falling from her face. "I missed you." He held her for a moment longer. Then with a gust of wind, he left the cavern. She stumbled forward, thrown off by the thrust and power of his movement.

She started shaking.

With Aidan gone, the reality of all that had happened was starting to sink in. She rushed toward me and threw herself into my arms. I smelled her hair, cupping the nape of her neck with the palm of my hand, pressing her torso to mine. "I'll keep you safe, Shea. Caelius will never take you from my grasp again. I'll train you. You'll get stronger—"

She pulled back. "There's time for that later. Now I just *need* you."

I looked around at the devastation. All I could smell was everyone's blood. The stalactites were dripping, but the darkness had lifted. All that had made this cave a prison, all that had made it torture for over three thousand years, had gone with Caelius. Now it was just a slash house in some horror film.

I brushed the back of my hand against her cheek. "I can take you anywhere. Just name a place, and it will be ours."

She leaned close to me, her chest resting on mine. I could feel the warmth of her blood pumping erratically through her veins. "I need you *now*."

For a moment I stared, confused. This wasn't like her. She grabbed a handful of my hair and pulled me in. She whispered in front of my lips before tasting them, "You could have died, I could have died, we still might die, but I know now more than I know anything else . . . you, Lucian, are *mine*."

A surge of passion rolled over me like a vacuum of air exploding a sealed burning building. Her breath. Her lips. Saying what I'd always said. *Mine*. It was a powerful word to a vampire. But it meant more than Caelius could understand. It was body, soul, and *heart*.

All of me.

I placed her onto the cold stone and kissed her neck. I didn't drink, I just held her there with my teeth while my hands peeled off the thrashed layers of her clothes. She moaned in ecstasy as I hissed, instinctually moving my hot mouth to hers. I kissed her like a man deprived of water in the desert.

And I had been.

All the years of feeling nothing, of being empty. She made me whole. But it was more than that. With her, I was more alive than I had been as a young man before I'd been turned.

She grabbed the necklace I was wearing and eyed it as she

kissed my ear. "This was from your safe place?"

I pushed the small of her back into my hips. "I've had it since I was boy."

Her breath was hot as it whispered into my ear. "I like it."

My fingers laced over the soft pressure points on her abdomen and into her thighs as I pressed her body deeper into mine.

Here, in the place Caelius had taken me in every way but one—love. Here, at the root of my torment, she was offering healing with the Light of her body. Amongst the blood and waste, she was planting a seed, a different memory to cling to.

I lunged deeper and she gasped as I licked a small trace of blood from her neck that had survived the battle. It was sweet like nectar. I wanted it. All of it.

My desperation, no, my *need* for her to fill my very being caused me to pull back. "Wait, Shea, I'm losing myself. I can't control—"

She grabbed my face and pulled me back in.

I hovered my growing fangs over the soft curve of her neck. It pulsed and I could feel my eyes lose their color, the pupils dilating, filling the irises to black.

Then she said my name. It was a whisper, but enough to make me blind. My teeth retracted. As much as instinct mixed with desire, my love for her was powerful, all-consuming. I'd never drink her. She was *mine*. I'd give up life and all its essence to never hurt her.

With every kiss, she penetrated the Darkness inside of me. She was in me as much as I was inside of her. My soul came alive, and it beat with hers.

I kissed her mouth, her hair, the small of her back. Everything stopped, like all of time was nothing but an illusion and we could speed it up or slow it down given our pleasures. I could move quicker than any human, but I hadn't moved this slowly before. Every breath, every motion was drawn out.

Before this cave had echoed the sounds of horror and pain, and now it was filled with the pleasured cries of two lovers.

It was terrifying.

More than any anguish Darkness could cause, losing myself completely like this . . .

A day passed until we both collapsed from exhaustion. The last thing she said to me was "France."

***

Shea was still sleeping in the apartment I'd bought for us in Paris. She looked beautiful, wrapped in white down blankets. Everything felt clean, new somehow, despite the relict architecture.

I sat on the terrace and braced myself as I looked at the Eiffel Tower. It was coming. There was no stopping it. It would come as it always had, except now, I wasn't going to hide. I would face it and myself.

Just beyond visible sight, I could hear it. The subtle shift in sound. All animals could. It was part of their internal clocks, knowing when night or day was approaching. Everything inside me shivered. Maybe the seal being broken had no effect on the sun. Maybe Aidan's brothers were wrong.

Either way, I had to know. I had to see it. As new as I felt on the inside, I wanted to drench my skin in the light, whether it would burn me alive or not.

I ripped the necklace off my neck. I'd kept it for so long, like an anchor keeping me where I was, keeping me who I'd been before. It had reminded me of all I'd lost. I'd sculpted it as a child, pressing the symbolic words of our tribe into the gold. I rubbed my thumb over the glyph of my name—my *real* name. Branded as it was, the necklace was never meant to be mine. It was *hers*.

And now that I was with Shea, I wanted to let it go with the coming of my first sunrise in centuries.

Light poured over the horizon. I winced instantly in pain. My skin felt warm, all of the hair on my body standing on end. Before I could back up, Shea grabbed my hand.

"It's okay, Lucian. You're okay."

She pulled the necklace from my fist and placed it back around my neck, smiling as only she could.

I stared at her face as the sun rose, casting oranges and pinks across her warm cheeks. Tears welled in our eyes. It was the first time in over three thousand years that I'd seen anyone look so warm. "You, Shea Harper . . . you are my sunrise."

EPILOGUE
CAELIUS

That worm. That insolent maggot. After all these years of fathering him, he'd turned against me. I laughed, unable to stop the feeling of pride welling in my chest. My son should've been wild and rebellious like I was. After all, he was *mine*.

I was still being dragged. I knew it wasn't Lucian because it didn't smell like him. I could hear the confusion of the beasts and their Light as they vanished back to the heavens above, back where they could protect their blessed maker. I spit and scowled. Only the Light would be happy with such obedient dogs. They didn't need any breaking or training. They came molded, sculpted, and created to serve.

I breathed in deep. They were nothing like my boy. He was over three thousand years old. Just a baby. And that Ur-Nammu . . . he thought I would have killed my Lucian. I laughed again, letting it ring through the sand as my body left a trail like a sidewinder in the dunes.

I would have kept Lucian inside me, totally consumed in Darkness, in all that I was. And when I spat him out, he would have been riddled with confusion. It would have taken him ages to put himself back together, and he'd be better for it. Stronger. And more mine than before.

That didn't matter now. One way or another, I'd have him.

As the sun rose above the pyramids, I scowled. I hated the light. I wanted to break free, but to break the seal meant that vampires could once again walk in the sunlight.

I only wanted free in order to spit at the Light itself. To walk under its brilliance, then kill and devour all that it loved. See—I was a good son, just like Lucian.

Those beasts, didn't they know I was allowed to live, that my very existence gave the Light pleasure? Or maybe the Light just didn't have the balls to finish what it'd started: to end Darkness completely.

I stopped. Or, rather, the person dragging me got tired. I casually looked up, eager to feed on the helping hand that had pulled me away from the fight.

I smiled, and she smiled back.

"Good girl," I said, moving my hand through her jet-black hair.

She heaved me up into her lap. "They thought you were torn to shreds, but I dragged you through the opening the Vessel left when she convinced Lucian to fight you. You came through easily because you drained some of her Light, but you are weakened. What can I do? You need your strength, Father."

I grabbed her wrist and took a long drink. She moaned in pleasure like she always did. My Eve to Lucian. I moved my thumb over her elongated black eye shadow. It was strange that even after all this time, she wore the paintings of Egypt. Strange, but fitting. She still matched those sculptures he'd made of her all those centuries ago.

"Now that I'm free, he belongs to us. We'll have our family like I promised. He'll just need some . . . convincing." We both smiled, baring our fangs at the sunlight. The desire in her heart matched mine. "Don't worry, Nefertiti. Lucian and this world are *ours*."

Other Books by Hina McCord

Ivory

Love & Dark Series (with Becca C. Smith):
Vessel
First Born
Gutian Code

Other Books by Becca C. Smith

The Riser Saga:
Riser
Reaper
Ripper

The Atlas Series:
Atlas
Grigori Returned
The Underworld

Alexis Tappendorf Series:
Alexis Tappendorf and the Search for Beale's Treasure
Alexis Tappendorf and the Search for Atlantis

The Dream Diaries:
The Dream Diaries
The Dream Diaries: Blood Ties

Love & Dark Series (with Hina McCord):
Vessel
First Born
Gutian Code

SHEA Chapters Written by:
Becca C. Smith

Becca fell in love with storytelling at an early age. The first book she read was The Lion, The Witch and The Wardrobe and she's been looking for the door to Narnia ever since! Becca is a passionate reader, consuming anything sci-fi or fantasy. Mix it in with YA and she is a fan for life. So it's no surprise that she writes in these genres as well. When Becca isn't writing, she loves to sew. From Mortal Instruments rune pillows, to elaborate Firefly/Serenity bags, Becca loves to create!

LUCIAN Chapters Written by:
Hina McCord

Hina McCord is a novelist, A.K.A. an avid bullshitter; that's why she lives in L.A.. She's been writing for as long as her ancient mind can remember, devouring tales like an anemic vampire roaming the streets in hot pink heels, always thirsty for more. When she's not writing, she's making steampunk weapons, sewing giant plant-eater Mario plushes, making costumes for some film bloke or cosplayer, and sculpting/casting movie prop replicas while gardening in her urban apartment. Her favorite tools? A soldering iron, a blowtorch, a band saw, a sonic screwdriver, a replicator and an active imagination.

www.ingramcontent.com/pod-product-compliance
Lightning Source LLC
Chambersburg PA
CBHW030656260626
47157CB00007B/2685